Homicide in Herne Hill

The Fourth London Murder Mystery

Alice Castle

From the same series:
Death in Dulwich
The Girl in the Gallery
Calamity in Camberwell

CROOKED CAT

Copyright © 2018 by Alice Castle
Design: soqoqo
Editor: Christine McPherson
All rights reserved.

No part of this book may be used or reproduced in any manner whatsoever without written permission of the author or Crooked Cat Books except for brief quotations used for promotion or in reviews. This is a work of fiction. Names, characters, and incidents are used fictitiously.

First Black Line Edition, Crooked Cat, 2018

Discover us online:
www.crookedcatbooks.com

Join us on facebook:
www.facebook.com/crookedcat

Tweet a photo of yourself holding
this book to **@crookedcatbooks**
and something nice will happen.

*To William, Ella and Connie,
with love*

Acknowledgements

Thank you so much to everyone who has been so generous in their enthusiasm for the first three books in this series, Death in Dulwich, The Girl in the Gallery and Calamity in Camberwell. Special thanks to my family and to Lucy and Clare, the New York Dolls. I owe so much to Christine McPherson, my wonderful editor. And thank you, Laurence and Steph at Crooked Cat, for making it all possible.

About the Author

Alice Castle was a national newspaper journalist for The Daily Express, The Times and The Daily Telegraph before becoming a novelist. Her first book, *Hot Chocolate*, was a European best-seller which sold out in two weeks.

Alice's first and second books in the bestselling London Murder Mystery series, *Death in Dulwich*, and *The Girl in the Gallery*, have topped Amazon's satire detective fiction chart. The fifth book, Revenge on the Rye, will follow next year.

Find Alice's website at www.AliceCastleAuthor.com. Alice is also on Facebook at www.facebook.com/alicecastleauthor and Twitter at www.twitter.com/DDsDiary

She lives in south London and is married with two children, two step-children and two cats.

Homicide in Herne Hill

Alice Castle

The Fourth London Murder Mystery

Chapter One

Beth Haldane lay under her flowery duvet, taking stock. Only a small nose – and a lot of unruly fringe – was peeking out into the chilly bedroom. It was 7.30am; she'd been semi-conscious for at least two minutes, and she was gingerly probing the furthest corners of her psyche to see where the looming sense of dread was coming from.

Unpaid bills? No, thanks to her job at Wyatt's, those were mostly a thing of the past. Problems with her beloved ten-year-old son, Ben? Nope, he was being a sweetheart at the moment. That could be suspicious in itself, but for the time being she was glad to embrace his apparent newfound maturity. Relationship? Much to her surprise, she sort-of had one, after a long period of lonely widowhood. And the thought of her boyfriend – ridiculous word for a woman in her mid-thirties – still gave her a tingle of pleasure, not the swoop of doom she was currently feeling in her solar plexus. So, what was the problem?

She opened her eyes and fumbled for her phone. An alert flashed up. *School Nativity, 2pm*. Ah, that was it. Instantly, she felt the tell-tale clutch of anxiety.

Normally, it wouldn't be an issue. Ben showed absolutely no signs whatsoever of being a budding Olivier, so he would be consigned to a spear-carrying role. She'd be lucky to spot him right at the back of the stage, where he and his best friend, Charlie, would inevitably jostle each other and lark about. She and Katie, Charlie's mum, would sit together and the afternoon would pass with the odd mild snigger at someone else's child having a tantrum, forgetting their words, or somehow comfortably making their own boys look really quite good by default.

But this time, it was all going to be different. Katie had already taken Charlie out of school, and by now they'd be halfway up a mountain in Courcheval, enjoying the first days of a luxury skiing holiday. Michael had swept his family off, declaring they all needed the break after the awful year they'd had, which Beth thought was a bit rich. It was she who'd had the year from hell, with Katie only peripherally involved as a concerned bystander and provider of cappuccinos, though Charlie had had a very lucky escape at one point. Michael was just using the recent goings-on in Dulwich and Camberwell as an excuse. Fabulous holidays were about the only thing that reconciled him to the long hours and high stress of his big-fish job in publishing.

So, Katie had stealthily sprung Charlie from school early, against all the rules, and they wouldn't be back until the New Year.

This wouldn't usually be such a crushing blow for Beth; she was capable of being friends with more than one person at a time, really she was. But today's Christmas show was coming hard on the heels of another ceremony – the small funeral for Jen Patterson. It was a week since they'd gathered at the grim municipal building, like a library gone badly wrong, in one of the farthest-flung bits of south east London. A celebrant who'd never clapped eyes on Jen in life had droned on about her many good qualities in death, managing to make her sound like a total bore, not the funny, feisty woman Beth had been so fond of. Jen's daughter, Jessica, and her ex, Tim, shell-shocked, slumped in the front row like second-hand soft toys.

A patchy congregation tried to do justice to *The Lord's My Shepherd,* said to be Jen's favourite hymn. But nothing could plug the most obvious gaps: the glaring absence of Jen's dodgy new husband, Jeff, who'd scarpered to Corfu; and, even worse, Tim's evil second wife, Babs, currently on remand in Holloway, charged with Jen's murder.

It had been a toe-curling experience. As if being killed at 36 wasn't bad enough, there was the impossibility of mentioning the absentees, the cruelty of the crime itself, and the awful situation Tim now found himself in. Then there was Jessica – motherless at ten and saddled with a spineless father. At the dismal wake afterwards in a nearby Wetherspoon's pub, there had been more elephants in the room than the entire cast of *Dumbo* put together.

All right, thought Beth. So at least today's show was going to be better than that. But she'd still miss Jen terribly. She had been one of the few women Beth had really gelled with at the school gates. Both working mums, and single for much of their time, they'd found a rare accord in SE21. Many of the other mothers floated around in a Marie Antoinette-style bubble, where the only things bigger than their houses and cars were their husbands' pay packets, and the astronomical private school bills which thumped onto doormats at regular intervals. Beth and Jen, though, had both had their feet firmly on the ground.

Now Jen's were six feet under and, well, Beth would just have to make some new friends, fill the gap. She put on the duck-shaped slippers which Ben had thought were an hilarious present last Christmas. It wasn't as though she didn't know enough people in Dulwich, Beth thought to herself sternly. She'd lived here her whole life, grown up here, gone to these self-same schools, albeit in an era when Dulwich had seemed much less shiny and perfect. Her mother, who still lived nearby, was very happily retired and played bridge with everyone from the lollipop lady outside Ben's nursery school to the last director of the Dulwich Picture Gallery. She did, however, draw the line at the current scary post-holder, Drusilla Baker.

No, thought Beth, she'd just have to make an effort. There were plenty of lovely people in Dulwich, loads of delightful mothers at the school. She'd just have to find them.

Sitting in the audience a few hours later, after skedaddling early from her job as archivist at Wyatt's School, Beth looked around hopefully. She'd been running late as usual, so hadn't got prime position. That, of course, had gone to Belinda MacKenzie, who was sitting right next to the harassed head teacher of the Village Primary, smack bang in the middle of the front row.

Even though Belinda had a bird's eye view of the stage, Beth knew that if not prevented, the woman would be up like a shot the moment the curtain rose, blocking the view of all the parents behind her as she captured the antics of her sons, Billy and Bobby, for posterity. Beth was pretty sure these boys were about as talented as her own lackadaisical lad, but it was a foregone conclusion that both of them would have speaking parts. Once, long ago, when Belinda's daughter, Allegra, had been at the Village Primary, the girl had been consigned to a role in the chorus. The memory of the terrifying series of altercations that had ensued could still bring on the deputy head's psoriasis. No teacher would ever make that mistake again.

There was a buzz of excitement as parents filed in and hailed friends or avoided enemies, haphazardly filling the rows of tiny, primary-size plastic chairs. Beth was halfway down on the right-hand side, with a goodish view, as long as no preposterously tall daddies appeared to block her sightlines. That was unlikely, though. Fathers were usually only wheeled out sporadically for parents' evenings, tending to keep their powder dry – from what Beth had heard – for the higher reaches of academe, rather than wearing themselves out by dashing back from important jobs while their kids were still at the colouring-in stage.

Beth was starting to have that paranoid feeling that always gripped her at these events. No-one was going to want to sit next to her, and she'd be publicly stamped a Johnny no-mates as every other seat got taken up. There were loads of people she knew piling in, but alas, no-one she liked that much. Why did she have to be so picky? It was all very well, on a day-to-day basis, but left her fearfully exposed at times like these. She could feel her cheeks heating up already, when a newcomer bustled in with not one but two bulging supermarket carriers, scanned the room for somewhere to sit, and lugged her shopping over to Beth's row.

'This taken?' she said perfunctorily, plonking herself down

next to Beth, and indeed, right on the corner of Beth's coat, with a heavy sigh. 'Bus was murder,' she explained. 'Should have walked but got all this, see?' she said, gesturing at the bags, which were now spilling open to reveal a cache of E-numbers, white bread, and multi-packs of crisps that would have had Ben thinking he'd gone to heaven. They weren't even Bags for Life, Beth noticed, but the 5p throwaways she tried to avoid in what she knew was a pretty feeble gesture towards dolphins. She looked at her new neighbour with a sneaking admiration. The woman was breaking at least five cardinal Dulwich rules already, and they hadn't even been properly introduced.

'I'm Beth, my son Ben is in Year 6,' she said, proffering a hand. Her new companion, busy rooting through the pockets of a puffy winter jacket, didn't seem to notice. 'Yeah, Nina,' she said. 'My Wilf's just started this term, Year 1. I know who you are. You're the one who keeps catching murderers.'

'Oh!' Beth was stunned. She'd realised she'd been getting a few sidelong glances in the playground recently. But were people saying that about her? And was it even true? 'I'm not sure that's really… I just seem to be in the right place. Or maybe the wrong place, if you know what I mean.'

Nina gave her a level look. 'Just as long as I don't get knocked off just for sitting next to you,' she said. Then, just as Beth started to worry she was serious, she let out a huge guffaw. 'Nah, you're all right. At least you're doing something interesting. I get the feeling that if I hung out with some of the other mums, all I'd get would be a bad case of baby brain. And that I can do without,' she said, nudging Beth sharply in the ribs. To her surprise, Beth found herself laughing. There was something infectious about the twinkle in Nina's eye.

Just then there was a loud call of '*sh!*' from Belinda in the front row and the beleaguered head got to his feet. He'd just cleared his throat and was about to speak when Belinda shot up and clapped her hands loudly, shouting, 'Silence please, ladies and, um, gentleman, our Head is *trying* to make himself heard.'

'Er, thank you, Mrs, er, ahem,' he said, accidentally delivering the best possible put-down to Belinda MacKenzie, who prided herself on being known by all. 'I'd just like to welcome you all to our little nativity play. As you'll know, the children have been practising very hard to make this a really special occasion for you. I'd like to thank...'

As the speech meandered through the roll call of long-suffering teachers who'd been attempting, since the first days of September, to knock the show into some sort of shape, the audience palpably zoned out. More and more parents started fiddling with their phones, ostensibly to switch the ringers off but often just to check that nothing major had happened on their Facebook feeds since they'd last looked five minutes ago.

To Beth's surprise, Nina didn't fish out an iPhone, but gazed into space, apparently perfectly happy to think quietly for a few moments, or possibly even to listen. Beth hastily switched her own phone to camera mode. Perhaps this year she'd be able to catch Ben doing something worth sending to her mum. She caught Nina looking at her.

'I've got five years' worth of blurs from this show stored somewhere in the Cloud. I'm hoping I'll get a proper photo this time. Aren't you going to take pictures?'

'Tell you the truth, my phone's as old as the mills,' said Nina with a shrug.

Beth was confused for a second. Nina certainly had a way with a phrase. Then her face cleared. 'Oh, I see what you mean. Mine's three years old. Practically a museum piece. My emojis won't even update.'

'No, I mean *really* ancient,' said Nina, taking a Nokia brick out of her pocket. Beth looked at it in astonishment. 'I haven't seen one like that for years,' she admitted.

'Yeah. It rings nice and loud. And I can text on it,' offered Nina.

Beth paused for a beat. 'Well, I can take pics and email them to you, if they come out. But I warn you, I'm the world's worst photographer.'

'Tell you what,' said Nina. 'Give your phone here. I'll take the pics. By the sounds of it, they can't be worse than your usual ones. They might even be better. Be nice to get some good ones of Wilf, too. He's the donkey.'

Beth didn't even have to think twice. 'Great,' she said, handing her phone over. To her surprise, Nina seemed completely *au fait* with the camera function, and rattled off a couple of surreptitious shots of Belinda, showing Beth the results. They were hilarious, capturing Belinda looking like Boadicea going into battle while, alongside her, the Head seemed even more shrivelled and careworn than usual.

She was just complimenting Nina when the speakers exploded with a recording of other people's children singing *O Little Town of Bethlehem* in tune, accidentally turned up to *Spinal Tap*-style volume eleven. The show was beginning.

An hour later, and Beth realised she had never enjoyed a Nativity so much. Liberated from the necessity of attempting to record it all for posterity, she was able to savour everything, trying and failing to suppress her laughter when the eager-to-please innkeeper declared there was room at his establishment after all, leading to pantomime-style calls of *'oh no, there isn't!'* from teachers offstage. Once the Holy couple was finally established in the stable, which was represented by one packet of fluffy rabbit bedding from the Sainsburys in Dog Kennel Hill, because no-one enjoys clearing up real straw, the fun really began.

The Angel Gabriel was extremely reluctant to hand over the Godchild to Mary, as it was her brand new Luvabella doll playing the pivotal role. Once that tug-of-war was over, one of the Year 1 oxen bit a shepherd on the leg and the Three Wise Men got lost, their Sat Nav having apparently failed in the desert. Billy and Bobby MacKenzie, playing the role of bouncers – characters who had oddly not appeared in the original Gospels – had a not very *sotto voce* fight over who was going to tether Mary's extremely uncooperative donkey, and only their mother's blistering intervention from the audience got events moving again. Finally, one of the angels absentmindedly lifted up her skirts to reveal she wasn't wearing any knickers, at which point many parents gave up live-streaming the event for fear of prosecution on public decency grounds.

Beth, wiping tears of laughter from her eyes, realised that, as usual, Ben had been just one of a herd of brown-clad, also-ran ruminants jostling for position at the back, belting out a surprisingly aggressive rendition of *Once in Royal David's City*. But he had managed to stay on the stage despite the outbreaks of pushing around him, and she was pretty sure that she'd picked out his singing from the crowd. He'd done her proud. And it had been so nice this year to have been able to enjoy being in the moment, instead of hiding behind a device while trying to capture the action. She owed Nina, she thought, looking round for her.

The moment the show had finished, everyone got up at once and bolted for the doors, despite years of experience of annual bottlenecks, proving that three hundred people couldn't get through a two-foot space at the same time. Beth tried to peer round the crowd in front of her, but as usual her field of vision was severely hampered. Being this height was no fun when you wanted to see what was going on.

She thought, briefly, of clambering onto a chair, but they were diddy little ones anyway, probably wouldn't take her weight, and the last thing she wanted to do was break school property and mortify her son. Just then, Ben rushed up to her, tearing off his paper crown with two pencils attached. She hadn't been able to see this detail against the fierce stage lights.

'Oh, you were a *reindeer*?' she said, hugging him tightly.

'Well, duh, Mum!' he said, shrugging out of her embrace. She supposed his nose should have been a giveaway, but instead of bright red it was this season's subtle must-have shade of iced peach and was hardly visible. It must have been lipsticked on by one of the yummier mums helping with the costumes backstage. And despite its delicious barely-there shimmer, it would probably be hell to get off in the bath tonight.

As they shuffled towards the exit, Ben listened with a patient smile to her paeans of praise for his performance, like a Shakespearian actor who acknowledges the audience's enthusiasm while accepting that they can't really hope to comprehend the depth of the performance they have just witnessed.

'Do you know Wilf, in Year 1?' Beth said eventually. 'I've just met his mum; she seems really nice.'

'Yeah, Wilf's all right, for a kid,' Ben allowed magnanimously, from the giddy heights of Year 6, the top of the school.

'She took some great photos of you. At least, I'm hoping she did,' said Beth, a germ of alarm suddenly growing. 'Oh no! She's still got my phone. And I've got hers.'

'Well, ring her then,' said Ben, as though speaking to a simpleton.

Beth supposed she'd have to get used to the fact that Ben was at ease with technology that hadn't even been a gleam in Steve Job's owlish specs during her own childhood. These solutions would always leap to him before she could hope to get her thoughts in order. Or that's what she told herself. It was plain disconcerting when one's children started coming up with clever ideas. She fumbled out the Nokia phone, looking askance at its blocky buttons.

'Cool,' breathed Ben, taking it from her with the reverence of an Egyptologist examining a rare papyrus. 'That's so... old.'

'Hm. Give it here, Ben, I've just got to—' But before she'd even finished the sentence, Ben had tapped out her mobile phone number on Nina's clunky keyboard and handed the phone back to her.

It rang three, four times, then was picked up. 'That you, Beth? Sorry, walked off with your phone, didn't I? And we're halfway home now. What do you want to do? Do you need it tonight, or shall we meet tomorrow, get a coffee?'

Little did she know it, but Nina had said the magic words. Beth's days tended to be punctuated with little pauses in lovely cafes over coffee (or tea, she wasn't fussy), and with Katie away now for two solid weeks, she'd been wondering where her next hot beverage would be coming from. She thought quickly. She surely wouldn't need her phone before the morning. Her mother would have forgotten that it was Ben's play today so wouldn't be calling, and she wasn't due to see her boyfriend – that word again! – until the end of the week. And she did have a landline at home, though nowadays the only purpose it served was as a hotline to cold caller hell.

'Great, let's meet at the playground. It'll have to be a quick one as it's my last day at work tomorrow before the holidays. Got to leave everything tidy,' said Beth, wrinkling her brow. As usual, the thought of work had her feeling a mixture of guilt and gratitude. Though the Wyatt's job had done so much to ease her financial woes, she was apt to dump it right at the bottom of her list of priorities, which was ungrateful, not to mention a bit silly. What if someone noticed how little work she actually did, and sacked her? But all that was going to change, she decided. She was going to work her socks off next year. It was going to be one of her resolutions.

'Okey doke,' said Nina. 'Got to go, Wilf's eating me shopping, straight out the bag.'

Beth realised she was smiling as she handed the Nokia back to Ben for him to switch off. Was she being disloyal to Jen, she wondered, feeling happiness again so soon? But her friend wouldn't have begrudged her a smile. She couldn't stay miserable forever; it wouldn't make Jen any less dead. Life was a precarious and precious thing, as events kept showing her. She had to make the most of her time, grab what joy she could.

It was, she realised, the reason why she'd finally decided it was time to make a go of things with DI Harry York. She felt the fizz of anticipation at the thought, something she hadn't known since her earliest days with her late husband, James, Ben's father. As she and Ben walked home under the coloured fairy lights in the Village, she felt her boy's sense of excitement at Christmas approaching. And for the first time in years, Beth shared it.

Chapter Two

There was nothing like the frozen wastes of a junior school playground to buffet the life out of you, thought Beth the next morning. As usual, she and Ben had made it by the skin of their teeth, and unless Nina had got here incredibly early and bombed off again already, she was even later than they were. Ben ran in and normally that would have been that, she could have toddled off, but today she'd have to hang about if she wanted her phone back. She sighed.

But wait a minute, there were loads of mums still left in the playground. Far more than usual at this hour. They were gathered in little knots, talking intently, the largest group around one of the Year 4 teachers. What was going on? Beth sidled over.

'...and they just couldn't wake her up. Poor little thing, she was only six months old,' one of the mums was saying, her nose pink and her eyes suspiciously shiny. Was that down to the cold weather, or had something awful happened? Beth instinctively moved closer.

'She was terrible at night, they said, always waking up and crying, so they were trying to train her, shutting her in the kitchen until morning.'

Beth had heard of draconian sleep-training methods, but this was going a bit far, wasn't it? But to her surprise, there was a murmur of assent from the other mums. 'It's the only way, break the pattern,' said one earnest woman, who Beth had always quite liked before.

'Then the kids bombed downstairs in the morning, and there she was, poor little thing, stone dead on the kitchen floor,' said the first woman.

Beth couldn't help herself, she gasped. The woman turned

to her. 'Oh, did you know Roxie, then?'

'Roxie?' said Beth, mentally scanning a roster of tiny brothers and sisters of Ben's classmates.

'Yes, Roxie, Pat and Sam's dachshund. She was such a gorgeous little puppy. They can only think that she might have eaten something while they were out in the park. She was such a one for munching down anything she found – you know, balls, plastic cups...'

A dog! Beth took a relieved breath. Ok, it wasn't great that someone's pet had died, but still, she couldn't help feeling, somehow, that it had been a close call. 'Poor little thing,' Beth murmured hastily, joining in with the others, shaking her head. There was a collective peeking at watches and tutting at the time, and people started melting away.

Soon, Beth was the last mum standing in the playground, and not enjoying the biting wind that swept across the deserted climbing frame and whacked straight into her. No sign of Nina. She got out the old Nokia, which was weighing down her bag, and poked at the keys, trying to get the thing to turn on.

Just as she was giving up hope, she saw Nina bustling up the street, Wilf running ahead, book bag waving frantically in the air. In Year 1, you didn't get much of a telling off for being late, Beth remembered fondly. The teachers tended to err on the side of cuddliness. It was in Year 2 that a more severe regime kicked in.

Nina puffed up to the gate, clutching her side. Her hugely padded white coat made her look a little like a snowball. 'Sorry, sorry. It's colder than a witch's bits, innit?' she puffed.

'Erm, yes. No problem,' said Beth, with the hearty relief that came from not being stood up, after all, added to the prospect of retrieving her phone. Though she wasn't as wedded to it as half the people she knew, she'd still feel better once she had her little window into the world safely back in her bag. 'Where shall we have coffee?'

This was a crucial question in Dulwich. You could tell a lot about a person from the place they chose to sip their lattes. Beth studied Nina as the other woman pursed her lips and went through the options. Though only an inch or two taller than Beth – and that in itself was a pleasant novelty; most people tended to tower above her, whether they wanted to or not – Nina seemed quite a lot wider. That shouldn't be comforting, but in the current fat-shaming culture, Beth didn't try to deny that it gave her a tiny glow. If she never had much of the high ground, height-wise, she could at least reclaim some points thanks to her naturally slender, some would say weedy, physique.

Perhaps there would come a time when she had to spend hours in the gym to ward the flab off, but at the moment, running around after Ben and her job at Wyatt's, plus her perennially high levels of anxiety, seemed to whittle away the pounds. They had quite a healthy diet, she supposed smugly, firmly shutting her mind's eye to the chocolate stash she kept in the bottom drawer of her desk at the school. That was a secret between her and the cleaners. Besides, she knew Nina's tastes ran to junk food, as she'd seen her bursting bags of Fanta and oven chips at the Nativity.

'There's a new place that's just opened up, where the Post Office used to be. Fancy trying it?'

'Good idea,' said Beth in relief. Nina had passed the first test. In many ways, it was a tragedy that one of the very few useful shops in the Village had closed down. It had been such a busy Post Office, too. Before Christmas, there were always queues snaking out of the door as far as the florists, as people patiently waited to send gifts to far-flung loved ones. Then, in the New Year, they'd all queue again to send their own unwanted swag back to Boden, Brora, and beyond. Now they'd have to schlepp as far as Lordship Lane or Norwood. But at least it looked as though the place wasn't going to be replaced by yet another chichi cushion emporium. Beth loved cushions, it was practically mandatory if you lived hereabouts, but at this point in her life she didn't possess a single chair that was unadorned. She refused to get to the stage some people seemed to have reached, of buying chairs just to put fresh cushions on. There wasn't room in her tiny house. And a new coffee shop was always a thrill.

It was chilly as they hurried through the grey December streets. From the outside, the little Post Office had been transformed. It was now a heavenly shiny turquoise, with a big neon sign – possibly a little *funky* for Dulwich – announcing the name, Puccini's. Beth rather liked it. The classical nod would no doubt appeal to opera aficionados, or those who aspired to know something about that rarefied world and had at least heard of the composer. It also gave a sense of multiple cappuccinos, which Beth, and most other residents of the borough, would firmly agree was a good thing.

The door opened with the familiar jangle of the bell, which had been such a nuisance when the place had been the Post Office and people had trooped in so regularly that the sound gave you tinnitus. Now it was a rather pleasing retro touch. There were about six tables crammed into the small space, but that again was very Dulwich. Both Romeo Jones, the miniscule deli, and Jane's, the much larger bakery café, were as crowded as an auction house's back rooms. Here, the walls were a slightly deeper shade of turquoise, and the art on the walls was colourful and not taxing – Matisse's snail, Patrick Caulfield's pottery, Andy Warhol's flowers. The tables and chairs were lacquered in mismatched corals, blues and yellows, and the whole thing was rather lovely. Crucially, it appeared to be pulling off the neat trick of appealing to Dulwich mummies, their nannies and au pairs, and the kids, too.

Both Nina and Beth turned to raise their eyebrows and nod approvingly. 'I'll get the coffees, grab a table,' said Nina. It sounded as though she'd handed Beth the best part of the bargain, but as usual hunting a space was no easy feat. As she stepped forward, Belinda MacKenzie, sitting in the centre of the room with five of her best pals around her, called over loudly.

'Beth! On your own again? Come and join us. Here, shuffle up,' she barked at the friends, who all obediently scraped their chairs in different directions.

'Oh, thanks, Belinda, but I'm with…' Beth said, gesturing

at Nina who was at the till, apparently deep in discussion about their coffees.

Belinda's head snapped over, took in Nina in her vast white coat, and immediately drawled, 'ohh!' With a rapid gesture to her cohort, she made it clear that plans had changed and they awkwardly closed ranks. Belinda had been willing to allow Beth into the favoured circle, but Nina was a step too far. There was a pause, then Belinda carried on talking as though nothing had happened, and the others went back to contemplating her vast handbag – today, a Marc Jacobs number bristling with studs and tassels, splayed on the table as though the high priestess was about to examine its entrails.

Beth sidled past them all with many a *sorry* and *excuse me*, and finally made it to the only unoccupied table, right in the corner, then sat down in relief. The chair was a lot softer than it looked, thanks to a cushion – of course – which looked as though it had come straight from the Village's fanciest emporium. As Beth leaned to one side to examine this gorgeous confection of turquoise shot silk, admiring its multiplicity of tassels and trims, she realised that this would be a good control experiment. If these cushions lasted more than a month before starting to look shabby, with all the wear that they were destined to get, then maybe they weren't such a batty purchase at £80 a pop and she might finally be able to upgrade some of her own boy-proof soft furnishings.

Just then, Nina arrived with two outsize earthenware mugs, cheerily glazed in coral pink and purple. The waiter brought up the rear with a plate bearing two *pain au chocolats*, each with a generous hoar frost of icing sugar.

'Yum,' said Beth, her eyes as big as saucers and her vocabulary suddenly shrunken to Ben proportions.

'I know, tuck in,' said Nina with a grin, picking up hers and sinking her teeth into it with a roll of her eyes. 'Better than sex.'

Beth, who for many years would definitely have agreed with this statement but had recently been shown the error of her ways, felt her cheeks flame and tore off a corner of the pastry, bowing her head over the plate.

'Aha! I see someone's getting some. Nah, don't look like that. Good for you, girl. 'S'all I'm saying,' said Nina, through a thick mouthful. 'That explains the number of missed calls you got last night. Phone was going like the clappers. I didn't bother to switch it off. Don't worry, it was all No Caller ID, so your secret lover is still secret,' she said with a wink, handing over the phone.

Beth, through her mortification, was much struck. She'd never been able to wink in that casually emphatic way. When once she'd been challenged to do it by Ben, she'd had to work up to it slowly, finally managing a sort of facial convulsion that moved all her features at the same time, not just one eye. She'd thought at the time that it was a male thing, but Nina's seamless usage had disproved this. Maybe it was practice.

But she knew that she was only dwelling on that wink to distance herself from the chaotic emotions aroused by Nina's oh-so-accurate guess. She was sorry that she'd missed Harry last night. He'd be worried, she knew. He had good reason to believe that she got herself into terrible trouble when he wasn't keeping an eye on her. She sneaked a quick look at the screen and saw four missed calls and a couple of texts. Part of her wanted to listen to her voicemails right away and luxuriate in the texts like a teenager whose crush has finally revealed his devotion. But she couldn't. She put the phone away firmly in her bag and applied herself to the coffee instead. Mm. Delicious.

'This place is really going to give Jane's a run for its money,' she smiled at Nina.

'I know, right? They'll have to up their game. Serve the odd drink above room temperature for a change.'

'Even get some non-wobbly tables,' agreed Beth. The two women were now skirting round, getting each other's measure, assessing whether a friendship could be born from their chance meeting at the Nativity. As far as Beth was concerned, she was ready and willing. Nina seemed fun and, best of all, she was irreverent. The way she'd semi-barged past Belinda's chair to get to their table told her a lot about the woman's view of Dulwich society and her place in it. Belinda, as ever, had been sitting with her chair pushed out from the table, just a little bit further than everyone else's. This was partly to dominate the space but also, Beth sometimes thought, because she wore such super-skinny white jeans that she couldn't actually bend her enviably long legs. She'd also been ostentatiously comforting one of her little gang, who seemed to be sniffling into a tissue.

'So, what's your story?' said Nina, breaking into her train of thought. She'd apparently tired of polite skirmishes and wanted to get down to brass tacks.

'Story?' said Beth innocently, looking into Nina's round face. Once her hood was down, the woman's flyaway, red-gold hair stuck up softly in all directions, a bit like the halo of curls sported by one of Raphael's renaissance putti. Her expression, though, was as far from angelic as you could get; knowing, cheeky, and full of irrepressible curiosity. Large gold hoops dangled from her ears and, under her white puffy coat, Beth could see the collar of a multi-coloured fluffy sweater which must have been rather hot in the steamy café. The windows had already misted up and Beth was feeling uncomfortable in her own coat. She shrugged it off onto her seat back, like a butterfly shedding its cocoon, revealing her less than thrilling work outfit which, as usual, consisted of jeans and a jumper. She loved Wyatt's dearly, but she'd never got her head around the dress code the other women all seemed to adhere to, featuring little frocks from the posher high street shops. Beth really considered it unnecessary to lash out a hundred pounds for a silk dress from Jigsaw in order to sit down on her own all day surrounded by ancient books.

'You know. Here you are, kid in the primary, little bit of a job. No husband, hence the keen boyf. Or is there a husband and you're just playing fast and loose?'

Beth gave Nina a sharp glance. She was usually the one asking questions, and they tended to be a lot more subtle than this barrage. She definitely wasn't loving being on the receiving end. There was only one thing for it. Turn the tables. She took a breath and plunged in.

'So, you haven't lived here long, have you? I haven't seen you around much, before this term started, anyway?'

Nina smiled. 'Sorry, I can be a bit full on. My mum's always telling me. I'll lay off. Yeah, haven't been here long, we live down Herne Hill. Not quite so posh as round here.'

'Oh, but Herne Hill's *lovely*,' said Beth quickly. 'I love the bookshop, Tales on Moon Lane.'

'Yeah, well, we don't actually live in the bookshop. More like the estates round the back of Sunray Gardens?' Nina said with heavy irony.

'I *love* Sunray Gardens,' said Beth quickly. Nina gave her a look, and Beth remembered that there were some not terribly prepossessing flats looming round the pretty little playground, and this was where she probably lived. Time to stop gushing.

'Well, I'm glad you've moved here, anyway,' said Beth with a smile. 'How're you finding it?'

'Yeah, not bad. Quite friendly. Some people friendlier than others, if you know what I mean. Good transport links and the school's nice. Came here really to be nearer to work, and make sure Wilf got a good start, you know?'

Beth did, indeed, know. The schools in Dulwich had been drawing people to the area since Sir Thomas Wyatt had finally hung up his swashbuckling seven league boots three hundred-odd years ago and strode into Dulwich. He'd had quite a change of tack, giving up his relentless exploitation of the unfortunate colonies and coming over all God-fearing, founding several churches as well as the first of the Endowment Schools, which now acted as such powerful magnets on those aspiring to secure a top-class education for their children. It was what had brought her own parents to Dulwich from Surrey half a century ago, and the same thought held her transfixed now, with Ben poised to sit the most important exams of his life in just a few short weeks' time.

Beth nodded, then added idly, 'So, where are you

working?'

'Oh, at Potter's, down near the station. You know, the solicitors? It's Paul Potter's place. His wife, Letty, is the stringy one over there, next to that MacKenzie bird,' said Nina, nodding at a willowy, breakable-looking ash-blonde whom Beth'd always thought of as Belinda's number two. But Beth had been past the shops in Herne Hill countless times and had never noticed a solicitor's office. She said as much.

'We've got frosted glass windows, quite a discreet sign. You might not have known what it was. Right next door to the off-licence, near that tapas bar that closed down.'

'Oh… yes,' said Beth, finally able to picture the plain office front, to which she'd never given a moment's thought. She'd usually been much too busy pulling Ben bodily out of the toy shop and into the book shop over the road, where he was a much more reluctant purchaser. The toy shop had a knife-edge business plan, doing a roaring trade in pocket-money priced plastic tat, sold directly to children, which it tried to combine with beautiful, traditional wooden toys which grandparents loved to lavish a fortune on once a year, and children rarely touched. If Beth had been in charge, a middle ground of moderately-priced popular nonsense would have filled the shelves, with a large computer games section, while the building blocks of yesteryear would be confined to a high and dusty shelf. But as long as the shop managed to stay open as things were, it was all fine, she supposed.

She looked at Nina a little quizzically. She didn't look like a natural fit in a solicitor's office.

'You're thinking, what's this big-mouth doing handling people's secrets?' said Nina with pinpoint accuracy. 'But actually, I can keep well schtum when I need to. Yeah, we deal with a lot of confidential stuff. Divorces, property, whatever. I'm just the office manager, keep everything on an even keel – I'm not the solicitor, in case you were wondering,' she said, going off into peals of laughter.

'I don't see why that's so funny. No reason in the world you couldn't do something like that,' said Beth staunchly.

'No reason, except no education,' said Nina succinctly. 'That's why it's all going to be different for Wilf.'

If Beth had had any lingering doubts about Nina, they were banished now. Any mother with ambitions for her child and a plan for her own life had Beth's vote, no question. She only wished she could be more forthright herself, half the time. *Was there anyone in the world as beset with doubts as she was?* she wondered. But Nina was continuing.

'You know what, it's probably lucky we bumped into each other. I've been thinking, for a while now...' Nina broke off, and stirred the dregs of her cappuccino energetically, her teaspoon clinking against the thick china.

Either she was angling for a refill, or she genuinely had something big on her mind, and was weighing up whether or not to spill it. As usual, Beth rose to the bait. There was nothing she loved more than a secret. And, of course, a fresh coffee.

'Something on your mind?' she probed gently, trying to catch the attention of the waiter as he hovered near Belinda's table. He was taking a lengthy coffee order which the Queen Bee kept amending.

'I insist you try the oat milk with your latte, Becky. It'll work wonders with your bloating,' Belinda was saying loudly to one of her acolytes, who blushed furiously and pretended to be looking for her purse, so she could stick her scarlet face in her handbag. Letty looked on, chilly and impassive. The one who'd been sniffing earlier was still pink-eyed, Beth noted.

Once again, Beth thanked her stars that she'd never been either boring enough, or exciting enough, for Belinda to bother with. She wanted yes-mummies who'd follow in her wake like ducklings, waiting for crumbs from her over-stocked table. Or scalps, who had interesting connections, high-flying jobs, or precociously bright children, so Belinda could lionize them at her endless dinner parties. There was a danger in both roles. The yes-mummies went quietly mad, as Belinda rode roughshod over their hopes and dreams; and the scalps inevitably became restless and tried to break away from her patronage, usually resulting in riveting arguments over the canapés, which Katie would tell Beth all about.

Beth, so far, had been too poor, plain and obscure, and much too little, to excite Belinda's interest, but the fact that Nina had known all about some of her adventures was a bit worrying. If she wasn't careful, Belinda might well start finding her a bit less dull. It was a sobering thought. Judging from the way Beth was failing to attract the waiter's attention, though, that time could still be a way off.

'Here, mate, when you've got a sec,' Nina said loudly to the waiter, who held up his fingers to say *two minutes*. He was frowning painfully with the effort of getting Belinda's ever more baroque coffee order down.

'So that's an oat latte, a soya frappuccino, a skinny filter, an Americano with hot milk on the side, and an Earl Grey with milk *and* lemon?' he said hopefully.

'No. Honestly, how hard can it be? I said an oat cappuccino, a skinny soya decaf…' Belinda droned.

'God, we might as well go round to the kitchen and make our own,' said Nina, not bothering to lower her voice.

Beth ducked a glance at the other table, but Belinda was still fully occupied, rapping out their list in crosser and crosser tones. 'It makes me want to order a simple mug of PG Tips and have done with it,' Beth whispered. 'Anyway, you were saying?'

'Oh? Was I?' Nina seemed confused, and Beth hoped the moment hadn't passed. She could never resist a mystery, and there had been something in the other woman's voice just now which seemed to suggest that something was up.

Nina's face cleared. 'Yeah, you know, as you're so great with the puzzles and all, I just wondered… thought I might run something past you. But maybe it's not the right thing to do.' Her brow furrowed, and she fiddled again with her spoon.

If there was anything destined to get all Beth's problem-solving instincts raring for the off, it was having an interesting conundrum dangled in front of her, then swiftly withdrawn. It was like teasing her imperious black and white moggie, Magpie, with her favourite catnip mouse. There was only so much playing you could do, before the cat would pounce and sink her claws into the little knitted creature – or your hand. She wasn't fussy.

Beth eyed Nina speculatively. She wasn't planning to attack the woman, but she did suddenly feel like giving her a mild shake. 'Oh, come on, you've said this much. What's worrying you?' she prompted.

'It's probably nothing,' said Nina, looking round, possibly to see whether any of the other mums were close enough to hear their chat. Belinda's table might be, but luckily they were all taken up now with chanting their endless coffee litany at the hapless waiter, who looked as though he was near to tears. If Puccini's closed down before it had even got going, Beth knew who she was going to blame. 'It's just that... well,' said Nina. 'I don't know if you know much about how a solicitor's office works?'

Beth shook her head. To be fair, it wasn't just solicitors that Beth knew nothing about. She hadn't a clue how most companies functioned. She'd been a freelance for years, and until she'd landed the Wyatt's job, her own workspace had been the part of her sofa not covered with Ben's Lego and Spiderman magazines. Journalism as a sector had been shrinking from the moment she'd entered it, in an Alice in Wonderland trick that never seemed to go into reverse.

She'd had a staff job, for about ten minutes, for a paper in Docklands. On her first day, she'd had her own corner and a phone, but a few weeks later a hot desk policy had come in, then she was working from home a couple of days a week, and before she knew it she was turfed out on a contract instead, her paid holidays consigned to history. If she'd known how short her time as a commuter was going to be, she'd have moaned more about it while she could.

'Ok, so I'm the office manager, basically,' Nina was explaining, 'so I get to sit in a smaller chair than the solicitor, but I do all the work to keep the office going.' Beth nodded briskly, this sounded par for the course. 'One of my jobs is to bung all the financial stuff in a folder. Potter pays extra for a book-keeper to come in and sort stuff out, for the year-end tax returns and so on, so I put that stuff on one side. Most of the time, it's just me and a whole lot of reports.' Beth nodded again. So far, so straightforward. 'Potentially, there could be a lot of work going through our office, though we're only small. We do the lot. Wills, conveyancing, family law, whatever. Well, they call it "family", but it's actually pulling them apart – divorce, in fact.'

'Must be a bit grim,' said Beth sympathetically.

'Been through it myself, and all I can say, girl, is – just get separated. Don't bother with an official bit of paper or you'll be caught, thousands of pounds later, wondering why you ever got married in the first place.'

'Is that how it was with you and your, um, ex?' Beth couldn't resist a little prod.

'Yep. Oddly, that's how I got into this line of work. Always loved legal dramas, been a secretary all my working life. Got divorced, ended up shagging the lawyer, you know how it is. Then got the job. Not the same firm, of course. Lawyer went back to his wife, bastard, but I've left all that behind. Very happy with the work, though,' Nina added insouciantly.

Beth, a little taken aback at the neatness of Nina's *précis*, smiled uncertainly. 'Sounds like it's going well. So, what's the problem?'

'That's just exactly it. I'm not quite sure. All I know is, there isn't really enough work on to keep it all going,' said Nina, her round face clouded for a moment. It was clearly an uncomfortable and unusual sensation for her. Nina's world seemed pretty plain sailing and, like Beth, she seemed not to be an ambiguity fan.

Beth, however, had lived in Dulwich long enough to know that it wasn't always possible to go straight down the line, however much it might appeal to you. 'Do you think there's something dishonest going on? Or... illegal?' she asked.

'Well, I think that's what I'd like to find out,' said Nina, falling silent as the exhausted waiter finally appeared at their table.

'Ladies, what can I get you?' he said faintly, turning over page after page of Belinda's detailed instructions in his little order book, before he finally found a clean sheet to write on.

'I'd just like a simple builder's tea, milk no sugar,' said Beth with an encouraging smile.

'Same here,' said Nina.

The waiter's tremulous gratitude was almost painful to behold. He dived back round to the kitchen, and returned a couple of minutes later, with a tray bearing a massive, steaming teapot, two mugs and a dinky milk jug, all in the same heavy, brightly-coloured earthenware as their coffee mugs. Belinda MacKenzie, whose order was still nowhere to be seen, attempted to waylay him as he passed, but the boy swerved gracefully and kept his eyes averted from her table. He was learning fast, Beth thought with approval. This place could well be here to stay.

By the time Beth and Nina had drained their surprisingly capacious teapot, they had agreed a plan. Nina would keep a watchful eye on things and try and narrow down exactly what was making her feel uneasy. This was no simple matter. She'd been feeling things were 'a bit weird' for a few weeks now, without being able to put her finger on anything in particular.

'But now that we've spoken about it, things will be different. You'll see things more clearly,' said Beth, with a lot more confidence than she inwardly felt. 'Just imagine that you're explaining everything you see to me. Then, if anything really is odd, it will really stand out.'

Nina had looked a little sceptical, but as Beth, with the best will in the world, couldn't really barge into the office on the basis of a *weird feeling*, it was all they could do for the moment. As soon as something leapt out at Nina, though, Beth would beetle on over and visit her *in situ,* making some excuse for dropping into the office. This bit of the plan was even vaguer than all the others, which was saying something. To the uninformed eye, it might all look a little like a portrait of a polar bear in a blizzard, but Beth knew she'd had real breakthroughs in the past on the back of even sketchier ideas.

In the meantime, she had to admit she was intrigued by the goings-on at Belinda's table, where the mummy who'd been sniffling earlier was now openly weeping, and being comforted by everyone, including Belinda, who was looking unusually sympathetic.

'Do you have any idea what all that's about?' Beth asked Nina, careful not to give herself away, simply sliding her glance towards the central table and raising her eyebrows. Nina turned her entire body and swivelled her head immediately, and Beth ducked down behind the teapot, hoping they wouldn't attract Belinda's basilisk gaze.

Nina turned back. 'Yeah, heard about that yesterday afternoon from Wilfy. Daphne, that's the daughter of that Beatrice over there, she was well upset. Their dog's been poisoned.'

Beth, who'd been idly musing on who'd call a five-year-old Daphne – a name she'd only ever come across before attached to one of her mother's oldest and frostiest friends – sat up in shock. '*Poisoned*? I thought it had dropped dead in the kitchen overnight or something.'

'Nah, not this one. This was a King Charles spaniel called Lola. Right as rain in the morning, dead as mutton last night. And been sick all over everything, that's why they think it had been given something.'

'Lola? Oh, of course, I knew Lola. She was so cute,' said Beth, for once not questioning a world where you could like a dog much better than its owner. 'Who would want to poison Lola?' Beth wondered incredulously, then thought about the other sad tale she'd heard in the playground this morning. She remembered now, it had been Roxie the insomniac dachshund puppy who'd died. *Two* different dogs dead? And in the same twenty-four hour period? Immediately, she couldn't help wondering if the dachshund had been poisoned, too.

She'd never had much time for Lola's owner, one of Belinda's more slavish devotees, but the dog, resplendent in a jaunty Schiaparelli pink jacket at the school gates most mornings, had been irresistible. She'd had one of those wise, sad, spaniel faces, and bottomless eyes the colour of treacle, which seemed to have seen and pardoned all that passed in this vale of tears, including someone naming her Lola.

Beth, not really a dog person – she found even the small ones unnecessarily *large* – had stroked her once or twice when she'd been a wriggling little pup. She couldn't help having a sneaking fondness for any creature that had legs stumpier than her own.

She shook her head. 'God, that is evil,' she marvelled. She'd seen a lot in recent months, but cruelty towards animals? If she'd been pressed, first thing this morning, she would have said, yes, people might stab each other occasionally in Dulwich, but hurt a pet? Never.

But it seemed she'd been wrong.

'Any idea who did it?'

Nina shrugged. 'Not as far as I know. I feel sorry for the kid. Wilf said Daphne's got her Grade 3 clarinet this afternoon – and I bet the mum will go ahead, even if the poor girl's in bits.'

Beth nodded. It was not only possible but probable. The mother was very upset herself – that much was clear, as Beth spotted Belinda handing her another tissue – but that didn't mean she'd contemplate bailing on the investment of time, energy and, frankly, money involved in dragging a child towards a music exam.

'Let's hope she doesn't have to play, *How Much is that Doggy in the Window?*' Nina added, then both women looked at each other, horrified, and burst out laughing. Sometimes something had to give.

Pouring out the dregs of the tea a minute later, when they'd collected themselves and ignored some sharp glances from the other table, Beth caught sight of Nina's watch and nearly had a heart attack. 'Oh my God, the time! I had no idea it had got so late. I've got to dash. There's so much to do at work. Sorry, Nina, look, this is for my half of the bill.'

With that, Beth threw down a crumpled note and dodged past Belinda's chair, thrust even further back now than ever as she really expanded into her morning's work, putting

Dulwich to rights, with particular reference to what poor Beatrice, Lola's owner, should have done differently. If Beth knew Belinda, there would be a strong suggestion that Beatrice had somehow failed her dog and family, and that if she'd only done everything Belinda's way, Lola would still be wagging her little tail right now.

Chapter Three

Beth was rather pink as she toiled up the road towards the gates of Wyatt's, which gleamed even on this dull and wintry day. The porter in his little glass sentry box smiled as Beth waved on her way past, almost jogging now as she heard the big clock on the tower looming over the lawn begin to strike the hour. Eleven o'clock! How had that happened? Now she felt all the more like Cinderella, rushing for her carriage. Though she had at least beaten Cinders to it. It wasn't twelve yet.

Beth was smiling at the thought as she finally puffed up to her office, in the Geography building. She'd just got the mortice lock undone, slung her bag onto her desk, shrugged out of her coat and flipped open her laptop, when there was a knock at the door. She took a harried glance around. Did it look as though she'd been here for hours? All the shelves were meticulously neat and tidy, her little conference table in the corner was ready and waiting, should the unlikely event of an archives meeting ever occur. True, her in-tray was bulging and there was a lot of filing building up in the corner of the room, but that just made her look busy and important, surely?

She quickly scattered the contents of one of the in-tray folders across her bare desk and picked up a sheet of A4 to gaze at studiously. 'Come in,' she called, her voice coming out in such an anxious squeak that she had to cough and repeat herself immediately. Her next 'come in' was ridiculously deep.

The door swung open heavily. Tom Seasons stood there, his bulk filling the doorway. An ex-rugby player, now a coach and the Bursar of Wyatt's, he was solid, beefy – and not Beth's biggest fan, since Beth's first investigation had revealed that his wife, Judith, had been having an affair with a murder victim.

'Ah, you're here,' he said, in tones of surprise.

Beth didn't rise to the implied jibe, merely swallowing once, giving her sheet of A4 – which turned out to be a stationery requisition form – a final, very intense appraisal, and then breaking off with what she hoped was a courteous, yet busy, 'And what can I do for you, Bursar?'

Luckily, her timetable was nothing to do with Seasons at all. Janice Grover was her line manager. Janice – the former school secretary, now second wife of the Headmaster – was definitely Seasons' kryptonite. He was powerless against her lethal combination of cosy cashmere loveliness, steely intelligence, and boundless influence over the very smitten Dr Grover, whose baby she was about to bring forth.

Seasons looked at Beth for a few beats, his small blue eyes seeming full of malevolence. Beth had heard rumours that Judith had finally left him. But that wasn't strictly her fault. 'Ah. Just checking how you're getting on with it all. The new exhibition?' he barked.

'It's all done, Tom. You've seen the outlines. Well, you should have done, I put them on your desk last week. We're all ready to start, beginning of next term.'

'I thought the exhibition was part of the Christmas concerts? Some disgruntled parents, I've heard rumblings…'

'Really? I'm astonished. We decided, in the end, that it wasn't very, ahem, tasteful to combine the themes of Christmas and slavery, don't you remember?'

'Oh, yes…' said Seasons, tailing off.

Beth could see a sheen of sweat on his forehead. It wasn't by any means hot in her office. What on earth was up with the man?

'Was there something else on your mind? Do you want to sit down?' Beth wasn't fond of him, but he seemed to be suffering. 'Is everything all right?'

Her concern seemed to jolt Seasons out of his trance. He wiped his forehead with a large white handkerchief and visibly pulled himself together. 'Oh, no, it's all good.' He stashed the hanky and started slapping one huge fist into the opposite palm, making a sound like a large, dead cod being thwacked down on a fishmonger's slab. 'Well, must get on. Glad we've had time to catch up,' he said finally, striding over to the door with a semblance of his usual energy, and closing the door as loudly as he'd opened it.

Beth was left staring at the space he'd so recently, and shiftily, occupied. 'Now what was all that about?' she wondered.

There was scarcely time to ponder it, though. For once, Beth really earned her Wyatt's salary as she churned through an in-tray that had been neglected for weeks and now resembled an alpine range. Once that had been whittled down to manageable proportions, she turned to the filing. Every autumn term produced a rich crop of Christmas concert and play programmes, a bit like a harvest festival just for the archives. Previous incumbents in her post had tended to shove this bounty wholesale onto the shelves, where it had mouldered in peace for many years – centuries, even – until Beth got her hands on it. But now there was no hiding place for duplicate copies. They were ruthlessly ferreted out and recycled.

Sometimes, Beth wondered what would happen if there was a huge fire and her shelves went up in flames. True, she could now digitalise everything – but she decided she was saving posterity by not doing this, as well as avoiding a lot of tedious and pointless work herself. Having cleared the decks today, she found she even had time to work on her cherished, long term project, the outline for a book on Thomas Wyatt's involvement in slavery.

In many ways, it was going to be difficult reading. Ever since she'd made the heart-stopping discovery some months ago that the much-lauded founder of the Dulwich Endowment Schools had had blood on his hands, she'd been alternately fascinated and repulsed by the knowledge.

It wasn't clear at what point in the past three hundred years Dulwich had decided that it didn't want to know about

Wyatt's activities. Wyatt himself had made no secret of the basis of his wealth. The ledgers Beth had first unearthed in the unloved and neglected archives she'd inherited from her predecessor had not exactly been hidden, they had just been lost. Whether that was by accident or design, it was impossible to know. All that was certain was that the silt of time had been allowed to pile up on the truth about Thomas Wyatt and, until Beth's discovery, no-one had much cared how he had made his money. He was just the rich founder of the Dulwich schools, and good for him and for all who benefitted from that largesse.

It was, without question, a sensitive issue. After an hour or so, Beth had written the opening paragraph of her proposal about twenty times, and she was more than glad to be interrupted by an imperious text from Janice, summoning her to the staff Christmas lunch. A few short months ago, Beth would have found an occasion like this extremely intimidating, involving as it did all the teachers who could be spared from the pupils' lunches. Now, although she couldn't say she'd chatted to each and every member of the staff, she certainly knew them all by sight. And besides, she had a place saved for her at Janice's right hand, so she had nothing to fear, except that Janice might go into labour before they got on to the crackers.

Glancing sideways at Janice's tummy, which now resembled a beautifully rounded Christmas pudding, she wished she'd picked 25th December in the rather naughty staffroom sweepstake on the birth, instead of a date far off in the New Year. Poor Janice was starting to get that look of occasional blank terror Beth had often seen on expectant mothers' faces, and which had no doubt been on her own, as the horrible truth dawned that two people couldn't continue in one body indefinitely, and there was only one possible exit route.

While Wyatt's sixth formers were notorious for smuggling in booze at the end of term and consuming it on the playing fields, far from the prying eyes of teachers, the teachers themselves got through a jolly, alcohol-free Christmas lunch in high good humour. The only thing that seemed dry was Dr Grover's speech, where he had everyone – luckily, apart from his wife – in stitches. When Tom Seasons stood to follow up, as was apparently the tradition, Beth felt a flutter of alarm. Was he going to be as odd as he'd been in her room earlier? Or would he have pulled himself together?

Thankfully, the Bursar was on autopilot. Beth had never had a Wyatt's Christmas lunch before, but those who had been at the school longer would have recognised his spiel as being well-worn, yet no less effective for all that. A favourite jumper of a talk – maybe not the one with the spectacular novelty light-up Christmas tree, but good and reliable and cosy all the same, like one of those Scandinavian snowflake knits, and a perfect note to end the term on.

Beth was sad when the last of the plates was collected along with the debris of paper hats and rubbishy jokes. The next time she had turkey, it would be one that she had reluctantly cooked herself at home or, more probably, had accidentally incinerated. She'd be pulling off a miracle if the only thing dry that day was the speeches.

Her cuisine, never particularly elevated, felt even more slipshod at Christmas when there were more than two people to cook for and the audience was slightly more demanding than a ten-year-old boy. Not that they ever really had anyone other than her mother, her brother, Josh, and his girlfriend of the moment, always such a fleeting presence in their lives that it scarcely mattered whether Beth impressed her or not. But still. For her, that was high pressure.

This year, though, there was also the rather tingly possibility that Harry might be joining them. This could be wonderful, or it could be the element that made her sprouts go extra soggy.

As they all filed out of the dining room, meeting up with the impossibly over-excited lower school children on the way, Beth wondered whether she'd take the plunge and ask Harry or not. She didn't even know what he usually did for Christmas. Maybe he was already expected at his parents' house. Maybe – gulp – he'd ask her and Ben to visit them at some point over Christmas? Or was all this just way too much, too soon? Did she need the stress of involving parents and siblings at such an early stage in their relationship? That's if it was a relationship at all?

Beth realised she'd better stop thinking about this as quickly as possible, or she'd be talking herself out of even having a boyfriend at all. Sometimes dreams were like water – the more you tried to grab hold of them, the more they trickled away. And she was enjoying there being *something* between her and the detective. He might drive her mad on a regular basis, but he also made her laugh. And sometimes he even made a half-decent cup of tea.

Beth rather pitied the teachers as they peeled off to take their ridiculously bouncy charges back for the last few desultory lessons of term. Though many of them would be taking refuge in that time-honoured teachers' get-out, the educational video, there would definitely be questions asked by the parents paying hand over fist for a jot of teaching, if all the kids came home having watched *The Polar Express* for the billionth time.

Back in the peace and quiet of her office, Beth glanced round fondly at the packed and ordered shelves, standing dust-free and purposeful, perpetually ready for the moment when Dr Grover would demand an urgent run-down on exactly what had happened at the Governors' meeting in 1923. Her in-tray had been vanquished, however briefly, and her to-do list was mercifully short: just come up with a proposal for the book and get it green-lighted by all the powers-that-be at the school. Peasy. She was just shutting down her laptop for the last time that year when there was a tentative knock on the door.

It was Janice, advancing bump-first and swaying like a heavily-laden camel train as she came into the room. Beth found herself wondering whether her friend was actually having twins. But surely they'd all know by now? Janice had been coy about the sex of the baby, but would almost certainly have said if it was two not one, wouldn't she? Especially as it would have been so wonderfully appropriate, for someone so into knitwear, to be producing a twinset.

Janice lowered herself slowly into a chair with a deep sigh, while they both ignored the protesting creak from its legs.

'Everything ok, Janice?' Beth asked. To her horror, Janice's pretty face crumpled, and she gave a loud sniff.

'No! It's not okay. Not at all. I'm fed up with being this siiize. I'm like a whaaaale,' said Janice, wailing all too appropriately. Beth grabbed her handbag and started searching for a tissue, but Janice already had one in her hand, and blew her nose noisily.

'Look, don't worry, I've been exactly where you are, and it's only temporary,' Beth said, coming round the desk and putting an awkward arm around Janice's shoulders. It was hard to hug someone when they were sitting down and you were standing up, but getting Janice out of the chair again was going to take some time, and a face-to-face hug was going to be very badly impeded by the bump. This was probably the best they were going to achieve. Beth carried on patting ineffectually while Janice gradually got her sobs under control.

'Once the baby's born, you'll feel brilliant,' said Beth, mentally crossing her fingers, and trying not to remember the weeks she'd spent staggering about in her dressing gown, sleepless, sore, and utterly shattered by the demands of a screeching infant. Maybe all that would be completely different for Janice.

'What if I'm a terrible muuuum?'

'Look, you won't be, Janice. You'll be a fantastic mum. This baby is really lucky to have you as a mother. It's going to be clever, and beautiful, and funny and capable, just like you and, erm, Dr Grover.' Beth had never quite got onto first name terms with the Headmaster. He was such an impressive man that she always felt she had just said, was saying, or was about to say, something incredibly stupid when she was in his presence.

'What if he doesn't like the baby? He never wanted children before, then this just, well, happened,' said Janice, mumbling damply into Beth's shoulder.

Beth thought rapidly. This explained the mystery, much discussed amongst the Dulwich mummies, of why Dr Grover had been childless in his long marriage to the quite successful actress whom Janice had supplanted in a bloodless coup. 'Well, whenever I've seen him, he's looked really thrilled and proud,' said Beth reassuringly. It was true, but was he looking at the bump, or at the wonderful Janice? That bit was hard to tell.

'Look, Janice, no-one is saying this part, or even the next little bit, is easy. But when the baby's here, you're going to love it so much that you'll forget all the heartburn and morning sickness…'

'And piles, and thrush, and stretch marks…'

'*Exactly*,' said Beth swiftly. Even she didn't want to think about all that, and for her it had been over long ago. 'And you'll just be a really happy family, all together at last.'

'Do you really think so?' said Janice tremulously, raising wet eyes to Beth's face at last.

'I absolutely know so,' said Beth. 'It'll be wonderful, you'll see.'

'I wanted to ask you, Beth, well, that's why I came in here, though I seem to have got side-tracked… Will you be a godmother to the baby?'

'Oh!' It was the last thing Beth had expected. But it was rather lovely. She was always wary of taking on emotional commitments, she seemed to have so little compassion to spare these days, after Ben's needs and her own were met, but she did love Janice and she was sure the baby would take only seconds to snuggle its way into her heart. 'I'd love that. Thank you, what an honour.'

'Then at least one of us will know what we're doing,' said Janice confidently. Beth, thinking of her own regular crises on parenting, and much else besides, decided this was definitely the moment to keep her mouth shut.

Chapter Four

It was day three of the Christmas holidays, and already Beth was counting the hours until the New Year. There was no escape from it – Christmas tunes playing in every shop they went into; decorations on everything except Magpie the cat; and endless adverts for gadgets costing hundreds of pounds that Ben vacuumed up every time the telly was on. She yearned to give him everything he wanted for Christmas, of course, but she could see that somebody was doomed to disappointment. Either it would be the bank, waiting in vain for its mortgage payment while she spent the money on ways to kill aliens on a screen, or it would be Ben, finding once again that Father Christmas didn't have very deep pockets in his beautiful red velvet coat.

And Ben was getting restless, too. Without Charlie to play all his games with, one of the consoles lay forlorn on the sofa, like a keepsake from a long-lost love. Beth occasionally tried to join in just to jolly him along, but she was so useless that Ben usually spent a few minutes laughing helplessly at her efforts, then she got annihilated and he had to carry on without her. So really, she needn't have bothered. After a morning spent in this less than satisfactory fashion, Beth decided there was nothing else for it. There were definitely times when children, like the worst manifestations of illness, were better out than in.

They were lucky they lived so near central London. If they walked down to Herne Hill station, they could be in Victoria in eight minutes, then it was a short tube ride to the museums at South Ken. She bundled a mildly protesting Ben into his coat, grabbed her own, and they were off.

Out of the door, they headed away from the Village for

once, and nipped down the wide cut-through road that connected up with Half Moon Lane. The houses here were banked up on a slight hill, and hidden behind high fences and long drives, as though watching passers-by from a well-defended vantage point. Already the place had a slightly different feel to it. It was much quieter than the main drag past Katie's yoga studio, Jane's café, and the other shops, which could be two solid lanes of traffic in either direction at the daily school run pinch points.

They were wandering past the dance school, closed now, but Beth sometimes saw clumps of tiny girls here, dressed in sugar plum fairy pastel shades, clobbering each other with ballet bags decorated with unicorns and cupcakes. Not for the first time, she wondered how different life would have been if Ben had been a Benjamina. Would she have enjoyed that rose-coloured world, or would she have drowned in all the saccharine trappings that seemed to go with girlhood these days? There was no compulsion to dress your daughter as a minor member of a Ruritanian royal family, she could have held out against princessification, but would she have done? The desire to cosset and protect girls seemed a natural one, and reliving her own fascination with fairy stories would have been hard to resist.

Mind you, she realised suddenly, she could still have more children.

This was quite a seismic thought. For years, she'd thought a lot of things were behind her forever. Love, certainly. More children, therefore, definitely. But if she wasn't now ruling out the first, then should she necessarily veto the second? She blinked a few times and tried to focus on Janice, sobbing in her office, an enormous cashmere mound pinning her to the office chair. It worked. The moment passed. The sudden baby hunger died away, as quickly as it had surfaced. But inwardly, Beth was a bit shocked. Apparently, all it had taken to set her off was the idea of a tiny pink tutu. She shook her head and looked around for Ben. He was marching on ahead.

'Come on, Mum, you're so slow,' he sang out over his shoulder.

'Cheeky,' she said, catching him up and grabbing his hand. He let her swing it back and forward once, then shook free and sprinted on up the road. It was partly his natural bounce. He did everything at twice the speed of an adult. And there was also the chance that one of his friends from school might be out and about, too. It definitely would not be cool to be seen holding hands with his mum.

Beth knew this was important, but she did pine for the days when his hot little hand had felt for hers, unbidden. Now his hands, larger already, were cool and elusive. They'd soon be bigger than her little paws, and he'd tower over her. Well, with any luck. James had been, not a giant, but at least not a titch like her. There was a good chance Ben would get to pretty nearly six foot, but she'd still be able to see him looming above her, on a clear day, if she used a telescope. She smiled to herself.

They'd now trotted down the least rewarding part of Half Moon Lane, lined on both sides with solid suburban houses, all worth a fortune these days, but not as fun as the shops. These were collected at the bottom of the hill, like the heavier, more elaborate beads on a necklace. Because of their position, they had suffered horribly in the flood of 2013, when a Thames Water main pipe burst and left everything three feet deep in water. Compensation claims had dragged on, but the spirit of the area remained buoyant despite the soggy circumstances, and most places had reopened. There was now even a thriving weekend market, with open air food and craft stalls doing a roaring trade.

As they reached the shops, Beth suddenly thought of Nina and looked around more carefully. Where was the blank façade that hid her firm of solicitors? Aha, that must be it, she decided, as she spotted an expanse of frosted glass, discreetly etched with a small sign reading Potter & Co, Solicitors. Next door was the off-licence, as Nina had said. Beth had sometimes bought a bottle of wine there for one of Belinda MacKenzie's dreadful dinners, knowing full well the woman had an encyclopaedic knowledge of all the nearby supermarkets' offerings and would turn her nose right up at

Beth's usual tipple, which was anything that cost under £5 a bottle.

'Ben? *Ben,*' Beth shouted at her son, who had run on ahead and was hanging onto the lamppost at the crossing, idly swinging himself backwards and forwards like a junior Gene Kelly. 'We're just popping in here for two minutes,' she said urgently, gesturing at him to come back.

Retracing his steps, at his mother's command, was always something that took Ben at least four times as long as the original journey. But as soon as he'd caught her up, Beth strode to the frosted door and turned the handle, sidling into a surprisingly spacious empty lobby, carpeted in thick beige seagrass matting, and with a frosted glass counter dead ahead. There were two sturdy, darker beige chairs in a little waiting area, with a spread of pamphlets on a glass coffee table between them. Beth scanned the depressing titles *Making a Will* and *Mediation in Divorce*, featuring photos of generic-looking models with mildly perplexed expressions. She moved to the counter, just as a door in the shadows beyond it opened.

A very, very, big, powerfully-built, middle-aged man in a suit dashed forward with the same sort of energy she could imagine might emanate from Ben, when he eventually reached his forties. He was as solid as Tom Seasons, but much taller. His face was deeply tanned, like the supple dark leather of an expensive handbag. Actually, it was a bit like Belinda MacKenzie's current favourite, Beth realised, with a tiny smirk.

His expression was welcoming but fairly neutral, though Beth could see small white lines radiating out around his eyes, like cat's whiskers, where the sun hadn't reached. She supposed she might well be here to enlist his help on a horrible divorce, and it certainly wouldn't do to be grinning like the Cheshire cat if she had a tale of woe to impart.

As far as his mahogany tan went, Beth would have diagnosed a recent skiing break, but didn't people usually wear goggles on the slopes? Maybe he'd just been to the Caribbean? Somewhere hot at any rate, and that meant spending plenty of money at this time of year. Beth didn't go on many holidays herself, but she certainly recognised the signs of a recent luxury break, on display year-round in these parts.

He put his hands down on the counter and Beth heard a clunk as his expensive gold watch connected with the surface. He was wearing a tie in a vivid turquoise and blue key pattern, the only man Beth had seen with one in an age, apart from the Wyatt's headmaster. And Dr Grover wore them as a semi-ironic flourish. 'Can I help you?' Mr Mahogany said. Even his voice sounded expensive, prep school, public school, top-flight university and years of pricey legal training oozing from every syllable.

'I was just looking for Nina,' said Beth.

Immediately, the wattage of the smile in front of her dimmed even further. 'She's not here today, you can catch her at home or probably tomorrow,' he said briskly, with no offer to take a message or pass anything on.

Beth, feeling put in her place, said thank you, though for what she wasn't quite sure, and rounded Ben up. In a few moments, they were out on the cold pavement again.

'What was that about? Why did you want to see Wilf's mum?' said Ben in a rare moment of curiosity. He'd inherited a lot from her, but his blithe lack of interest in the mundane came straight from his father.

Beth wasn't sure she could really have given him an answer, even if she'd tried. 'Oh, it's not important,' she said. 'Quick, let's get to the station before we miss our train.'

Inside the office, Paul Potter stared at the door Beth had just walked through, without seeing it or anything else. Now there was no-one around to observe him, his face had fallen, sagged even. The smile lines seemed a ghastly irony around eyes that looked lost and helpless. Below them dangled pouches large enough to contain any amount of excess baggage.

Had he had anything real to smile about for years? But no, that was harsh. He loved the kids, he loved Letty. It was just... so difficult. She wanted so much: to live in a certain way; to bring the kids up right. He couldn't argue with any of it – he'd been through it himself at their age, the piano lessons, the tutoring. He hadn't loved it, and much of it had been a stupid waste of money – he couldn't so much as play Chopsticks now. But wasn't it a parent's duty, as Letty was always saying? To discover and develop their kids' talents? Even if it looked as though they didn't actually have any? No, that was unfair.

They were good kids, certainly beautiful to look at, with their pale skins and blonde hair, just like their mother. But they were... ordinary. Bright enough, reasonably sporty, healthy for sure. Just not exceptional. Yet. It was the 'yet' part that Letty stuck to like glue. For such an ethereal woman, she had surprising tenacity, he had to admit.

When he'd first met her, he'd been bowled over by her fragility, her gentleness. She was like a beautiful long-stemmed bloom, she needed careful handling, the utmost attention. He'd have to spend a lifetime protecting her, he'd decided, and he'd been happy with that. He'd dedicated himself, his whole life, to keeping her safe, loving her. He'd felt almost like a medieval knight on a quest, and she was his fair lady. He had never once told her this, in case she laughed at him, which made the quest all the more sacred in a way.

Time hadn't altered the way he felt about her, but over the years he had realised that in some ways she was the strong one. She had survived childbirth, which he'd feared would kill her, and she fought like a tigress when her children were threatened. She was a wonderful mother, home-maker, wife. He was a very lucky man. But... but. It did all come at a price.

That was the problem, the circle that couldn't be squared. Money. Maybe if she'd gone back to work or would even contemplate it now... but he knew how dedicated she was to bringing up the children the right way. It was something they both believed in, had discussed, right from the start. Latch-key kids, the strain of both parents being busy, dealing with the pressures of careers – they saw it among their friends' families (or heard about it happening somewhere near) and they agreed it wasn't pretty. Truancy, drugs – it didn't bear contemplating. Though he privately thought half her fears were a little absurd. After all, despite recent events, that sort of thing didn't really happen in Dulwich, did it? Not to people like them.

The girls involved in that incident at the College School, well… he didn't want to cast aspersions, but maybe their parents hadn't been quite as vigilant as he knew Letty was. He couldn't fault her on that. Or on anything, for that matter. And if she knew the real situation, he was sure she'd reign things in… but he couldn't tell her. Could he?

In all these years, he'd been the dependable one, the one who'd held the centre when she had one of her meltdowns – all perfectly justified, he was sure. Bringing up children was a stressful business. Even tiny suggestions – Sainsbury's not Waitrose; Clarks not Lelli Kelly – were met with tears, incomprehension, and accusations of mental cruelty. It was so tiring, so distressing – for him. It was easier to play along; it always had been. And he couldn't turn on her now, could he, when she was always so vulnerable? He had so much to lose. More with every passing year.

This was no good. His thoughts were becoming gloomier and gloomier. He recognised the pattern, needed to break it. Rapidly, he wiped a hand across his face and seemed to gather himself and remember where he was. He took a paper out of his pocket and read it through again. And again. As though he could scarcely believe what he was reading, though he'd read it so many times now. He shook his head, rubbed his hand over his eyes again. Was there moisture gathering there?

But if he'd learnt anything at all those fancy schools of his, it was that big boys don't cry. He took a breath, squared his shoulders, and stuffed the paper back in his pocket. As his fingers touched the cool silk lining, he shook his head. A fallback option, safety net, whatever you wanted to call it. Coward's way out, maybe.

He shivered. Not yet. No, there was still a chance. So

much to play for. He squared his shoulders. Yes, they – and he – bore a heavy burden, but that was the price you paid for love, wasn't it? Was it worth it? He couldn't even ask himself that question. He was gambling everything on the fact that it was.

Chapter Five

It wasn't long before Beth and Ben were tramping the dank underground tunnel which connected South Ken tube station with the museums. They passed the entrance for the V&A, and Beth had another pang. She was being really silly, she knew, but she couldn't help thinking that if she'd had a girl, they could have looked at costumes and jewellery all day.

Beth stopped herself. That was terrible pigeonholing. Ben would probably be quite happy there, she was sure. To him, museums were mostly about lots of space, not the small print on the display cases. But as she looked at him, running on ahead as usual, doing aeroplane arms and swerving from one side of the tunnel to the other between knots of bemused tourists, she decided today wasn't the day to try it. They'd stick with the tried and trusted dinosaurs at the Natural History Museum.

There was nothing like a Tyrannosaurus Rex to inspire awe in both boy and diminutive mother, she decided later as she craned her neck to look at the display. How many seconds would she have lasted, back then, if people had been around at the time of the dinosaurs, when she only came up to this T-Rex's toenails? At least the beast wouldn't have been able to spot her, with his tiny eyes so many metres above her. She would have spent her entire life hiding under leaves and waiting for the baddies to go away.

She smiled. Sometimes life in Dulwich still felt like that. Things were getting better and she was growing in confidence all the time, but there had been moments, at the school gates, when a handy bit of foliage would have felt like quite a refuge. Why was it that standing up to Belinda MacKenzie and her ilk always seemed so much harder than venturing into dark alleyways in search of murderers? Oh well, at least Ben would never suffer her crippling nerves. There he was, right now, making friends with another boy who was similarly transfixed by the dinosaurs.

Beth smiled tentatively at the boy's mother and got a slightly worried glance back. Judging from the woman's pristine Burberry and the small mountain of luggage parked by the information board, they were tourists who'd stopped in at the museum en route for other parts.

Beth gazed round at the hall, with its high ceilings and intricate brickwork. She did love the Victorians for building these great palaces to knowledge. For her, this part of Kensington was just chunk after chunk of wonder, places stuffed with treasures to delight, entertain, and educate. Of course, half the time it hadn't quite been theirs to take, which reminded Beth of Thomas Wyatt's cavalier ways. The chutzpah needed to amass this stuff seemed to be allied to huge insensitivity over where it came from and who rightfully owned it.

Walking back up Half Moon Lane later, the slight incline was transformed into a mighty hill for both of them by the exhaustion of a full day out and about. They were just plodding past the off licence, hampered by a brisk wind blowing down from the direction of the Village, when the frosted door of the solicitors opened, and Nina straggled out, festooned once again with carrier bags. Did she take them everywhere? Beth wondered. Mr Mahogany Tan didn't look like the sort of employer who'd turn a blind eye to shopping cluttering his pristine waiting room.

'Blimey, it's you! Ben's mum with the secret lover,' said Nina loudly.

Ben, for once, looked up from the game he was playing, jumping from paving stone to paving stone without touching the cracks, and gave his mother a suspicious glance before leaping onwards.

'Oops! Sorry,' said Nina in a now-redundant stage whisper. 'I forgot he's at the listening age. I could tell the world I was shagging the whole cast of *Hollyoaks* and Wilf wouldn't bet an eye.'

'That's the difference between six and ten,' said Beth a little sharply.

'Don't get the hump, hon. It's not like he isn't going to find out sometime, is it?' Nina said simply.

It was a good point. In fact, Ben already knew something was going on between his mother and the big policeman. It was just that no-one had quite spelled it out. Until now. Beth sighed inwardly. She'd probably better have a little chat with Ben tonight. Though, come to think of it, she hadn't heard from Harry today. Maybe she didn't need to stir things up, if there was nothing much to tell?

But then she realised that it was she who owed Harry a call, or several, as they hadn't spoken since Nina had gone off with her phone. He was probably feeling quite shirty and neglected.

In her years of widowhood, she'd forgotten how tiring a relationship can be when it's in play. Who calls whom, who makes all the arrangements, who puts themselves out more? All these little signs seemed to be ways of jockeying for power, determining who had the upper hand. The person who loved the most was vulnerable; a hermit crab minus its shell. It was a feeling she didn't like at all. But that had to be balanced against the good things, of which there were so many.

She'd shouldered all the responsibility for Ben for so long, with only the nominal help of her mother and brother, who really were additional passengers on the weary boat she'd been paddling upstream. She envied her mother's Teflon-coated ability to avoid distractions and her brother's rootless drifting, and she hoped Ben would inherit some of their cunning propensity to live life on their own terms. But it wasn't her own way. Having shared her life so successfully and joyfully with James, she realised that all these lonely years she had just been searching for the same again, please. Like a regular in a favourite pub.

She wasn't sure, yet, whether that was what she'd found. But just having someone to discuss Ben's foibles and funny ways with was such a relief. Plus, there was all that fantastic sex, too.

Just thinking about it brought a rosy flush to her cheeks, and Nina gave her a knowing look and nudged her with her elbow, inadvertently whacking her shin in the process with a bag full of hard, lumpy boxes of stuff which, from what Beth could see, were largely composed of breadcrumbs and batter. Delicious, she thought with a pang of hunger.

'Seeing him tonight, are you? Can't wait, by the looks of you.'

Normally Beth would have found this ribaldry hard to take, but as it was, she laughed a little reluctantly. There was a lot in what Nina said.

'Listen, hon, why don't you come back to ours for tea? I've got to pick Wilf up from the childminder's in Red Post Hill on the way, won't take a minute. It'll save us both cooking. Leave you a bit more energy for later, eh?' Nina snorted.

Beth gave her a sidelong glance and then smiled a yes. She'd never willingly turn down someone else's offer to cook, and she was curious about Nina. There was something irresistible about her approach to life, that was for sure.

They chatted away as they passed the newsagent's and fish and chip shop, then the white post-and-chain fences of houses that swelled in size and importance as they approached the SE21 postcode. At the top, they turned left at North Dulwich Station, and Beth felt the first flicker of alarm. She only knew one person who lived over this way. Surely, it couldn't be?

But, inexorably, Nina came to a halt outside a house with a steep flight of steps in front and, sensing Beth's hesitation, looked questioningly at her. 'What's up?'

'It's just that I know someone who lives here. If it's still the same lady…'

'You know my childminder? It's a small world, innit?' chuckled Nina, unfazed.

And why should she even have an inkling of Beth's distress? The events that had brought Beth to this house had been done and dusted, thank heavens, for months now. That didn't mean that she was any keener to reopen old wounds. Just seeing her face was bound to be upsetting, and she hated to be the cause of pain. But it was too late now. Nina had shed her bags at the bottom of the flight and had nipped up, surprisingly fleet of foot when not impeded by what looked like a week's shopping, and the door swung open more or less straight away. Beth stood at the bottom of the steps, staring wordlessly upwards.

Jo Osborne, a smile of welcome dying on her lips like a spring bud blasted by frost, didn't quite take a step back in horror, but she did falter the moment she looked past Nina, down to the small figure on the street.

'Hi, Jo, how are you doing?' said Beth nervously.

'It's you, Beth.'

To Beth's huge relief, Jo's face cleared. She'd been placed, and not blamed. 'Come up, come up,' she said, gesturing to both Beth and Ben, who'd been watching the antics of the grown-ups from a safe distance. It wasn't the enthusiasm of someone greeting a long-lost friend, that was for sure, but neither was it the repulsion or anger that Beth realised would have been more than understandable.

As Beth climbed the steps, toting the discarded shopping bags, Jo turned to Nina, whose eyebrows were now raised into perfect arches. 'Beth was the one who found my Simone, my daughter. How've you been, Beth?'

In the streetlight, Beth saw the sudden shine of Jo's eyes.

'Fine, fine,' said Beth, guilty that her life had taken an upward turn while Jo must have struggled to put one foot in front of the other. 'I'm sorry if seeing me brings it all back.'

'Don't be silly. Never goes away, does it? But I'm keeping on, as you see. Childminding now, so I get more time at home with him,' she said, gesturing behind her to where her young son peeped out from the kitchen, with Nina's Wilf.

'Orlright there, Wilfy? Let's get going then, hon. Get home for our tea,' said Nina, and Wilf bounded towards them.

On an impulse, Beth reached over and hugged Jo, the

woman's tense frame melting a little just as they broke off the contact. 'See you soon,' she said, though in truth she'd be lying if she pretended she'd seek her out. Even if Jo could never forget, it must make it harder for her to see someone who'd been through those hours and days with her. Beth remembered the time she'd spent sitting in the hospital, holding Simone Osborne's hand, and hoping against hope that the girl's eyelids would flutter and she'd come back to life. Sometimes dreams did not come true.

'You ok?' said Nina, looking at Beth shrewdly as they walked on.

Beth, now swinging one of the well-stuffed shopping bags, while Nina had the other, just nodded. She didn't want to have to go through the whole story with Nina. It didn't feel fair. If Jo wanted to tell her, she'd have ample opportunity when she saw Nina at drop-off and pick-up times.

Wilf, liberated from the small flat where he'd spent a happy but contained few hours, now bounded around in a style which left even Ben looking sedate. Beth suppressed a small smile. She was so used to Ben having enough energy to supply the National Grid. But, she supposed, the time would soon be coming when she'd have to pitchfork him out of bed in the mornings, instead of the current situation, when she'd stagger downstairs only to find that he was already soaking up illicit hours on his PlayStation. But no matter how early he was up, they were still never ready to leave for school on time.

Once they'd left Jo's, it was only a five-minute walk to Nina's place – a maisonette with a balcony that seemed to be as bursting with good things as Nina's habitual shopping bags. Though they'd only been there a matter of months, Nina had made the place very homely, with wide, pale, squashy sofas and the biggest telly that Beth had ever seen. It took up almost a whole wall of the sitting room, standing on spindly legs that seemed hardly strong enough to support such a weight. There were toys everywhere, and a large shaggy rug in the middle of the room, with a ginger cat sitting dead centre who was almost as big as Nina, let alone

Wilf.

'What's his name?' said Beth, meeting the unblinking amber stare of the cat, who seemed to swivel his head to watch her as she followed Nina into the tiny kitchen.

'Oh, that's Tom. Not very original but I wore myself out thinking of Wilf,' said Nina. She flipped the switch on the kettle and rooted around in the sink for mugs, which she rinsed quickly and gave a perfunctory swipe with a tea towel dangling from the draining board.

Beth, who knew she was far too much of a stickler in these matters, willed herself to rise above minding, but when the cup of tea was passed to her, she was relieved to see it was as clean and dry as though it had been given a much more thorough going-over. Nina might seem slapdash, but she was surprisingly efficient.

Beth took a cautious sip. Ouch. She set the cup down on the little table, just the right size for Nina and Wilf but which was going to be a squeeze for the four of them. 'Shall I give you a hand with the cooking? Help put stuff away?'

She watched as Nina stowed the shopping in a way that looked haphazard to her, but which no doubt involved a method too obscure for her to detect.

'Nah, you're all right. You just sit there. I'll just shove this lot in the oven.' Nina took a large red plastic pouch out of the freezer, ripped the corner off with her teeth, and shook a sunny yellow cascade of oven chips onto a baking tray. Next, a box was hacked apart with the bread knife, and four dark oblongs, like old-fashioned brown paper parcels, thudded onto the tray. Nina poked everything around with a finger until it was arranged to her total satisfaction, then slammed the oven door. She turned to Beth, every bit as smug as Nigella Lawson after knocking up passionfruit soufflé.

'Hey presto, we're done. Now, tell me all about life here. Why's that Belinda MacKenzie got such a massive stick up her arse, for example?'

Beth nearly choked on her tea, which had now reached the perfect temperature. Not for the first time, she wondered why tea couldn't be made at this point; why one had to wait so long for it to reach this ideal state, which was perilously easy to miss if you weren't concentrating. But maybe that was the joy of tea drinking – there was a skill to it.

'Belinda, well, what can I say? I'm not sure anyone can do her justice. Or understand what drives her. Really, she should be running a small country, not harassing her family and the rest of Dulwich.'

Nina laughed. 'Why doesn't she just go back to work, then? Give everyone a break?'

'She's always trying to prove something, being the best mum, the best hostess, whatever. There can only be one winner; she has to make sure it's her and no-one else. Maybe she's scared to go back to work?'

'Scared? Scary, yes, for sure, but I can't see her being frightened of anything.'

'Well, she's been out of the workplace for years. Her eldest is thirteen. Things must have really moved on. The people she was working with when she first went on maternity leave must all be the big bosses now, so she would lose a lot of status if she went back. No-one would take her on at the level she should be at after such a long break, so she'd be right back where she started, and I don't suppose it would suit her to be rushing around getting other people cups of tea.'

'Ha! I'd pay good money to see that. And I bet that poor bleedin' waiter from the other day would as well,' said Nina, passing Beth a fistful of cutlery and plonking glasses down on the little table. 'I bet it wouldn't take her long to claw her way up again.'

'Well, that's true.' Beth started arranging knives and forks, making the conjunctions tighter and tighter until they all fit in. 'But maybe she's too chicken to try. I know I was actually terrified when I started my job. I'd been working from home for years, but that's different, somehow. You're less exposed. When you're in an office, you sort of feel you're being judged. Or maybe that's just me?'

Nina snorted. 'You need to grow a thicker skin, babe. And you'll be having me feeling sorry for Belinda in a minute.

Not sure I've got that much love to go round.' She darted a fond glance at Wilf, who was now showing Ben his extensive collection of knights, in shining armour, on horseback, waving lances and shields and, in one case, duelling with quite a large plastic dragon.

Ben, though officially way too grown-up to show even a modicum of interest in such things, was actually having a whale of a time, playing with physical objects in a way he hadn't for ages, Beth realised with a shock. So much of his life was online, he scarcely handled a toy these days.

'Didn't you feel out of practice when you went back?' she asked Nina. 'Not at all? I mean, it's great to be with our kids, but I did feel that I couldn't talk about anything except computer games and who said what to whom at break time…'

'I know what you mean, but in my case, it's not like I had a choice, did I? It was either get back out there or starve. And talking of starving…' Nina shot up and opened the oven door. Thick black smoke billowed out, but Nina waved it away. 'Don't worry about that, it's from ages ago, cake mix spilt. I just haven't got round to cleaning it up. Well, to be honest, I'm not going to. I think it'll get burned off in time; they're self-cleaning, ovens, aren't they?'

Beth looked sceptical. True, she didn't spend a lot of time with her head in her own oven, that would be much too Silvia Plath for her taste. Usually it would tell you in the instruction manual whether there was one of those clever self-clean linings or not. But in a rented place, would you even get instructions? She couldn't blame Nina. And there was probably a grain of truth in her theory. After all, once the cake had been thoroughly carbonised, it would just be ash, wouldn't it, and would stop burning? By the looks of things, though, they were some way off that stage. She got up. 'I'll just open a window, shall I?'

Nina, who was busily engaged in wafting a tea towel up and down in the vicinity of the oven, like the sail on a storm-tossed frigate, shook her head. 'Nah, sit down, babe, it'll be gone soon, don't worry.'

Wilf seemed unconcerned and Ben, having glanced up once and looked over to her for reassurance, was happy enough to go back to his dragon, though she noticed he'd pulled his T-shirt up over his nose.

'I 'spect you're fretting about vegetables, but don't worry, I'm doing beans,' Nina smiled over.

Beth, who hated to admit that this had indeed been on her mind, tried to look airily unconcerned. 'Oh, I knew you'd be doing something…'

With a flourish, Nina opened a cupboard, got down a can and yanked the ring-pull back, dumped the contents in a bowl, and shoved it in the microwave. Beth smiled and tried to pretend that she had not been thinking of green, runner, or even broad beans. She also tried to imagine what Katie would say.

Was it going to make any difference, in the long term, that Charlie was brought up largely on carefully sourced, free range organic greens, while Wilf's food, judging by today's plate, was always fried as deep and crisp and even as St Wenceslas's snow? There was one obvious difference. Wilf attacked his meal with gusto, while Charlie was often to be seen listlessly pushing mountains of fearfully expensive kale from one side of his plate to the other.

For a second, Beth thought of them as a brontosaurus, chewing slowly and thoughtfully, versus a tyrannosaur, ripping his cod limb from limb, the ketchup on his plate as bright as any small creature's blood.

Ben, meanwhile, was in total heaven. 'Can we have this at home, Mum?' he asked, chewing blissfully.

Beth, who'd been tucking in just as enthusiastically, nodded, her mouth full of delectable batter, and he smiled happily. Who knew fish technology had moved on so far? Though they ate fish fingers by the truckload, Beth hadn't tried anything that more nearly resembled an actual ocean-going shape. That was because she remembered slabs of frozen fish as horrible, dry, grey things, lurking in the nastier bits of her childhood. Now it was even better than the stuff you got from the fish and chip shop.

Pudding was a choc ice each for the kids, which they ate on the sofa while Wilf took over the monstrous remote – almost as big as the wall of telly itself – and fired up the machine. They were soon splayed in front of a restless parade of cartoons. Again, at home Ben would have turned his nose up at such juvenile pursuits, but here he showed every sign of loving his temporary regression and catching up with old favourites.

Nina, unlike Beth herself, had a dishwasher, and it didn't take a moment to stack everything and sling the food boxes away – ta-dah, a clean kitchen. With another strong cup of tea in hand, they retired to the table where Nina thoughtfully stirred sugar into hers.

Seeing her plump paw of a hand, bare of nail varnish and rings, jogged something in Beth's memory.

'Oh, nearly forgot to say. I saw your boss today.'

Nina stopped stirring. 'Really? Where?'

'Your office. I just stopped by in case you were there. Wanted to get the lie of the land, after what you said, you know.' Beth looked over at the boys, but both seemed absorbed by the flickering images on the screen.

'Oh, and you met him? Paul Potter? I was out today, mostly. Wanted me to "work from home", didn't he?' Nina gave the phrase heavy air inverted commas. 'Suspicious in itself, that.'

'Why? Loads of people do that for a couple of days a week.' Beth thought guiltily of the hours she herself had clocked up recently, very much not working, but also very much at home.

'Yeah, fair enough. Just a little problem. See anything missing?'

Beth looked around the small living room again, with its kitchen corner, its comfy seating, and the small table. 'Looks like you've got everything sorted.'

'Yeah but – no laptop? And you've seen my phone. Unless I had a quill pen here and a stack of parchment, not much I could be doing in terms of work.'

Beth laughed. 'But that's crazy! Does he know you don't

have a PC here?'

'I told him at the interview. And he's seen my phone. Telly's the only bit of tech we've got, and I let Wilf talk me into that. Hardly know how to turn it on, myself. But still Potter insists, every now and then, that I bugger off out of the office and "work from home". I reckon it's just an excuse to get me out of the way.'

'And I don't suppose you're going to turn him down, are you?' Beth was thoughtful, then saw Nina give her a sharp glance. 'Oh, I don't mean anything by that. I'd be exactly the same,' she added, thinking Nina didn't know the half of it. Beth might be many things, but a shining example of the Stakhanovite work ethic, she most definitely wasn't.

'So, what did you make of him?'

Beth thought for a moment. She couldn't say exactly why, but she hadn't warmed to Paul Potter. The obvious signs of wealth in the tan, watch, and vowels, were always going to wind up someone like her, who'd been born in easy circumstances, but who had always had to work hard to stay in the middle. There was the on-off charm, which had been abandoned when it was clear that she wasn't a potential client. And then there was just an indefinable sense that something was out of kilter, either about Potter himself or the set-up he presided over. But would she have felt that if she'd just wandered innocently in off the street, or was she being unduly influenced by Nina's suspicions?

'I can't really say why, but I didn't take to him.'

'Nah. He's a tosser.'

Nina was nothing if not succinct, thought Beth, darting a glance over to Ben, but he was as absorbed as ever. On the screen, a five-foot *SpongeBob SquarePants* was doing some sort of dance, his radioactive yellow colouring not a million miles from the chips they had just consumed.

'Are you any further on, working out what seems to be wrong?'

'Nah.' Nina stirred her tea thoughtfully. 'Been thinking about it, and it's got to be some sort of scam. He's just back from a week in Dubai with the missus, and she's quite the shopper. The whole thing must have set him back a fortune. They stayed in some swanky hotel that's in the shape of a pineapple or something, ten billion storeys and gold taps everywhere you look. He left the window open on his computer. Yeah, I don't love the tech, but I can work it when I have to.' Nina raised her eyebrows.

'Well, I suppose everyone's entitled to a holiday,' said Beth.

'Yeah, but where's the money coming from? We're not doing that well. There hasn't been a juicy divorce in Dulwich since Dr Grover got shot of whatsername, that one from *Holby*. Potter handled that. Before my time, but I looked at the file. Even that wasn't hammer and tongs like you'd want. All nicey-nice and wishing each other the best. No wills coming in, neither. We need a really good cold snap, like this but worse, get the oldies dropping off their perches,' said Nina thoughtfully.

Beth, a little taken aback at this gruesome thought, had a brainwave. 'Maybe he was just using savings for the holiday? Or maybe his wife's rich?'

'Savings? I don't think so. We're dodging the bills most days. And Letty? Well, you'd know better than me.'

Beth thought for a moment. She'd only ever seen Letty Potter with Belinda. And the trouble was that Belinda dominated everything. Not just the conversation and the space, but also the view. She was centre-stage, glossy, and beautifully packaged, her face just a little blander and less mobile than you might expect for someone her age. It was hard to focus on her friends. They were Michelles, compared to Belinda's triumphant Beyoncé. But wait a minute, was Letty the Kelly of the group? Someone who, with her silvery hair and wafty clothes, had enough personality to stand out from the also-rans in Dulwich's answer to Destiny's Child? Well, maybe – but not enough for Beth to remember anything salient about her background.

'It's weird but I've no idea about her. I'd ask Katie, but she's away...' said Beth wistfully.

'All I know is, Letty's tougher than she looks,' said Nina.

'What makes you say that?'

'The way she's got Potter running around, doing all this stuff for her. The holidays, cars, house, you know, the full Dulwich monty. Those jumpers with the sleeves miles too long, f'rinstance – it's all from Amanda Wakeley, costs an effing fortune.'

Beth couldn't help laughing. 'Really? I just wondered why she couldn't find the right size. But I suppose it explains why Belinda keeps her so close. She *loves* the money side of things.'

'Yeah, and I think they've got a place in Norfolk, and a chalet in some skiing resort somewhere.'

'I don't know a thing about skiing,' Beth confessed. She'd never tried it, though James had been keen to give it a go, way back when. Although she'd reckoned her low centre of gravity would mean she wouldn't have as far to fall as virtually everyone else she knew, this had not been enough of an inducement. She didn't like being cold, and though she was prone to moments of recklessness, she liked to think she usually had better motivation than simply the desire to scare herself out of her wits by throwing herself down a mountain into the white unknown.

'Me neither. As you can imagine, me bowling down a slope is an invitation to an avalanche,' Nina said dryly.

Beth tried to look supportive, but the image of little round Nina, on skis, hurtling down a black run was, she had to admit, reasonably comical – almost as funny as the Shetland pony on ice that Beth herself would be.

'I suppose a chalet would be quite a draw for Belinda, though,' Beth mused. Belinda, for all her showy ways, did rely on her acolytes for a lot of freebies, which were willingly given in return for a place at the top table. This was despite the fact that her husband, Barty, was an investment banker and, if only one quarter of Belinda's boasting was accurate, he owned all the chunks of the British economy that were still making a profit. A corner of Beth's mind added this nugget to a store of information which sometimes suggested that Belinda, like so many people in their postcode, was not exactly what she appeared.

'Well, maybe she does have family money or something? Everyone seems to, round here,' said Nina.

At this, Beth's cheeks flamed, and she blessed the fringe that swung down heavily and hid her expression. Though she was hardly an heiress, her dad's untimely death, coupled with sensible investment in life assurance while he'd had the chance, meant that there'd been enough for her Pickwick Road house. She didn't feel guilty about it, but she didn't feel entirely comfortable gossiping about other people in similar circumstances, either.

'Anyway, it all seems to be financed by him,' Nina went on. 'And it's a constant drain. I don't know how he does it. And when I say that, it's not an "*oh, I really admire him*" kind of compliment. I mean it's just *not possible* to do it on our income. He must have another business, some really successful investments somewhere, or...'

'Or?'

'He's diddling the firm. Simple as,' said Nina, draining her tea.

'Hm. Finding out about stuff like that's hard, though, isn't it?' Beth was thoughtful. She knew enough to cope with her own tax return once a year and usually remembered to stump up Ben's pocket money, but she was by no means a financial genius. Anyone trying to pull the wool over her eyes in money matters could use egg cosies, not enormous fluffy jumpers and scarves.

'Nah. I've done some book-keeping before. Not in this job – they never wanted that, just reception, filing, all that crap.'

Beth automatically darted a look over at Ben, as she was wont to do when there was swearing. She didn't disapprove of it *per se*, and was prone to let rip a few choice four-letter zingers when heavy objects inexorably sought out her unguarded toes, but she didn't want him picking up too many bad habits. Time enough for all that when he was at big boy school. Ben, though, seemed to be glued to the cartoons, now showing a talking dog effortlessly upstaging its owner.

Nina, noticing Beth's sharp glance, rolled her eyes a little and carried on.

'That's a bit odd in itself, doncha think? If you'd got a qualified book-keeper sitting around, would you send out all your accounts to an outside place, costing more?'

Beth swung back to face Nina. 'That *is* odd. And they know you can do it?'

'S'on my CV, large as life. I'm not going to hide my lights under any bookshops, that's for sure.'

Beth, puzzled for a moment, moved on. 'Who does the finances then?'

'Dunno, really. Just a firm. Everything gets picked up by a courier.'

'Could you find out where it goes to?'

Nina looked doubtful, her normally confident features seeming suddenly vulnerable as she seemed to calculate the possibilities. 'Dunno. I could give it a go. Ring up the company, maybe? Ask a few questions? But I'm no great actress. I'd be worried they'd smell a cat. That's where Wilf gets it from.'

Wilf's star turn as the donkey in the Nativity was fresh in Beth's mind. Rarely, over the past two thousand years, can Mary have been equipped with such a recalcitrant animal to bear her in the ninth month of her pregnancy. It was a wonder the Holy Child wasn't born several miles shy of the stable, throwing out the plans of the shepherds, kings, angels and, indeed, God himself, so frisky was her mount.

'I wonder if I could come into the office and help out or something, then? Or make some enquiries from home? Must be possible to just check…'

Beth was still meandering gently through various half-formed plans when Nina yelled out. 'Brainwave! Listen to this, you'll love it. And it should work. How about if I suddenly get ill, and you have to cover for me? I can say you're from the temp agency, Potter's never going to check. So, you get to sit in the office, have a shufty around, get on the trail of the couriers, and Bob's our lobster. What do you think?'

'Do you think Potter would buy that? That I'd just arrived

from a temp agency? He wouldn't check up? Or be surprised later when there isn't a bill from this mythical agency?'

'Have you ever had a boss who's complained because he *didn't* get a bill? He'll be over the moon, if he even remembers about it. He thinks he's so far above me, with all his billions of qualifications, that we're barely in the same universe. He leaves all the grunt stuff to me, and getting someone to sit in my chair for a while is very grunty, as far as he's concerned, believe me.'

'The only thing is, he sort-of knows me. I popped in today looking for you.'

Nina was silenced for a second, then her face cleared. 'Did he actually ask you what you wanted?'

Beth thought. 'No. As soon as I said I was there to see you, he lost interest.'

'Typical, but there you are then! We can say that was your interview.'

'Interview? For covering for you when you're going to be ill, some time in the future? But you weren't even ill today, were you? Isn't it going to look a bit fishy, or at least like you've been planning to take time off, behind his back?'

'Nah, you're over-thinking it. He honestly doesn't really care who sits there. Anyway, I've been feeling peaky for days, I really have,' said Nina, breaking into a very unconvincing, high-pitched cough. Beth could see what she'd meant about her acting skills. 'He never asks me how I am, so he's not going to know exactly when I started to feel rough, is he?'

'I don't know, Nina. It sounds a bit dicey to me. Quite a lot could go wrong, and if he starts to suspect anything…'

'What's the worst that could happen? He'll just sack you. Sack us both probably, which wouldn't be so good. But I could find something else,' Nina said with bravado.

Beth thought for a moment. There was a lot at stake for Nina. She'd only just moved here, but had already got a little nest sorted out for her and her boy, and a job was central to feathering that. There didn't seem to be a Mr Nina in the picture, to take up any potential slack. Surely she could just turn a blind eye to whatever was going on at the solicitor's, and get on with her life?

'Do you really want to risk this, Nina? You never quite know what you'll find, or what effect it will have on everyone...' Beth didn't want to labour the point, but she was speaking from bitter experience now, not least from her last adventure in Camberwell. She didn't regret getting involved. She couldn't, or the mystery of what had happened to Jen might never have been solved. But it had not been without its costs, for all concerned. And now they all had to live with the consequences.

Nina looked thoughtful, which sat ill on such cherubic features, made for laughing and seeing the sunny side of life. 'Thing is, you see, at the end of the day it's a solicitor's. If it was a newsagent's, for example, and they were selling a few knock-off sweeties, then fine, I suppose. I can turn a blind lie if I have to, same as the next person. But this is the law, see? If he's fiddling the law, well, that don't sit right with me. What's the point of all this, trying to bring our kids up proper, telling them about truth and lies, if a man like that is bent? It's worse than a crooked policeman, that's what it is.'

It was a long speech, and at the end of it Nina's cheeks were like Pink Lady apples, clashing frantically with her auburn curls, though whether the heat came from passion or just embarrassment, Beth couldn't quite tell.

But she was thrilled that Nina seemed to share her moral compass. Often she'd thought she was the only person in Dulwich who was driven by anything more than the desire to inveigle their children into good schools, though she certainly shared that need, more than ever with the entrance exam for Wyatt's looming. But she did also care about abstract notions like good and evil. She smiled approvingly at Nina.

'I know just how you feel, I really do. And I'd like to help. But I'm not sure how it would work.'

She thought about Potter. She hadn't exactly taken a dislike to him on sight, which she was more than capable of doing, but she definitely hadn't warmed to him either. What she had noticed, above all, was the trappings of wealth, which he clearly used as a currency to prove his credentials in a high-achieving world, to intimidate less successful mortals and maybe to bolster an ego that might be more fragile than it looked.

'First, I'm not convinced that we can just tell him I'm a temp. I don't know one single thing about being a receptionist, for starters. And if I just turn up, what if he asks for my CV, or rings the agency to check up on me?'

'Look, I think you're way over-estimating the number of fucks he gives,' said Nina, while Beth automatically swivelled to check where Ben's ears were now. Still being filled with inane, high-pitched cartoon storylines, and still oblivious to grown-up chat, or so it seemed. 'Honestly, as long as there's a live body in that chair, he's happy,' Nina continued. 'We can do you a bogus CV if you like, that's no prob. And being a receptionist, well, I don't want to do myself down, do I, but it's not rocket salad, know what I mean?'

Beth did a slight double-take. The more she talked to Nina, the more she realised that sometimes, she *didn't* exactly know what she meant – but she did rather love the way she said it.

'Could you tell me every single thing I'm likely to need to do, as a receptionist, before I go in? *If* I do. It's a big "if"; I haven't decided yet. Imagine how awful it would be if he took one look at me and called the police, saying I was completely bogus? Seriously, it's probably some sort of offence, impersonating a receptionist…'

'Nah. Don't take this the wrong way, but I wouldn't be mad keen for you to do surgery on me, or even to mend my car – not that I've got one – or fix the electrics in here or something. But sitting there saying, "Can I take a message?" all day long? I kind of think you can do that. Hell, Ben could probably manage.'

Ben, hearing his name, now did look round, and Beth could see he was drooping slightly. There were only so many cartoons that even her son could sit through. Wilf, meanwhile, seemed to have gone into a sort of trance, which was probably going to end in sleep very soon judging by the way he was sliding down the leather settee. Beth could see this was a pretty handy way of ending the evening for Nina, but she still had to get her own boy home and sorted out. His bedtime, he was sure to protest, should be hours after Wilf's. But it was cold and dark outside. Time to make a move.

'It's been a lovely afternoon. Let me give it a bit of thought, the receptionist thing. It might work, but I've just got to think it through. I'm not even sure if I could spot what was going on with the financial record stuff even if it was all lying there in front of me on the desk, that's the trouble.'

'No, but you could keep an eye on Potter. You've got some experience of crooks – you can tell me if I'm going loopy-loo or not. Even that would be good. I don't want to stay there if he's up to something well dodgy. I *need* to find out, and if I'm right and he is, well, then I need to think about moving on. While you're in the office, I can be brushing down my own CV, getting onto some agency books, doing all that stuff. Anyways, it's a mystery, innit? And I know you love those. You'll be bored, otherwise, sitting at home. Nothing much else going on... except maybe the dogs dying.'

'Have you heard any more about that?' asked Beth, immediately curious, though it was very hard to believe such a thing could have been deliberate. Who could possibly have wished any ill to little Roxie, or Lola? They must have eaten something that had gone off. Maybe in Dulwich Park? That was where everyone aired their pooches. And as they'd died so close together, it was possible they'd scoffed the same thing.

'Nah, only that the families are beside themselves. Dogs don't usually go from fine to dead so quick, do they? I'm no expert, though, cats are more my line,' she said, as Tom wandered over and butted her with his huge orange head.

'I don't suppose I could get anywhere with that mystery, anyway. I don't know either family really, and I couldn't just poke around without being asked,' Beth said.

'Couldn't you?' Nina said innocently. 'But no, don't worry

about that whole business when you've got mine to sort out.' Her voice was as near pleading as Beth suspected it ever got.

'Well. All right. I suppose it wouldn't hurt just to look into it a bit, for a couple of days. There's just one thing. What would I do with Ben? He's off school, and I don't have a childminder.'

Nina thought for a moment. 'Leave that to me. Wilf's nearly finished at Jo's for Christmas, and when he has, then I can take both boys, do some great stuff with them while you're ferreting away in the office. He'll have a whopper of a time, your lad, don't you worry about that.'

Beth smiled. Ben had certainly enjoyed the afternoon. He always loved company, and with Charlie away and her own limited enthusiasm for unbridled boys' activities all day long, staking out the office could well turn out to be an oddly satisfying option for both of them.

But sitting on her sofa later that night, Beth wondered if she'd let Nina's irrepressible bounce sway her into a pointless, and potentially dangerous, operation. Harry hadn't come round after all; he was busy on a case, and it was tempting to distract herself from her disappointment by thinking she might soon have one of her own. But, despite herself, she listed the potential hitches with the plan.

One, getting caught out by Potter in seconds flat, as she knew absolutely nothing about being a receptionist, then being unceremoniously slung out on her behind, possibly in full view of passers-by from Herne Hill, many of whom she might know.

Two, getting caught by Harry himself. He would almost certainly go nuts at the idea of her embroiling herself in another Dulwich contretemps.

Three, what about Ben? For all Nina's promises about great outings, Beth was willing to bet he'd just end up watching far too many cartoons and eating far too many battered suppers, at the exact moment when she should be getting his mind finely tuned for the looming exam.

She sighed. There were certainly enough possible pitfalls arrayed against her to make this sound like a very bad idea indeed. But when had she ever let that stop her? If she'd stuck with doing the sensible thing in life, then she wouldn't be on the verge of writing a book about slavery, and she wouldn't have a handsome policeman boyfriend either. A little voice whispered that she wouldn't also have woken up in hospital several times, or felt the dread that came with being pretty certain your last moments on earth had just arrived. But the trouble was that such adrenalin rushes were quite addictive. And her curiosity and obsession with the truth were, as all who knew her could vouch, quite unbounded.

Would Ben really be any the worse for having the odd ready-meal for supper? And anyway, fish was supposed to be brain food, wasn't it? She scooped up Magpie, who'd been contentedly shedding all over her lap while she mulled, and snapped off the lights. Time for bed. Maybe by morning, the way forward might be clear.

Chapter Six

Beth woke to the sort of grey day, garnished with a relentless mean-spirited drizzle, that had mothers everywhere groaning. Especially mothers of boys. Without regular airings, Beth had rapidly discovered that even Ben's cheerful disposition tended to fray round the edges, causing the disintegration of her own mood. He needed exercise, like a puppy, and it was down to her to provide it.

She sat at the kitchen table in her dressing gown, clutching a cup of tea as though her life depended on it, and tried not to jump a metre as Magpie clambered in through the cat flap and proceeded to wipe her cold wet fur lovingly all over Beth's legs, like a particularly affectionate car wash.

'Hm, strange the way you're so keen to cuddle up when you're sopping wet,' said Beth resentfully, pushing Magpie away and getting a reproachful glance from glinting green eyes for her pains. Something about the water jogged a thought, though. *Swimming.*

Yes, they'd go swimming. It was a perfect wet weather activity. Beth was by no means a mermaid: the school trips she'd endured, to a crumbling Victorian baths, with a coachload of classmates who'd all been sportier, taller, stronger, and more enthusiastic swimmers than her, had been enough to put her off forever. And that was without the horror of the changing rooms. But Ben wasn't bothered by any of that stuff. He was unspectacular but competent in the water, didn't care what he or anyone else looked like, and was just out to have fun, thank goodness. And once they'd been outside and slogged over to the public baths, Beth was willing to bet they'd be so wet and cold that being wet and hot in the pool would be a nice change, even for her.

There was an ace up Beth's sleeve. She'd heard tell, via a friend who sometimes saw chums in Greenwich, that there was a newish pool there that was rather fabulous. It was quite a drive away, but for Beth it had the inestimable advantage that it was not likely to be full of half of Dulwich. She might be a fully-fledged grown-up now – something she still felt quite surprised about a lot of the time – but she still hadn't lost her horror of being gawped at in an unflattering swimming costume by people she then had to chat to the next day on the school run. It was just a little too much like an *'I didn't recognise you with your clothes on'* moment from a 1970s farce.

When Beth finally unearthed the swimming kit in the under-stairs cupboard, she had a bad feeling that Ben's hadn't been washed after his last visit to the pool with the school at least six weeks ago. The towel felt suspiciously crispy and she only hoped his trunks, folded into the middle of the sausage-shape poking out of the nylon bag, had not gone mildewed. Well, even if they had, she supposed the industrial strength doses of chlorine used in public pools would kill it off, and much else besides.

Once they'd shoe-horned the tiny green Fiat into a parking space, they jumped out into fine rain that was now coming down at an elegant oblique angle. The building was rather space-age, looked newly finished and incorporated a library. If Beth had been in charge, she knew she would have worried about the books getting wrinkled.

There were two pools – one shallow, and one for more serious swimmers – and there was a row of seats behind a glass wall for spectators. For a moment, Beth was sorely tempted to sit it out, pretend to be watching Ben, and spend a quiet session on her phone away from the squawks and splashes. But a look at him, eager now to get in the water and without any friends to play with, was enough to convince Beth that she had to do the decent thing.

If there was anything she hated more than actual swimming, it was getting into her cozzie, thought Beth in the cramped changing room, with Ben sighing with boredom in his blessedly mould-free trunks, forbidden to plunge on alone thanks to Beth's nameless fears. She yanked crossly on the shoulder strap of a sturdy black suit, identical to the school one she'd had all those years before. How did it manage to be simultaneously too tight and too loose in so many places at once? And how on earth did other women ever manage to look good in these things?

Finally, having tugged and squished as much as she could, Beth was ready. She carried their goggles and swimming caps, and Ben dashed out of the cubicle like a Grand National winner hearing the starting pistol.

'Ben, don't run!' she yelled after him a little hopelessly. Sure enough, he hadn't even gone a furlong before he'd crashed headlong into another boy, and both were sprawling on the slick blue-tiled floor.

Beth darted forward just as another mother emerged from her cubicle. At first, all Beth could see was yards of tanned leg and a blindingly white one-piece that looked as though it should be on the cover of this month's *Vogue*. Then the woman bent over her child and Beth's field of vision was blotted out by a close-up view of a bottom, like a harvest moon rising. Though not inconsiderable size-wise, it would certainly have been considered to be in fine shape, even by yoga guru Katie. Beth, who now felt she knew much too much about this person, was also forced to consider that her own depilatory regime was distinctly lacking in finesse by comparison.

'Oh my goodness, Billy, are you all right?' cooed the mother to her child. 'Some people should *look where they're going*,' she continued, dropping effortlessly into a terrifyingly frosty tone, and delivering her rebuke directly to Ben.

Beth, gripped by a sudden horrible misgiving about the owner of the perfect bottom, sidled past it to Ben, who was sitting on the floor in a heap, none the worse for wear and oblivious to the telling-off he was receiving, giggling wildly with the other boy. From this angle, she was able to appraise the front view of the beautiful swimsuit, which had a plunging neckline, gold clasps on the straps, and even a mini-belt around its owner's enviably small waist. It was gorgeous and wouldn't have looked out of place in a James Bond film.

Unfortunately, it was being worn by Belinda MacKenzie, who was working herself up to a gale force ten rage.

Beth decided to get in first. 'I'm so sorry, Belinda,' she said, hating to be on the back foot with the most powerful mummy in Dulwich, but recognising the situation could only be salvaged by a speedy grovel. 'Anyway, looks like there's no harm done,' she added as the boys darted off together, neither slowing down a jot after their collision.

Belinda straightened up in a fluid movement, and stood, one hand on hip, raking Beth with one of her disapproving X-ray glances, taking in the ageing swimsuit, the thick hair tied back haphazardly, the fringe now sticking to Beth's hot face in the tropical warmth of the changing rooms.

Beth knew Belinda had never really been able to work her out. Treating her harshly didn't make her come to heel the way some of the more submissive mummies did, because Beth had no interest in being in Belinda's gang. On the other hand, Beth was quite often party to the chunks of gossip that were Belinda's stock in trade, thanks to her Dulwich roots, and nowadays she knew the inside track on most of the surprising number of dastardly crimes that kept unfolding in the area. Belinda needed Beth much more than Beth seemed to want Belinda. Beth could see an inner struggle going on, then Belinda broke out into as much of a sunny smile as she could manage.

'Oh, don't worry, Billy's fine. Great to see you here! And you've come with…?' Belinda looked around.

'Oh, we just came on our own,' said Beth. 'And you?'

Belinda seemed puzzled, unable to compute why anyone would venture out on a solo mission when they could go in a pack and dominate the space. She paused, then remembered. 'Oh yes, I brought Letty. Letty Potter, you know?'

'Yes, yes, of course.' How interesting, Beth thought. This could be a chance to see Letty, with the silvery hair and elusive personality, in close-up. But wait a minute. This could put a serious crimp in the plan for Beth to work at the solicitors and get the lie of the land. Belinda was bound to introduce her as the Wyatt's School archivist, and Letty would then think it was odd if she suddenly turned up as a receptionist at her husband's office.

Luckily, Belinda was still talking.

'...But she had to go home. One of her kids was sick. And to tell the truth, Letty herself didn't look too clever. She's started a bit early on all that Veganurary stuff and I don't think it's agreeing with her. So now we're on our own. Tell you what, why don't we team up?'

Beth had a moment of relief, followed by cold horror. She would still be fine to take over at Nina's work – if she survived being Belinda's handmaiden for the afternoon, that was.

Swimming was already one of Beth's least favourite activities. Swimming with Belinda MacKenzie, she would have thought, could have gone down in history as one of the worst few hours she'd ever spent. But once she'd got over the shock, to her surprise she found herself enjoying the woman's company. There had to be a reason why Belinda was so popular. Yes, she was daunting, but she could also be great fun. She knew so much about so many people that her every utterance was smattered with nuggets of fascinating gossip, usually accidentally.

'Of course, you know about Beatrice's dog. So sad. Poor little Lola. Though I did tell her she ought to have trained it better. That dog was such a greedy little thing, always snuffling around in people's handbags, looking for treats. Though even Lola wasn't as bad as Sue Rand's chocolate Lab, Truffles. You know, he's just died, too,' Belinda added in a lower tone.

'Not another one? Poisoned, too?' Beth was agog. The third dog to die in Dulwich in quick succession.

'No. Honestly, Beth, you see crime everywhere these days, it's as bad as having a policeman in the playground,' Belinda laughed scornfully. 'And talking of policemen...'

To Beth's horror, it looked as though she was about to undergo a thorough inquisition on her least favourite topic –

herself, coupled with Harry. Could anything be more cringeworthy? Just then, thank goodness, Billy did an enormous belly-flop into the water and Belinda jumped up and ticked him off. By the time she got back to Beth's side, she'd lost track of her line of questioning and Beth started in immediately. 'You were saying about Sue's dog, Truffles?'

'Oh, poor old Truffy. Well, he was terribly ancient, you know. Such an old sweetie. He was actually the uncle of my chocolate Lab, Twix. The children named him,' she said. And, before Beth knew it, she was deep in the genealogy of every gently-bred dog in Dulwich, most of which Belinda had of course owned herself.

Sitting next to her on the edge of the pool, legs dangling in the warm turquoise water with the welter of words lapping over her, Beth found she was accidentally basking in a sort of reflected glory, with passers-by darting her envious glances and a couple of mothers at the other end of the pool staring hard in her direction.

She'd never been in the cool gang at school, or at uni, or at any time in her life. While she'd always told herself she didn't want to be, that didn't mean she hadn't sometimes wondered what it would be like to be among those groups of exotic, tall creatures (they were *always* tall) who strode around, cynosures of all eyes and slavishly copied by so many.

Today, she was getting a tiny taste of it. All the sidelong looks they were getting were full of admiration, and Beth could see why. The beauticians, personal trainers, and wardrobe consultants who worked so tirelessly on Belinda did do an excellent job. Her light all-over tan was flawless, and even this close, Beth couldn't really tell whether it was from their last holiday to Bali or fresh out of a can. Her hair was swishy beach-blonde, her make-up-free skin was glowing, her fingers and toes were as shiny and red as the Grade Two-listed letter box in Dulwich Village.

Beth knew that most of the parents at the pool, male or female, would have killed to be sitting where she was. And she could see how it could become addictive. As someone who loved beautiful things, Beth was enjoying taking in the marvellous symmetry of Belinda's face, the planes and angles reflecting the light so well that even the harsh neon made her look like Botticelli's Venus rising from harshly chemical waves. But then Belinda pushed things just a little too far.

'So, what's up with Katie? I hear she got into *dreadful* trouble yanking Charlie out of school like that, for this skiing holiday she's just rushed off on,' she said casually.

Beth, who'd been smiling over at Ben and Billy, immediately flashed a glance at the other woman and felt her shoulders start to hunch defensively round her ears. 'Oh?'

'The Head was *not* impressed,' Belinda added smugly, showing off her connections at the school and a holier-than-thou attitude towards term time which, as Beth knew full well, had never precluded her taking her own children out of school whenever it suited her.

'Do you think Letty's all right?' Beth said desperately. Part of her was undeniably intrigued to see how far Belinda might go in her bad-mouthing of Katie, but she felt disloyal listening without sticking up for her friend. She had to change the subject. Luckily, Belinda was easily distracted.

'Oh, she's always peaky. I put it down to her super-picky diet, I mean, how ridiculous to put your kids through that,' said Belinda.

'I thought you were vegetarian, now, though?' Beth was surprised. The gossip was that Belinda ate nothing but chickpeas these days.

'Oh, yes, a couple of days a week. But vegan? No. *Don't tell anyone*,' – despite herself, Beth thrilled at hearing this well-worn Belinda mantra – 'but I really think making kids go vegan is tantamount to child abuse. I mean, that's all *so* over, anyway. "Clean eating", *tsk*. Half those waifs who've written the vegan cookbooks have actually just got eating disorders,' Belinda whispered.

Beth, who'd read a long article on this very subject in last weekend's papers, nodded along, unsurprised. It was a well-known Belinda tactic to adopt *The Sunday Times*'s view as her own diligently researched position. She seemed to have a touching faith that no-one else read any of these treatises, perhaps because she never got challenged on her sources.

'But Letty, bless her, well, she will just persist with things. I've told her, but oh no, will she listen?' Belinda went on, and Beth instantly felt a little sorry for the wan woman. You crossed Belinda at your peril. And Letty didn't appear capable of blowing the skin off a chia pudding. But if she was holding out against Belinda's 'advice', maybe she was stronger than she looked?

'Do you know her husband? What's his name, Paul?' said Beth disingenuously.

'Oh, lovely man, just so great with his kids,' said Belinda. She was always hugely enthusiastic about husbands. Those who deigned to notice their progeny, in addition to paying for them, were right at the top of her list.

'They must come from a wealthy family, do they?' Beth attempted to keep an airy, not-really-interested, just-making-conversation tone going, but Belinda gave her a sharp look. Talking about money was not really done. Yes, the whole of Dulwich revolved around who had the most of it, what they did with it, and particularly how they showcased it, but discussing where it might have emanated from was distinctly bad form.

'Well, I'd have thought you'd have known, if anyone does. They're an old Dulwich family, after all.'

'Are they?' Beth felt doubtful. She'd never heard her mother mention either Letty or Paul Potter, which definitely suggested they were incomers.

'Anyway, their business is doing so well. Paul's a whizz with all his contracts and things, really busy at the moment,' said Belinda.

Hm. Beth wondered. This sounded like the sort of half-information that wives extracted from tired, bored, and unwilling husbands after 'a hard day at the office, dear', and then spread amongst themselves when asked. Did anyone really know what their husbands, or wives for that matter, were really up to? Did they care? And what about Beth herself? Half the time, Harry wouldn't tell her what he was working on, for obvious reasons, and so she'd started to forget to ask him. Already. That wasn't good, surely? She made a mental note to ask questions, and even listen, when they next saw each other. And that reminded her that she needed to make a date. Unless that was always supposed to be the man's job? She was so new to this dating lark.

'So, how's Ben getting on now, after all the tutoring?' It was Belinda's turn to use a deceptively casual tone. Beth knew that Belinda was determined to get Billy into Wyatt's for Year 7, which unfortunately made Ben the competition. She'd been happy enough to suggest her own tutor to Beth, once another friend had dropped out, but she'd be even more thrilled to hear that Ben hadn't learned a thing in months. Beth didn't want to join battle, but she wasn't going to roll over either.

'It's so hard to tell, isn't it? I must say I have no idea how he'll do in the exams,' Beth replied quite truthfully.

'Oh, you're surely not thinking about those exams, are you? Really? It's the holidays, after all. We're not doing a thing until the next term starts,' said Belinda. 'Oh, must be time to take a dip now. I'm getting all sweaty sitting here.'

Beth looked over at her. Belinda looked daisy-fresh, no sign of perspiration at all, and her hair was as shiny and well-behaved as a timid child on its first day at school. Beth, meanwhile, was puce, her fringe spreading like seaweed over a rock pool, and her ponytail was busily slipping its moorings. Worse of all, her swimsuit seemed to be getting baggier by the second in the humidity. Maybe it would be good to have a quick swim; at least it might somehow cool her down and bring her costume back under control. Her ancient Speedo really wasn't holding up too well against whichever eye-wateringly chic designer Belinda was currently championing.

'All right then,' Beth conceded, and attempted to slide gracefully off the side into the pool. But she hadn't realised they were dangling their toes in the deep end. Her feet scrabbled for the bottom of the pool, but it wasn't there, and the world was suddenly falling away, choppy turquoise waters closing over her head, the shouts of the children abruptly muted as she sank like a small stone. After the first shock, and the horrible sight of bubbles streaming upwards as she opened her mouth to shriek, she pulled herself together, closed her eyes against the sting of the chlorine, and concentrated on scrabbling upwards. It seemed as though agonising hours had passed, before she finally clawed her way back up to the surface, coughing and spluttering.

'Did you slip? Are you all right?' said Belinda, a concerned tone failing to mask her amusement.

'Absolutely fine, it's lovely in here,' said Beth, lying through her teeth, holding onto the side with one white-knuckled hand while trying to wipe away the hair that was now laminating her face with the other. God, she hated swimming pools.

Belinda was taking advantage of her moment, solo in the spotlight. She rose up to her full height, did one of those clever flicks with the fingers of both hands that gently disengaged her suit from her bottom and simultaneously drew lots of attention to the area, then played the same trick with the golden links on the shoulder straps, holding aloft the impressive bosom which was the subject of many unconfirmed rumours in the playground. This chest was unusually self-supporting for a mother of three who'd been a vocal advocate of breastfeeding, especially to those finding it hard-going.

From Beth's angle, several feet below in the water, Belinda's breasts looked like the pyramids of Giza. Good for her if they were real. And good for her if they weren't, Beth thought, trying to be fair, though she felt a moment's sadness at any woman choosing surgery over nature. But at her age it was all very well thinking that way, she realised. She might have an entirely different take on it in a few decades when gravity had done its worst. Though she still probably wouldn't have the money to change things.

Belinda's perfectly executed dive sliced through Beth's thoughts and, after a couple of lengths of flashy crawl, which displaced shoals of small children in its wake, she zoomed into the spot next to Beth's clinging hand and bobbed elegantly in the water, smoothing her hair back from her face with an effortless rake of her red nails.

'Isn't it fabulous?' she smiled.

'Mm,' said Beth, scanning the pool for Ben and Billy, and waving to them.

'Ugh, you're wrinkling up like a prune,' said Belinda, catching sight of Beth's fingers, which were indeed looking pretty wizened. 'Maybe it's time we got out.'

She put her hands on the side of the pool and levered herself out in one smooth movement, water dripping off the blinding costume in perfectly orchestrated rivulets. A daddy swimming nearby crashed into a group of old age pensioners and could be heard apologising profusely.

Beth abandoned any ideas of getting out like Belinda, and chugged round to the steps instead, her usual doggy paddle seeming even less elegant than usual today after her fright. Getting up the stainless-steel stairs was quite an effort, water flying in all directions from her suit, which she tried to hike up around the now alarmingly baggy crotch. This thing was definitely going in the bin the moment she got home, she decided. She looked down for a second, only to be confronted by escaping straggles from a lady garden that was definitely more of a wilderness than a pleasure park. In dread of showing off much more in public than she'd had to even while giving birth all those years ago, and in front of Belinda MacKenzie of all people, Beth yelled to Ben.

Luckily, he was quite docile as Billy, too, had been ordered out of the water, and he stood patiently by the steps, screening her from most eyes. Beth was then able to follow very closely behind him all the way back to the changing rooms, as her costume sagged in every conceivable place.

'Want to come round tomorrow?' she heard Ben asking Billy, somewhat to her chagrin. She had nothing against the boy; surprisingly enough, he was quite a sweetie, especially when he wasn't with his brother, Bobby. But she wasn't sure if she could cope with another dose of Belinda.

'Nah, can't. I've got an extra session with the tutor, then Mum says I've got to do at least two practice papers, then my piano lesson…' The poor boy looked downcast.

Belinda, leading from the front, as ever, affected not to have heard the exchange, but Beth smiled to herself. So much for not doing a thing during the holidays! But did that mean she ought to up Ben's game, get him slaving, too? The poor lad. She did feel he deserved a break. But it was now (or in a couple of weeks) or never, for Wyatt's, wasn't it?

True, they could attempt to get him in later, if Year 7 didn't work out, but would they? One humiliation was probably enough. Beth sighed. She'd have to give it some serious thought. And there was really no point trying to discuss it with Harry. He wasn't from Dulwich. He didn't understand. He'd gone to a normal school, and that was fair enough. But she'd always dreamed, probably stupidly, that Ben would go to Wyatt's. Had she just been setting him up for failure, all this time? She hoped not. She really, really hoped not.

Chapter Seven

Beth was scarfing down her second mince pie in the kitchen the next morning, and vowing that she'd start a new keep fit and grooming regime the moment the clock struck midnight on New Year's Eve, when the phone rang.

'What you up to this afternoon?' said a perky voice that was becoming familiar.

'And hello to you, too, Nina. Um, I was just wondering what we'd do,' said Beth, a bit indistinctly through the last mouthful of Mr Kipling's pastry. 'Park, maybe?'

'Tell you what. Pop down here to the office. Himself's going to be out all afternoon, he's just told me. One of his mysterious meetings that I'm not allowed to ask about. You can come round, I'll show you what's what, then we can take the boys for a run-around in Sunray Gardens.'

It sounded like a lot more of a plan than Beth currently had. They rapidly agreed timings, and Beth put down the phone. It left just about a big enough window to drag Ben through his paces on a timed paper. English, maybe, that was definitely his Achilles heel. Or one of his heels. Unfortunately, she rather suspected that both their bodies were entirely made up of heels some days. Or should she have another mince pie and just let him lie fallow for a while longer? Maybe, like a medieval piece of land, he'd do all the better for being let alone for a spell. And that would give her time to catch up with Harry.

She dialled his number quickly, before she had time to worry too much, about him, Ben or just life in general, and was about to burst into speech when she realised she wasn't listening to Harry live, but Harry recorded. He had one of those deceptive answering machines that sounded just like his normal telephone manner. She left a quick message, but there was no telling when he'd get back to her. He could be round the corner, dealing with a break-in at one of the enormous houses near the Picture Gallery – the ones she'd had an envious eye on her entire life – or he could be sorting out the aftermath of a knife fight in Deptford. It had been over four hundred years since Christopher Marlowe had come to grief in an argument over the bill in a tavern there, but some things never changed. She hoped Harry had his stab vest on. Then she smiled at herself. It was the equivalent of making sure Ben wore a jumper on a cold day. She just wanted to keep them all safe, happy, and warm.

They hadn't managed to see each other now for days, which niggled at her. The relationship was in its fledgling stages; some would say the honeymoon period. Surely, at this point, they should be so wrapped up in each other that the outside world barely got a look in? But instead, they seemed to be involved in an endless game of telephone tag, with the occasional gooey late-night text message which, Beth admitted, made her heart beat faster.

In some ways, she was quite grateful for the snail's pace progress of the romance – it meant that ticklish issues, like her recent dilemma over whether to invite Harry to the school Nativity, had been taken out of her hands. Bringing him with her would have been tantamount to announcing their engagement by loudhailer in Jane's café on a Saturday lunchtime. Was she there yet? She'd been worrying about it for days when, as it turned out, he was on shift all along.

And they were, of course, playing it very carefully with Ben. So far, he showed every sign of thinking the sun shone out of Harry's notebook – but Beth worried (of course) that all that would change once he finally sussed the nature of Harry's relationship with his mother. Any nocturnal visits had been cut short by Harry tip-toeing out of the house long before dawn like one of the criminals he was always trying to catch, and romantic suppers had taken place only twice – both times when Ben was on a playdate at Charlie's.

In some ways, Beth felt ridiculous keeping the whole thing

from her son, as though he was a potentially psychotic, jealous rival. But the boy had had his mother all to himself for years now, and as an only child, he already found the concept of sharing a little mysterious. It was probably no accident that his greatest friend, Charlie, was a singleton, too. The boys did share well together, but both treated the act of taking turns like a massive favour one bestowed upon the other, in a rather ceremonial fashion. It wasn't instinctive.

Secrets were definitely not good. Beth had had concrete experience of the trouble they caused in families, and she resolved that, as soon as the time was right, they'd be open about the situation, especially given that Nina had already made a few indiscreet comments within earshot of Ben. There was a bit of a frisson, though, in having an illicit fling. She could see how people could become hooked on the sneaking around, the sidelong glances, the snatched messages and hidden *rendezvous*. It was like a naughty game, with some grown-up perks thrown in for the moments when they finally did manage to be in the same place at the same time. But she didn't want to be a guilty secret forever; it felt a little grubby.

Grubby could be good – and the corners of her mouth twitched upwards as she reminisced about their last encounter – but she didn't want Harry to be ashamed to be seen with her. That wasn't it, was it? The reason why everything was still under cover, as it were? She shook her head, alone in the kitchen, apart from Magpie who was watching her through slitted eyes, glinting green. She was being silly.

And anyway, she was hardly after a huge declaration. She still felt quite tentative herself, at this point. If it had just been the two of them, she and Harry, then sure, she wouldn't have minded sauntering down the street with him, hand-in-hand. But as it was, they needed to be circumspect. And maybe this was just destined to be a short fling? There'd been no sign from Harry, so far, that he harboured any long-term ambitions for them.

Beth had ample experience of commitment-shy behaviour

from her brother, Josh, who'd avoided long-term entanglements as efficiently as oil declining to mingle with water. It wasn't that he'd never fallen in love, just that he did it with extraordinary regularity, and it always lasted exactly two years from beginning to end. The first six months were perfection, bliss, and – for all she knew – endless sex. The next year was an escalation of misunderstandings and disagreements as the object of his affections realised they'd get so far and no further. And the final six months were consumed in the flames of resentment, anger, and bitterness. A couple of months off, once the relationship was well and truly dead – sometimes reduced to a couple of days – then Josh would be away again, having learned absolutely nothing at all, and with the next unfortunate girl thinking this time she'd found the one.

Beth had never discussed this cycle with Josh. What was the point? He was quite happy with the situation. Even the six-months-of-hell part was a thousand times harder on the girl (whichever one it was at the time) than it was on him, because he knew the score while she was just trying to piece clues together and work out where she'd gone wrong and how she could do things differently. One of the hardest things for Beth was that, ultimately, her sympathies had to lie with him, and not with whichever heartbroken woman he had in tow. He was her brother, after all. Blood was thicker, as they said. That wasn't to say she approved, though. And if asked, which she tried to avoid if humanly possible, she would be as honest as she could with the girlfriend of the moment. She just hoped that Harry wasn't in the same mould as Josh.

There was nothing at all, yet, that suggested he was or ever had been. His behaviour around colleagues had never hinted that any of them were exes (whereas Josh, as a photographer, had to avoid certain newsdesks these days as they were staffed by the ranks of the fallen), and she'd never noticed Harry giving any other woman the eye when she was around. Sadly, this couldn't be said for Josh. Much though she deplored it, his internal workings were set to auto-flirt.

She hoped Ben hadn't inherited any of the same

propensities. He bounded into the kitchen, still in his Spiderman PJs and with his dark hair tousled, looking heartbreakingly like his dad. Beth felt the usual lump in her throat but converted it swiftly to a big smile. 'Nearly time for you to get dressed, what do you think?'

'Same to you, mum,' Ben said, pointing to Beth's ancient M&S dressing gown, which was now scattered with mince pie crumbs.

'All right, I'll do you a deal. First one to get dressed chooses what we're having for lunch,' and they both charged up the stairs, while Magpie moved with stately dignity towards her cat flap and all but rolled her eyes.

Ben was still running when they followed the road down to Herne Hill later. After the hideous drizzle of recent days, the blue sky was a treat, though the lack of cloud cover meant a piercing cold, which cut through Beth's down coat with surgical precision. She sank her chin into her scarf and felt her eyes watering as the wind gusted up the hill and seemed to pass through her body. Thank heavens, they were soon at the frosted glass office. Beth paused with her hand on the door, trying to see whether Nina was right, and Potter was out. It was impossible to tell anything from outside. Yes, there was a blurred shape inside, but it could have been a yeti for all they could tell from here. She pushed their way in and the door gave a merry jingle. Nina bustled forward.

'Wilf's going to be so pleased to see you, he's blimmin' dying of boredom over there,' she gestured at her son, who on the contrary was hunched over a phone and moving slightly from side to side as his fingers, in a blur, vanquished unknown foes.

Beth sighed as Ben looked up at her, eyes limpid with appeal. 'Oh, go on then,' she said, handing her phone over.

'Wait, Nina, I thought you only had a brick phone?'

'Yeah, that's Potter's old one, believe it or not. Wilf downloaded the app himself, he's great with all that stuff. But come over here, let's show you the popes.'

'You are sure Potter's not going to be coming back?'

'Nah. Gone for the day, he has. Never comes back if it's an

afternoon appointment. Sometimes he's barely in at all anyway. Acts like he owns the place.'

Beth raised her eyebrows at Nina.

'Yeah, well. All right then, so he *does* own the place. But how does he keep it going, if he doesn't do anything? I'm not exactly working my arse off while he's out, I can tell you that much.' She tapped a big slab of a paperback on the countertop to prove her point. It was Beth's favourite type of reading matter, as long as she wasn't being observed, that is. The cover was all menacing silhouettes, a shouty title and the statutory quote from another million-selling author saying, '*I'm jealous I didn't write this,*' or something similar. As a single mum who was solely responsible for checking under the beds for bogeymen, and as someone who could easily be kept awake for hours by an unauthorised creak from the floorboards, Beth knew she should give these books a very wide berth. But they were a guilty pleasure.

She turned the chunky volume over and read the blurb, the hairs rising pleasurably on the back of her neck. She shouldn't let herself get distracted, though – potentially there was just as interesting a conundrum right here. She slapped the book back down and turned to Nina, all business. 'So where do you think Potter is this afternoon?'

'That's the sixty-four-rupee question, innit? It's a great big blimmin' mystery, that's what it is.'

Beth paused and wondered whether, at some stage, she would be able to work out whether Nina's unique way with phrases was an accident or design thing. Now was probably not the moment. She didn't feel she knew the other woman well enough yet to cross-question her and, as she'd just said, they had something else rather pressing on their hands. Despite Nina's confidence, Beth was terrified that Potter would make a reappearance, so they needed to get on with it.

'Ok, then, for now, how about you just show me the, erm, ropes, then I'll try and work out what's going on – if anything is. It could just be, well, something that has a perfectly reasonable explanation.'

Nina gave her a sidelong glance. 'And that's how things

usually pan out, is it? It all turns out to be perfectly "reasonable"?'

Beth blushed, though it was hardly her fault that so much had happened in Dulwich recently, and that so little of it came under the heading of *reasonable.*

'Well, no. There's often more to things than meets the eye. And if you really think something's off, well, then it's worth investigating, isn't it? Just in case.'

Nina nodded briskly, seemingly satisfied. But neither of them clarified what would happen if her suspicions did indeed prove correct. Beth, by this stage, felt she was quite used to flying by the seat of her not inconsiderable pants – and that reminded her, she really ought to go underwear shopping if things with Harry continued. Nina, who seemed a little bit more of a planner, although that perhaps wasn't saying an awful lot, didn't reveal her thoughts about next stages. Instead, she got down to brass tacks.

'Right,' she said, yanking open the top drawer of her desk. 'Here's all the stuff you'd usually find – stapler, hole punch, calculator, pens, Post-its, paperclips... all that jazz. Gets a bit more interesting in the next drawer down.'

Beth perked up, only to sag again as Nina opened the next drawer on three of her current author's previous works, all dog-eared and looking as though they might well have been read in the bath, as well as the office. She'd have to use all her strength to resist this much junk fiction. 'In case things get dull. But down here, here's where we finally get down to it. The files on current cases.'

The third drawer of the desk was arranged as a deep filing cabinet, taking full-sized A4 files containing loose-leaf sheets about current projects Potter was working on. Beth was looking forward to reading these. Not just because here might lie the solution to the mystery nagging at Nina. She hated to admit it, but she was, as ever, agog with curiosity. Who in the little charmed circle of Dulwich life was consulting a solicitor at the moment, and what for? And could anything here be at the root of Nina's sense of unease?

The afternoon pottered on, with the boys fighting invisible

enemies on their phones, and Beth getting increasingly irritated by Nina's explanations of office processes. The only thing she didn't pick up in seconds flat was the complicated telephone system. Even though the office was so small and there hadn't been a single call since they'd got here, the switchboard was an enormous piece of apparatus, taking up half the counter, with buttons and switches galore.

Beth gazed at it in dread. It looked a bit like Lieutenant Uhura's fearsome bank of instruments in the original (and best, in her opinion) *Star Trek*. But she supposed if Nina could work it, then so could she, and she tried valiantly to keep concentrating on the many protocols necessary to transfer calls, put people on hold, and take messages. In the end, she decided, as long as she wasn't getting calls from the Klingon high command, she'd probably be ok. And the bonus was that she didn't have to wear skin-tight Lycra and a wig while she was doing it.

'Let's have a bit of a practice run. I'll be a client, you be me,' said Nina, getting out her brick phone and dialling the number by heart. The phone on the desk promptly rang and Beth jumped a mile. 'Hope you're not going to do that every time, love, or this job will be taking years off you,' Nina quipped.

Beth smiled weakly, leant forward, studied the array of buttons and pressed one because it was flashing wildly.

'No, handset first, then you press… oh, I'm not going to tell you,' said Nina.

After the first five calls, Beth had it down to a reasonably fine art, and was even attempting some of Nina's sassy style. 'Potter and Co, how may I direct your call?' she lilted, as though she were sitting at the hub of a multinational, not just a tinpot office in downtown Herne Hill.

Then the phone warbled again, and Nina turned to her, both palms upwards, and the Nokia brick lying unused on the counter. It was a real live phone call! Immediately, Beth panicked, and nearly pressed the off switch.

'Nina? Neeens? That's not you! Here, she's never been sacked and not told me, has she?' came a woman's insistent voice in her ear, shrill with worry.

'No, no, madam, she's right here,' said Beth, and passed over the handset with relief.

Nina listened for a few moments. 'Nah, Mum, it's all good, just showing a temp how everything works,' she winked hugely at Beth. 'Between you and me, I'm not sure she's cut out for it,' she added, giving Beth a playful shove that nearly pushed her off her swivel chair.

Just at that moment, there was a jingle from the door and a tall, slender woman walked in. Her silvery hair and floaty clothes seemed to betoken an other-worldliness, but the look in her eye was far from ethereal as she took in the scene. Ben and Wilf were sprawled in the seating area, shoes and socks lying discarded across the tasteful beige carpet. Nina was still on the phone, now trying to wind up her call quickly, and Beth, blushing like a guilty schoolgirl, was sitting in the hot seat, surrounded by stationery and a few folders from the desk drawers.

'Nina? Are you having some sort of party? Is Paul in?'

The woman made to bypass Beth and Nina at reception, but Nina, who'd hung up, spoke rapidly.

'Paul's had to pop out, but he said he'd be back later. Anything I can do for you, Letty?'

Beth knew Letty Potter from the playground, and just about every café in Dulwich, where she was always seated at Belinda MacKenzie's right hand. But somehow, without Belinda, she seemed a stronger presence. Or maybe that was just because she was in a filthy mood. The anger beaming out from her pale blue eyes was at odds with her dryad looks, the hair straight out of a Norse fairytale, and the wafty ice blue dress, a floating panel of which was now snagged on one of the complicated levers on Beth's chair. Beth stooped to try and disentangle it, but Letty leaned forward with an angry exhalation of breath and yanked it free with both hands. Beth could see an ugly grease stain on the fine silky material. She averted her gaze quickly.

'And what on earth are you doing here, Beth?' said Letty sharply.

Surprised, Beth was silent for a beat. She'd had no idea that the woman even knew her name. Letty had always blanked her whenever they chanced to meet in the street, at the shops, the park – everywhere, really. If she was with Belinda, there'd be the merest trace of a glacial smile, as Belinda did always say hello to Beth. But if Letty was on her own, she'd sweep past without acknowledging Beth's existence. They'd had children at the same school for, what, four years now? Letty's son, Jacob, was in Year 6, with Belinda's Billy and, of course, with Ben. But that was no guarantee of friendliness – none at all.

Beth had never taken it amiss, particularly. Yes, it wasn't pleasant, but it was possible that, from Letty's lofty position – she must be at least five foot ten or eleven – she couldn't even see the likes of Beth, so close to the ground. And, crucially, their children had never been pally. For many women, this was the factor that made all the difference, and in her heart of hearts Beth knew she was as bad as anyone about this. There were quite a few people that she didn't bother to chat with, as Ben simply didn't like their offspring. She'd never fail to smile; she wasn't a horrible person. But if there was no rapport between the kids, it made an effort at friendliness seem a little misguided, unless there were other factors at play.

She and Nina, for instance, had really hit it off, despite the fact that their children were years apart. But the circumstances were unusual: Beth had been shorn of her everyday friends, thanks to death and Michael; and besides, Nina had dangled a promising mystery in front of her nose. But, exceptions aside, there was only so much time for everyone to scurry through the basics of life, and being overly chummy with all and sundry was probably as alien to Beth as it clearly was to Letty.

'Well...' Beth started, not really sure at all how her sentence was going to pan out. Thank goodness, Nina interrupted her before she got too far.

'I asked Beth to come in. Well, I begged her. I've got to take a couple of days off and wanted Beth to cover for me.

She's brilliant at this stuff. I was just showing her the popes.'

'What are you on about, Nina?' Letty's tone was withering, as she looked down her nose at both women. 'And don't we usually get temps for this sort of thing? I fail to see why—'

'Erm, yeah, usually, but Beth asked me if she could help out. I didn't have the heart to say no...' said Nina, to Beth's consternation.

Feeling her jaw start to sag open, and also realising Letty's cold eyes were upon her, Beth struggled to think of something convincing. 'Ah, yes...' she started haltingly, but Nina was off again. At first, Beth was relieved to have the baton wrested from her grasp, but as Nina's story unfolded, she wished she'd staggered on.

'It's the bills, you see, really mount up, don't they? Basically, she needs the money, she'd never say so herself,' said Nina, giving Beth's hand a pat and continuing briskly on while Beth made a strangulated sound and went puce in the background. 'We need a couple of days' cover, so, as she's qualified, *years* of experience, I'm doing everyone a favour, really,' Nina added smugly.

'And this is all agreed with Paul?' said Letty in surprise.

'Oh yes,' said Nina. 'I gave him the memo ages ago. Whether he read it, or remembers it, is another thing. You know what his memory's like,' she laughed.

Letty's lips moved in the merest suggestion of a wintry smile. She gave Beth a sharp glance and said grudgingly, 'Well, if it's agreed... we can't have these kids around, though,' she said, looking at Ben and Wilf as though they were pond life.

''Course not. They'll be looked after, don't you worry.'

'And *not* on the premises?' Letty, unlike Paul, did not seem the type to let the finer details evade her. 'I don't want any clients, er, discouraged...'

'Absolutely not,' said Nina equally firmly.

'Well, I suppose that's in order, then. Sorry to hear that things are so... difficult, Beth,' said Letty, with a gleam in her eye.

Beth, scarlet now, tried to avoid looking at Letty, but couldn't entirely escape that speculative glance. Then, with a smooth turn that was almost a pirouette, Letty moved to face the boys again, didn't quite shudder, then wafted out of the door, which closed behind her with a haunting ding.

'What did you say that for?' Beth exploded.

The boys looked up briefly from their games, then their heads bobbed down again like birds pecking up seed.

Nina smiled, unrepentant. 'Well, she's not going to check up on that story, is she? It makes sense, too. Who in their right minds doesn't want a bit of extra cash before Christmas, anyway? Don't tell me it won't come in handy. I've actually done you a massive favour. Before, you were going to get diddly-squat. Now you're being paid, and you've got a bona fido reason for hanging about. Stroke of genius, I call it.'

Beth sighed deeply and rubbed her hands over her face. Her cheeks were still flaming, with mortification and, she had to admit, with anger. 'You don't understand, Nina. Letty's going to tell Belinda that I'm broke. Belinda will tell everyone, *everyone* in Dulwich. Everybody will know and they'll all be discussing it.'

'So what?' said Nina. 'It's true, in't it? Well, you may not be exactly broke, but I bet you're not rolling in it either. Why wouldn't you want to get a bit of extra dosh in while you can't go to your other job? That must only pay peanuts, over at Wyatt's. I mean, you're hardly ever there.'

This stung. And was rather worrying. The job at Wyatt's, which she did love, was certainly supposed to be full-ish time, allowing for school drop-offs, pick-ups, and the holidays and so on. 'I... I work from home a lot!' said Beth defensively.

Nina smiled. 'Yeah, right. Like I was the other day. But you'll have plenty to keep you busy here, with all the ferreting around you'll be doing.'

Beth had been wondering if she should make a start on Paul's office, as he wasn't there at the moment. But she was so riven with a toxic combination of anger and guilt that she knew she wouldn't be able to read a word of any of the files, even if they said *Paul Potter is guilty of fraud* in huge letters.

She hardly recognised her own voice as she said, 'Right, well, we'd better be off,' and started collecting her own bits and bobs with jerky hands, averting her flushed face.

'Look, wait a minute, missus,' said Nina. 'Don't go off in a massive huff. I'm sorry if I said the wrong thing. It was spur of the moment – Letty really put us on the spot there. I just wanted to tell her something she'd understand, that covered both our arses. I didn't realise I'd be leaving yours out to dry. Is it such a big deal? Will the whole of the village really be talking about it?'

Beth stilled her hands and took a breath. 'That's ok, Nina. The trouble is that people really do talk around here, and I don't want anyone feeling sorry for me, for us,' she said, looking significantly over at Ben. 'What if he gets teased or something?' she whispered.

'Seriously? You think anyone would do that?'

Beth shook her head. 'You don't know Belinda MacKenzie. Letty was loving it, but Belinda will be shouting it from the rooftops. I bet I'll have my mother on the phone this evening, worrying if my house is going to be repossessed.'

Beth knew she was exaggerating. Even if she did fail to make her mortgage payments, her mother would be one of the last people to interfere. That's not to say she'd want her only grandson out on the streets of Dulwich. Just that any gossip that didn't pertain first and foremost to bridge was of minimal interest.

But there'd be plenty of other people who'd be agog at the news that Beth was struggling. And, perhaps more importantly, the thought cut right into Beth's own fragile self esteem. She'd worked so long and so hard to keep their chins above the water. She really didn't want people pitying them, especially now when they were finally doing a little better.

'I'm sorry, hon, I really am,' said Nina, her cherubic features crumpling and her eyes becoming suspiciously shiny.

Oh Lord, thought Beth. That was all she needed, having to

comfort someone else while she was hurting so much herself. But she hadn't reckoned with Nina's doughty side.

'Look at me, snivelling, when it's you that needs the hug. Here,' she said, enfolding Beth in surprisingly consoling arms. Before she knew it, the boys had rushed over.

'Love sandwich,' called out Wilf. Beth looked at Nina.

'That's what we call a hug,' she shrugged.

Beth loved it, and finally started to feel a little more like herself. The trouble with having had to protect herself and her precious boy for so long was that she had built up a carapace that even a hermit crab would have been proud of. She needed to relax. So everyone in Dulwich would think she was a pauper. Well, as Nina had pointed out, a few days in Potter's office, being paid, would actually sort that one out. And maybe she'd be able to afford the latest bit of ludicrous plastic that Ben had his covetous eye upon. It was, as her new friend had said, win-win, particularly as she'd soon be solving a mystery as well.

Beth disengaged herself gently, and realised she'd learnt a lot today. She was now *au fait* with the switchboard, with office procedures, with Letty's surprisingly well-developed mean streak, and with her own innermost fears. Not a bad day's work, in fact. She pulled on her coat, chivvied Ben back into his shoes and socks and was helping Nina tidy the office until it looked as though they'd never been there, when she heard her phone beep and pulled it out to take a look. A big smile spread across her face.

'Hm, lover-boy, is it?' said Nina much too loudly, though Ben, wrestling with the straps on his trainers that she'd told him in the shop were way too complicated, seemed oblivious.

'Might be,' said Beth with a grudging smile, which concealed the fact that her stomach was already aflutter. The heart emojis at the end of Harry's message looked promising. Very promising indeed.

'So, tomorrow then? You'll bring Ben over in the morning, and we'll compare notes when you pick him up?'

'All right then,' said Beth decisively. It looked like the investigation was on track.

Chapter Eight

The morning seemed to have lasted a thousand years already. Beth was trying to resist the lure of the paperbacks, but it was hard. Paul Potter had been in, an hour before, and had smirked at Beth in a way that told her that Letty had not spared one detail of Nina's explanation for her presence. She'd be lying if she didn't admit she found her position humiliating. Letty was all too ubiquitous in Dulwich and now Beth had been pushed into the position of being her 'employee'. And at one remove, too, which somehow made it worse.

Mind you, they hadn't exactly had a golden friendship before, so really it was going to make no difference, Beth decided. Anyway, no good thinking about all that. It just got her hot under the collar. Her only hope was that the three-day-wonder of her apparent grinding poverty would have blown over by the time everyone had to reconvene in the playground at the start of the spring term.

Potter had said he'd be away for the rest of the morning, but Beth had been giving him a bit of time to forget something and rush back for it, something she was known to do herself. Then the phone had gone a few times. Each peal had caused her a minor heart attack, not just because the ring tone was so strident, but also because she was so worried about pressing the wrong thing and losing the caller in the ether. Now she was twiddling her thumbs, just gearing up for her first attempt to prise the secrets out of Potter's inner sanctum.

The back office was separated from Beth's work area, sheltering under the main reception counter, by only a couple of metres. That included a tiny toilet cubicle, so miniscule it must be contravening some sort of health regulations, and on the other side a sink, kettle, and two cupboards – one above, one below, for all the teabags, mugs, and cleaning equipment.

Beth slipped off her swivel chair, took an entirely fruitless glance at the frosted windows in front of her, through which she could see nothing, and slipped past the kettle and loo. She gently turned the handle to Potter's office. It was locked.

What an anti-climax. For a second, Beth was stymied. There was no point at all in her being here if she couldn't look through Potter's papers.

But wait a minute. Nina must have known that Potter had the habit of locking his office door – unless he'd only done it because there was a newbie around. That was a bit unlikely, surely? So, there must be a way of getting in there. She had a brainwave.

Her own desk in Wyatt's archive institute had the usual catch-all gubbins drawer on the top left-hand side, but also had a spindly little plastic tray that slipped out, which contained all the really small bits of office crap that would be lost in the depths of a bigger space. Maybe Nina's was the same? She slid open the drawer, not really daring to hope, but there it was. The shallow tray, almost, that you had to fish out separately. And in it, amongst the used but un-franked stamps, the bent paperclips, and the business cards handed over with high hopes but destined never to be looked at again, was a small collection of keys. Two of them, joined together on a tiny silver circlet, were the tiny ones that opened cash boxes – and she hadn't seen one of those around, she reflected – but one was a normal, office door-type key. Eureka! She grabbed it and made for Potter's office again.

But it didn't fit. It was like one of those dream sequences where nothing works properly. It looked like the right sort of key, the keyhole seemed right, too, but they stubbornly refused to mate. She sighed, reached for her phone, and dialled quickly.

'Hi Nina, Ben ok?' she said automatically, nodding to herself in the empty office as Nina gave her a full rundown of all the tremendous educational activities she'd been offering Ben and Wilf this morning. It would have been more convincing if Beth hadn't been able to hear the all-too-familiar theme tune of PlayStation's FIFA 18 in the background. 'Anyway, I rang to ask you about the key to Potter's office,' Beth broke in, lowering her voice to a whisper and looking around her in the empty office.

'What? You mean he's only gone and locked it?'

'Yes. Doesn't he usually?'

'Nah. Never. You must be giving off a well suspicious vibe.'

Beth felt a little stung. She was doing her best. Granted, she probably wasn't a natural at the role of receptionist, as she generally felt quite prickly towards new people and she definitely loathed the switchboard, but that didn't seem to matter as hardly anything at all seemed to go on in this office. They hadn't had a single visitor so far, and precious few calls either.

'Well, I'm doing my best. But yes, he's locked it. Is there a spare key anywhere, do you know?'

There was a pause. Beth couldn't quite hear the cogs whirring in Nina's brain, but she could tell that a lot of concentrated thought was going on. 'Nah. No idea, mate,' said Nina eventually.

Beth let go of her breath, disappointed.

'But you're there, on the spot, Beth. And I bet you're not exactly rushed off your feet. You'll just have to search for it. Oops, looks like Wilf's knocked over the Coke, got to go…'

Beth didn't have time to say that Ben was only allowed Coke on Friday nights, as a treat. Just as well, probably. She could just imagine the sort of snort Nina would emit at this news, and also, she did want Ben to have some fun while she was tied up with this almost-certainly doomed quest.

Putting the phone down, Beth scanned the empty office. The chairs, the coffee table, the expanse of carpet, were all still pristine despite Ben and Wilf's efforts yesterday. This office wasn't very promising, as far as providing potential hiding places went. And it was quite possible that there was only one key to Potter's office, and it was on him now, wherever he'd gone. Short of stalking him to his secret meeting and then mugging him, she might never get her hands on it.

On the other hand, maybe, like the teeny cashbox keys, office keys came in pairs. It made a sort of sense. She tried to think of the keys at work at Wyatt's. Were they supplied singly? But it was all a bit different at the school. The buildings were ancient and venerable, and all the offices had served spells as other things in their time. She and her archives were now in the Geography building, but when the school had been smaller, a century ago, her block had housed the whole of the lower school. It was probably only the Headmaster's office that had never been tinkered with, as the years added to the roll of pupils and the inexorable upward glide of the school.

The office doors here, though, were Johnny-come-lately things, cheaply made of veneered MDF in a factory, and there were identical specimens up and down the country. It seemed quite likely that, for a new lock on a new door, there would be at least two keys given as standard. She pushed herself back from the counter, her swivel chair gliding smoothly on the beige seagrass, then stood up and looked around. There was nowhere in the loo to hide a key, unless it was in the toilet brush container – an idea that made her feel quite sick. She took a quick peek, long enough to confirm her suspicion that Nina's duties included those of office cleaner, and that she didn't like this side of her job very much. That left the kitchen/cupboard area.

It didn't seem promising. Apart from the kettle, which she did squint into but which was void apart from a few interesting rock formations growing from south east London's notoriously high limescale content, there was only the Lilliputian fridge. It stored a brace of squat plastic containers of milk – an organic skimmed, which she was willing to bet was Potter's; and a full fat from Lidl, which had Nina's name all over it, in spirit if not in deed. She even checked the wincy little freezer compartment, which had an ice cube tray growing a furry beard of icicles, but nothing else.

The cleaning materials were dusty, comprising some dried-up sponges and cloths that looked as though they might crumble at her touch – she raised an eyebrow here at Nina. Then there was only the mug cupboard, above the kettle, still to check. Beth wasn't hopeful. And it was high up. Well, high for her but fine for most people, she thought a little crossly.

She could reach the bottom shelf easily enough. There was no key in the box of tea bags, and nothing else there but expensive mugs which matched the seagrass matting, which she recognised from the cushion shop in the Village. She was willing to bet they were Letty's contribution to the ambiance. There were also a couple of plain glasses and a lonely egg cup. How that had made it in there – and why – seemed the biggest mystery she was likely to stumble upon today, unless her luck changed. But there was another shelf to go.

She dragged her chair over from the counter, and positioned it in front of the cupboard, gingerly stepping onto it and relaxing a little when it didn't immediately career across the carpet. She leaned forward to scrutinise the contents of the top shelf – another, larger collection of cups, more glasses, and a milk jug that wouldn't have looked out of place in a charity shop. There was plenty of dust here, as well – no surprise, by now. It looked as though Letty had been shipping mugs that she didn't like out of her house. There were a few Pantone colour mugs, and some Penguin classic covers, *A Room with a View*, *The Body in the Library*, *Pride and Prejudice*. She obviously wasn't a big reader. There was also one, clearly daubed by her children when they were a lot younger, unless they were remarkably ungifted artistically. It hailed from one of the ceramic cafes nearby, where you could pay for your children to decorate a plain china object, which would then be fired and glazed at terrific expense.

Beth remembered a few trips there with Katie. The results, from Ben's paintbrush, were really horrible. She'd given one mud-brown model of a rabbit to her mother, who had promptly broken it – accidentally on purpose, she was sure.

Beth couldn't really blame her. Letty's kids had at least managed a wobbly 'Dad', written in red, on this fine example, which for some reason had been put back upside down. It was really a bit sad it had ended up here, amongst the unused flotsam of the office cupboard, thought Beth sentimentally, reaching up for the handle and sliding the mug forward to have a closer look. But there was something in it, grating against the shelf and the mug as she pulled it forward. She lifted it. Sure enough, where the mug had been, there was the silvery gleam of a key.

She thought immediately of Simpkin, the cat in Beatrix Potter's *The Tailor of Gloucester*, one of her favourite stories as a child. She'd adored the watercolour of the embroidered waistcoat, worked so exquisitely in cherry-coloured silk – and been horrified by Simpkin's habit of hiding such industrious, supremely talented mice under teacups, a sort of impromptu porcelain larder, to come back and eat later.

So, Potter was a sort of Simpkin, was he? Beth wondered if he shared any other qualities with the cat who, as well as being murderous, was spiteful, too – but ultimately redeemed himself. But she was wasting time. She grabbed the key and hopped down from the chair, which lurched at the last moment like a rodeo beast making a terrifying bid for freedom. The key's hiding place was so close to the door itself that she could see it made a lot of sense, particularly for an absurdly tall person.

Holding her breath, she shoved the key into the lock, and turned it – hearing a satisfying click. Which was rapidly followed by the much less satisfying sound of the street door bell jangling. With fumbling hands, she re-locked the door, then realised too late that, since her chair had lurched away from the cupboard, she couldn't nip back up and replace the key.

She was throwing herself back behind her own desk, key palmed in her hand, when Potter breezed past her with a quick 'Hello!' and an even quicker on-off smile. She hoped he was a bit less insincere with his clients, otherwise the business really would go to pot.

Thank goodness, he must have the second key to the office on his own keyring, as he bypassed the kitchenette and in a moment had surreptitiously opened his door, perhaps not wanting Beth to know he trusted her so little that he'd locked it earlier.

Five minutes later, he stuck his head round the door. 'Er, um...'

'Beth,' she reminded him, her turn this time to do the fake smile bit. He definitely knew her name, unless he had the worst memory on the planet. But maybe he was just embarrassed at knowing her circumstances? She probably had as good a degree as he did, yet here she was, doing his bidding. Even if it was just for a few days, it was an ignominious position to be in. Especially as there was something a little tacky about him. She could see his gold cufflinks gleaming from here as he leaned out.

'Yes, yes, um, could you rustle us both up some tea? I don't think there's any coffee, is there?'

She gritted her teeth. There was no way to refuse and, in any case, after the last few minutes she could do with one herself, if not a double brandy. Besides, it gave her the perfect opportunity to replace the key. She wondered why he'd asked about coffee, surely he knew there was no coffee machine? Or did he seriously expect her to magic one up from her bag, like Mary Poppins? She tutted.

Potter, coming out while the kettle was boiling, seemed surprised to see her standing on her chair, but she hastily put the Dad mug back over the key and turned round clutching the small milk jug, which she then made a big show of filling with the organic milk – a completely unnecessary palaver, in her view, but he wasn't to know that she never bothered at home. She hoped he wouldn't catch on that she'd been sniffing about in close proximity to his spare key. With any luck, he'd put it there months ago and by now had semi-forgotten his clever hiding place.

'Oh, Beth, I just had some invoices I wanted typing up... do you do that sort of thing?'

Beth thought rapidly. Well, she had a laptop with a Word

programme on her desk, so yes, she had the capability. But she was willing to bet he did too. Maybe this was part of her duties, though? Nina hadn't mentioned it, but then it was hardly going to be rocket salad, as she'd said. Also, it could be a way to get to know the workings of the business better.

'Yep, no problem. I'll bring my notebook through, shall I?'

'If you would,' said Potter, more sure of himself now she'd conceded the point.

Beth scanned the desk for a notebook. There wasn't one. She hunted through the drawers, clogged up with blockbusting fiction, then finally gave up and fished a few sheets of A4 out of the printer, trotting to Potter's office with these bunched in one hand, and a red biro in the other. It didn't look quite as polished as the full Miss Moneypenny shorthand-notebook-and-pencil that he seemed to be expecting, but it would be fine for jotting things down. She breezed in and took a quick look around Potter's office.

After all her efforts to get in earlier, it was disappointingly bland, though it was much larger than she'd expected and extended back further than she'd imagined. There even seemed to be a small outside area beyond the floor-to-ceiling windows at the end of the room, but they were shrouded with opaque blinds, so it was hard to be sure. There was more of the same seagrass flooring everywhere, a large desk in a blond wood that dominated the room, and a promising bank of filing cabinets on the other wall which, Beth suspected, she ought to get rifling through as soon as she could.

Everything was extremely beige, and Beth wondered if this was down to Letty. She seemed such a stylish woman, with all her layers camouflaging what Beth was beginning to suspect was quite a tough core – the floaty disguising the flinty. Surely she could have been a bit more imaginative? Then she caught sight of a print, facing Potter's desk – a large Rothko. An orange square, suspended in space, with a smaller yellow lozenge beneath, the colours hazy. Beth turned away from it.

'You like Rothko?' she said, taking the seat in front of Potter's desk. It was an upright chair, comfortable but very solid, not as padded as Potter's throne-like tan leather number. She bet his had all kinds of clever levers you could pull to get the best lumbar support. It was the chair equivalent of, if not quite a Porsche, at least one of the lovely, shiny Audis in the Village showroom.

Potter looked blank, until Beth gestured to the picture on the wall.

'Oh that. Yes, very cheery.'

Beth hid her astonishment as best she could. Anyone who could sit opposite a Rothko and find it *cheery* was either a natural born optimist, had their eyes firmly shut, or was impervious to atmosphere.

'Did Letty choose it?'

'What? Erm, yes. That is, she got in a firm to do the refurbishment when I opened the office... um, shall we get on?' Potter was transparently irritated by the art history quiz, and Beth couldn't really blame him. She braced her wad of A4 on her knee, poised her pen, and looked up expectantly. Potter glanced at her, cleared his throat once or twice, then leaned back in his chair and started to declaim.

Three-quarters of an hour later, Beth was exhausted, the red biro was on the point of running out, and her A4 stack was covered, front and back, with scribbles that were going to be hell to decipher. Some people loved the sound of their own voices, but Potter was passionate about his in a way which Beth had rarely encountered before. If he could have married it and had children with it, then Letty would never have got a look-in.

On the plus side, if Beth ever managed to finish transcribing these endless reams of notes, then the filing cabinets – and she now saw why there were so many of them – must be stuffed full of more of the same. If there was something dodgy going on, then she was now willing to take a bet that Potter would have rambled on about it at enormous length, got someone else to type it for him, and was now storing it for posterity in his office. The wonder was that Nina herself hadn't come across whatever it might be. The only explanation had to be that it was before her time. Maybe this was why her predecessor had been let go? Had she known too much?

Beth, now sitting back at her desk, had no sooner set up her first document, when he popped his head out of his office again. 'How about another of those great teas, Beth?'

Luckily, she had her back to him, so he couldn't see her ferocious expression. But she got up and switched the kettle on. It was almost a 'what did your last slave die of?' situation – except she knew full well that his last slave was alive and well, probably sniggering a little and chomping her way through a family bag of Quavers on her very comfy sofa right now with Beth's own son, whose brain was at least halfway to total stagnation. On the other hand, he'd no doubt been having a lovely time.

She sighed and sloshed the boiling water over two more teabags. At least it would be time to go home soon, wouldn't it? Please?

But many hours seemed to pass before Beth had knocked her notes into some semblance of sense, printed them up, presented them to Potter, and done the last of the washing up at the miniscule sink. As she stowed the cleaned and dried mugs back into place, ready for tomorrow, she glanced up at the Dad mug, now safely restored to exactly the spot she'd found it in. Tonight was not the night for exploring Potter's office – she was exhausted. She'd just have to hope that he went out again tomorrow. At least, now she knew where the key was, she could jump right to it.

But as luck would have it, it was three full days until Potter left the office on an appointment again. Three full days during which Beth had brewed tea with a regularity that stumped even her own enthusiasm for the stuff, and three full days when she'd typed endless reports so rammed with legal jargon and abstruse bits of phraseology that negotiating them was like wiggling through a barbed wire fence. And they were also days in which she began to wonder exactly when all these meetings were supposed to have taken place.

All the reports were undated: once she'd taken down Potter's endless burblings and neatly formatted and typed them, she printed out the reams of pages and gave them to him, placing them on his desk in a folder. And that was the last she saw of them.

Presumably, he then filed them himself. But where, how, and according to what system, she still had no idea. Worse still, she was now willing to bet that when Potter did finally step outside the office, she was only going to find that the filing cabinets were also locked.

Her hope was that the keys to the cabinets would be as easy to find as the office keys had been. After all, if Potter was locking up his office every time he left it while she was there, would he really need to be so careful with his cabinets? This wasn't Fort Knox, this was Herne Hill. Anyone breaking in would be after his laptop, maybe the printer, car keys or house keys left lying around. They wouldn't be interested in a billion tedious reports on legal meetings, would they?

That brought Beth back to the real puzzle – what these reports really represented. Was Potter working through some enormous backlog? He'd only been away from the office once during Beth's brief tenure, and unless he'd had back-to-back encounters with clients every ten minutes during that absence, it was hard to see where all these details were coming from.

Beth had initially been a bit sceptical about Nina's suspicions. And after the first day, she'd been wondering whether she'd just been roped in to give Nina a bit of a break from Potter and his indefatigable dictation. But the more she thought about it, the more the realisation grew. There definitely was something very odd going on at the solicitor's. The annoying thing was that she still couldn't quite work out what it was.

That evening, picking up Ben from Nina's, was the first time that she wasn't so exhausted that she'd just grabbed him and straggled back home. It seemed she was getting used to the frankly punishing routine of office life. That's not to say she wasn't tired. But tonight, she could still string a sentence together. The exhaustion wasn't physical; most days she'd barely strayed from her swivel chair. It was more the strain of being constantly with another grown-up, even if his door was often closed, and on her best behaviour. No jokes, no fun, endless tea and dictation – it was weird. No doubt Nina was more successful in melding the job round her own strong personality. But Beth was only there for a short time. Her job was to fit in, observe, and – hopefully – get out in one piece.

She flopped down on Nina's sofa, squashing up against Ben, who to her astonishment was reading a book. Then she saw to her horror, it was a lurid paperback. She grabbed it from him and scanned the blurb. 'I'm not sure you should be reading this,' she squeaked, conscious that, not having seen her boy all day, she didn't want to come across as the fun-sucking parent. But on the other hand, nor did she want Ben immersing himself in a world of serial killers amassing piles of hapless women victims. To her relief, she eventually realised it was a re-issued Sherlock Holmes, with a cover from the recent TV series and a back page that made the hundred-year-old story sound more like a bodice-ripper than a three-pipe problem.

Ben snatched it back. 'I'm enjoying it,' he remonstrated.

For a second, she was on the point of explaining herself, then realised she'd accidentally given the book enormous extra cachet by appearing to disapprove. For once, she did the wise thing and kept her mouth shut.

Looking over his head, Nina caught her eye. 'Cup of tea?'

'God, I'd love one, and what I'd love most is a cup of tea I haven't made myself. Potter drinks tea all day long, and keeps asking me about coffee, even though he must know there isn't any kind of coffee maker, not even a cafetiere or any instant or anything. It's his office, he or Letty must be buying the tea bags in industrial quantities. You don't think he's got Alzheimer's, do you?'

To Beth's surprise, Nina burst out laughing, her red-gold curls bobbing. 'Oh, that's a good one. No, he's just trying to make you offer to go down the road to the deli and get him a cappuccino from there.'

'You're kidding! Why doesn't he just come out and say it?'

'Well, that's probably a bit of a tribute to the fact that he sort-of knows you... he can't quite order you around the same way as he does me. You know his wife, you probably all have lovely dinners together and discuss your mortgages...'

'Not if I can help it,' said Beth, thinking grimly of an awkward, oh-so-apparently casual kitchen supper at Belinda's that she'd been summoned to a few months ago, presumably because someone had dropped out at the last minute. It featured lumpy artisanal bread that Belinda swore she'd baked herself (although they'd all seen the poor au pair covered in flour when they walked in), and a *velouté* of artichoke soup that had had the duvets of Dulwich rippling with its painful gastro-intestinal consequences for days to come. Beth had made her excuses and left as soon as she could.

'Right, well, if he thinks I'm actually going to *volunteer,* he can... just wait, then,' said Beth, glancing at Ben and Wilf's innocent ears and manfully swallowing a series of choice Anglo-Saxon syllables.

'He does pay me back,' said Nina. 'And if I'm out of the office, he can't dictate those reports to me,' she twinkled.

'Yes, the reports. Thanks very much for warning me about *those.*' Beth's heavy irony briefly weighed down her end of the sofa. Nina, however, seemed cheerfully untouched by nuance, so Beth ploughed on. 'And that reminds me, do you have a notebook anywhere? I'm just writing on loose sheets of paper and he keeps giving me these looks, like he's declaiming the works of Shakespeare and I'm scratching them out in mud with a stick.'

'He got through the last batch of notebooks. Got some on order, they'll arrive soon,' said Nina, getting up and turning on the oven. 'Shall I do the tea? You're knackered, I can tell.'

'I don't know how you do it, full time. It's a mixture of unbelievable boredom and really hard typing,' said Beth, yawning as widely as a hippo.

'Welcome to my world.' Nina delved into the freezer and brought out a selection of boxes. Beth didn't really feel like beige food after a day in the beige office, but she definitely didn't feel like cooking for herself either. She smiled at Nina. 'Thanks for this.'

'No, thank you – and have you managed to find anything, yet?'

Beth sat up a little straighter. She didn't mind admitting she was quite disappointed with that side of the exploit, but the tiredness she was feeling from the routine work was acting as a sort of buffer. If she wasn't careful, she'd start forgetting why she was even there in the first place. She could see now how people got trapped for years in jobs they hated. There was something about office life that sucked your sense of agency from you.

Tomorrow, she was going to have to try to rise above it, keep her eye on the prize, watch carefully for anything that pointed to genuine wrongdoing and wasn't just mild exploitation of office staff. As long as he didn't start dictating at her again.

Chapter Nine

As it turned out, it was a visit from Letty that finally put Beth on the right track. Everything had been plodding along as usual in the sea of seagrass. Potter was firmly in his office and hadn't even been out for lunch. Beth had eaten a sandwich of her own concoction at her desk, trying to economise after three days of pricey offerings from the deli or nasty processed meal deals from the Sainsbury's Local. There'd been oceans of tea. There was a ton of dictation. And now, in the mid-afternoon, there was the soothing tip-tap as Beth converted Potter's legal circumlocutions into neat paragraphs. Their meaning still escaped her, but she was beginning to find the neatness of the finished product disturbingly satisfying. If she wasn't careful, she'd go into a trance and wake up fifteen years later, her youth behind her, and only oceans of gobbledegook legal reports to look forward to.

Suddenly the office door burst open and Letty stood there, quivering. As usual, she was dressed in clothes that brilliantly accentuated the slightest movement, drapey crepe fabrics, a waterfall coatigan against the December chill, layers of scarves, and a cashmere hat crowned with the *de rigeur* fur bobble on the top. All these elements seemed to be moving independently, as Letty herself swayed from side to side, her voice rising to a wail.

'Lancelot! *Lancelot!*'

Beth sat for a moment, stunned, and wondering if she'd somehow found herself in a Knights of the Round Table drama. What on earth was the woman on about? Letty would make a stunning Guinevere, it was true. That left Potter as a rather surprising Arthur. He had the physical stature, she could see that, but he'd hardly have time to pull Excalibur from the stone, what with all the report writing. And where did that leave Beth herself? Some sort of troglodyte peasant, presumably. She felt like touching her forelock to Letty now, but luckily, she was saved the bother as Potter rushed out from his inner sanctum.

'Letty! Darling? What is it?'

'It's Lancelot,' said Letty, swaying into Potter's arms and collapsing on his shoulder. Beth ducked behind her laptop so that she was as inconspicuous as possible, wondering whether she should get up and leave them to it. But it was much too fascinating. As Potter murmured, petted, and soothed, Letty broke out of Potter's embrace and looked up at him, a tear tracing a leisurely route down her long, pale face.

'He's dead,' Letty intoned.

Potter took a step back. 'What? How?'

'He wouldn't wake up this morning. I've just come from the vet's. She thinks it might have been some sort of h-h-heart attack.' More tears joined the first.

By this time, even Beth felt sad. She didn't know what Lancelot was, or had been – it could have been anything from a fish to a ferret. But the mention of the vet told her he was a pet. She couldn't bear to think what would happen when Magpie eventually… but no, she didn't want to go there. Couldn't, in fact. Luckily, she'd made a deal with Maggers when she'd been just a feisty kitten that she'd live forever, and as far as she was concerned, they were both going to stick to that.

'Can I get you a cup of tea, Letty?' she asked, leaning forward out of her hiding place.

Letty started. 'Oh, Beth, didn't see you there. Um, yes. Or actually, no, I should get back to the children. I've got to break it to them,' she gulped down another sob.

Potter leapt into action. 'Right, I'm coming with you. It's too much for you on your own, Lets. Give me a minute, I'll just get my…'

He hared off towards his office, leaving the two women awkwardly contemplating each other. Beth gazed at Letty, still fragile and beautiful despite, or maybe even because, of the tears. That slight hint of steel seemed to have been submerged in salty water. Letty sniffed and tried a weak smile. Beth rummaged in her bag and passed over a tissue.

'Thanks. You know how it is…' Letty said tremulously.

'Absolutely,' said Beth, heart wrung. 'We have a cat…'

'A cat? Oh, but it's not the same at all, is it?' Letty was dismissive.

'Sorry, what kind of animal was…?'

'Lancelot?' said Letty sniffily, seeming cross that Beth didn't know. 'You know Lancelot. Everyone knows him… *knew* him. My Great Dane?'

And suddenly, Beth realised that she did, of course, know Lancelot. It would have been extremely hard to miss him, as he was, had been, almost as tall as Beth herself. A dappled grey, exactly like the sort of rocking horse that Beth had loved when young, he was a huge beast of a dog who'd lolloped through the Village at Letty's side. Beth had always given him plenty of space, in case he mistook her for a chew toy. At one time, Letty used to bring him to every school pick-up and drop-off, but gradually the rules about Dulwich's schnoodles, cockapoos, and labradoodles being paraded in front of the children in the playground were tightened up. It wasn't so much the dogs biting – the mummies, however, had definitely been known to snarl over who had the cutest four-legged friend.

'So sorry, Letty. He was… quite a dog. What happened? Was it an accident?'

Letty raked Beth with a glance, a look which instantly made Beth wonder if she had lipstick on her teeth (no, because she never wore any), or had her shirt buttoned up the wrong way (a distinct possibility, but not the case today), or was just wearing something hopelessly out of date (a certainty). She didn't deign to reply, which left them both in silence.

Beth felt increasingly awkward. Letty, meanwhile, stood gazing off to some unseen mid-point, swaying very slightly, the fluffy hairs on her pom-pom hat trembling slightly with her movement. Hours seemed to pass. Beth cleared her throat, struggling to think of something to say that might ease the situation. Maybe she should offer another platitude about the dog's death? And attempt to make it a bit more heartfelt this time?

Potter emerged at that moment, coat on, briefcase in hand, and she was spared the excruciating task.

It wasn't that Beth didn't care, she really was sad for poor Lancelot. There'd certainly be a large – very large – gap in the Dulwich dog population from this day forth. The children would no doubt be devastated. And she knew how terrible she would feel if she had to tell Ben... but she wasn't going there. She did get the feeling, though, that nothing she could have said or done would have appeased Letty, short of weeping, wailing, and slashing her own wrists. None of which she was mad keen to do on behalf of someone else's dog in the middle of the day in Herne Hill.

Taking Letty by the arm, Potter ushered her towards the door as gently as though she were made of thistledown and might blow away at any second. 'Beth, you can lock up, can't you? Just finish up what you have there, get the copies ready for the morning, finish off that filing – and whatever you do, don't forget to put the phone on answer mode,' he said abruptly over his shoulder as they rushed out.

'Yes, boss,' muttered Beth under her breath to the closing door. Though why he was getting her to bother with the answering machine, she wasn't sure. No-one ever seemed to ring, even during office hours. Was he seriously expecting a rush of divorces and wills to overtake Dulwich in the hours of darkness? She supposed he must be living in hope. They needed the business, after all.

She'd give the couple a good five minutes to get clear of Herne Hill and zoom off in their enormous Volvo, all the way from SE24 to SE21. It was a distance of less than three hundred yards up the road, they'd be lucky to make it into second gear, but of course it was essential to make the trip by car. They lived in a very nice house indeed, not far from Beth's own, but probably four times the size. What was it about the Potters and scale, she wondered? Both were outrageously tall, in her view – though admittedly she had a paradoxically low benchmark for tallness – their kids already promised to be similarly rangy, and even their dog had been ridiculously big.

Beth couldn't help it, but she wondered what on earth one did with a dead Great Dane. Burying him in the garden would be almost as troublesome as disposing of a person, surely? She'd never been in the Potters' garden – or the house, come to that – but it was lucky it was sizeable, to accommodate a corpse like that. Maybe they'd opt for cremation.

Even more of a mystery was what had actually happened to the dog. By her count, this was the third to have died recently in Dulwich. What on earth was going on?

Chapter Ten

Paul Potter opened the front door and ushered his wife in. To his relief, she seemed to have calmed a little on the journey, and by the time they'd crunched to a halt on the gravel drive in front of the house, she was quiet, a tiny sniff the only sign anything was out of the ordinary. He turned to her and tenderly undid her seatbelt, noting the delicate pinkness of the tip of her nose where she'd rubbed it with his tissue. He couldn't help it, he slid a hand possessively down her cashmere arm, and leaned in to kiss her cheek. She moved away, imperceptibly, and he straightened up.

'You're right; no point putting it off. The kids have got to be told.'

'I wish you'd call them *children,* kids are baby goats,' said Letty grumpily, but the reprimand was automatic.

The poor woman was distraught, he thought, stepping out of the car and slamming the door. Normally, he'd listen to that satisfyingly heavy clunk with an almost paternal pride, he loved this car, but now there were more important things to think about. He scrabbled to open the door before Letty did, and held it open for her courteously.

'No, no, you go in first. I just can't face them,' she said tremulously.

He stepped forward, blind for once to the stunning décor that took most people aback. The house, from the outside, was not exceptional; large and imposing, yes, but architecturally without enormous merit. Inside, though, Letty – and an extremely expensive interior designer, who never got a shred of credit for the hardest project of her working life – had created a massive open white space, dominated by a glass staircase soaring up to the next level, juxtaposed against a silvery two-metre-wide mural of trees in a forest. A spectacular pendant light fell twenty feet from the ceiling, shards of brightness splintering from its custom-made, Nordic-inspired shade. It was this house, as much as her dead-straight blonde hair, that made people think Letty must have Scandiwegian blood. The truth was more prosaic – she was from Dalston, but she hadn't watched three seasons of *Borgen* and four of *The Bridge* for nothing.

Hearing their parents clattering around below, the three little Potters ran forward and pressed their dear tiny noses against the glass balustrade, to their mother's audible distress. Paul, imagining it was the prospect of breaking the dreadful news about Lancelot, immediately wrapped a protective arm around Letty's slim shoulders and hugged her tight. She gave an infinitesimal smile and shrugged him off, announcing loudly to the children, 'Come down here, Daddy's got something to tell you.'

Then she strode rapidly into the kitchen, where Potter could hear her opening the fridge, unscrewing a bottle, and glugging its contents into one of their enormous crystal glasses, big as a goldfish bowl.

The children scampered downstairs stairs, happy to see their daddy so early in the day, and clustered around him. He hugged them into his waist, pressing a kiss onto each blonde head. Letty had been angelically fair at this age, too; he'd seen the pictures. She'd only needed chemical assistance after having children. She'd told him it often took women that way.

'Listen, my darlings, Daddy's got something very difficult to tell you. Let's sit here on the stairs and I'll explain everything,' said Potter, looking into each face in turn. They were such beautiful kids – children. The same oval faces as their mother, with eyes of precious *lapis lazuli* fringed with sable lashes and lips like blush suede. He drank in their features, the unblemished skin, the world of possibilities within each little head, struggling to see any of his own clunky DNA in these miraculous creatures.

'I'm so sorry, my loves. It's very sad news.'

Chapter Eleven

Beth slid off her chair. The Potters were long gone, and the office was quieter than the grave. She might not have another opportunity like this for days, given Paul's propensity for sitting tight. Still moving stealthily, which she realised was quite ridiculous given that she was alone in a place which hardly ever attracted a visitor, she popped to the tiny kitchenette, opened the cupboard, then realised in annoyance that she'd have to wheel her chair over again. That shelf was just too high for her. Still, it was the work of only a few moments to hop on, delve, and hop off, and she soon had the cool, hard shape of the key in her hand. She was almost tiptoeing as she made her way the few paces over to Potter's office, slid the key in the lock, and opened the door.

The room was slightly less immaculate than usual, which was not surprising given the crisis that had seen Potter bolting for home. There were a few papers out on his desk, including, Beth was amused to note, *The Daily Telegraph* turned down to that day's crossword. So, he really wasn't as busy as he liked to pretend to be. She also saw, to her annoyance, that he'd been annotating one of her beautifully-typed reports, changing things around and even challenging the spelling of a couple of words. Where did the man get off?

But Beth was wasting time, allowing her blood pressure to rise when she should be keeping icy cool and finally plumbing the depths of the filing cabinets. She turned to face them, also getting an eyeful of the Rothko, its sullen yellows and dirty ochre shades seeming to hum with meaning across the room. Perhaps Letty had chosen the picture because she, herself, seemed so rarely to be entirely still, with her shimmering hair and fluid clothes.

Beth stepped over decisively and pulled at the top handle of the cabinet. Not surprisingly, it held firm. So, he had locked everything; she'd rather thought he might. Potter, outwardly so confident and commanding, seemed to be strangely paranoid about his working life, or at least he was now she was there. But maybe that was normal in legal offices? Beth supposed this bank of information was full of details about people's lives, estates, even loves, certainly their wishes about who would get what and, perhaps more crucially, who wouldn't.

There was nothing for it but to give his desk a thorough search. Beth stepped back over to the blond slab of wood and slid behind it, preparing to sit in the tan leather chair. But before she got settled, she had a clever thought. She quickly jammed the door open with the wastepaper basket, just in case anyone came in from the street while she was busy snooping. That way she'd be able to hear them, sprint out again while the front door was doing its chiming thing, and more or less be back in position at her own desk in time to pretend she wasn't up to anything.

Settling into Potter's chair, Beth luxuriated for a moment in the plushness of the seat and inhaled the scent of very expensive leather. If she sat here all day, she'd probably be firing off reports left, right, and centre. It was the kind of chair that appealed to the inner, lurking Donald Trump in a man – or a woman, too, if she was anything to go by. But she mustn't get distracted by fantasies of world domination. She leaned forward from the sumptuous depths and rattled the desk drawers. Locked. Of course. Why would Potter stop at two locks, when he could have more? He probably locked his briefcase, too, and for sure his iPhone would have an elaborate code, whereas Beth's was open for anyone to snoop into. Maybe she should change that now that she had a few texts she felt less than comfortable about Ben reading, she thought suddenly with a blush.

But that was neither here nor there at the moment. The question was, how to get into Potter's drawers, as it were. She stared in front of her. If she was a paranoid, entitled, 40-

something show-off, where would she hide her keys? Given that she knew a little about the man's *modus operandi* from having found his Simpkin office key hiding place, Beth pondered, drumming her fingers on the smooth, expensive, bland desk top. There was an in-tray right in front of her, bristling now with her own impressive output of reports, all neatly stapled. She lifted them out carefully, dragged the tray towards her and scanned it. Nothing there, save a broken rubber band.

She shook out *The Daily Telegraph*, just in case, then rearranged it back in its original folds, an annoying piece of origami. There was an A4 size, tan leather-bound desk diary, for the year they'd so nearly dispensed with but, leafing through it, she could see it was untouched. Either Potter made his appointments straight into his phone, as most people did these days, or the diary represented the true state of the firm's business.

Wait a minute. The pen pot. It was an Orla Kiely ceramic, with an orange graphic pattern on a white background, discreetly designerish, but not enough on its own to do much against the preponderance of beige in the room. The desk key would be here, surely. Beth grabbed the pens with one hand and put them down in a neat pile, then upended the pot onto the pristine desk, unprepared for the pencil shavings that fell out everywhere, with that fine accompanying graphite dust that always drops out of sharpeners. Yuck.

With a tut, she swept the fine powder off the desk into her palm and took it over to the door to dump into the bin. Well, she'd caught Potter out in the nasty habit of sharpening pencils into his pot during quiet moments, but that was hardly a crime, or not one of the magnitude that she and Nina were looking for. What else? She looked hopefully into the depths of the neat cylinder. Had he fixed the key to the bottom with tape, maybe? That would be smart and add a James Bond touch. Nope. Aside from an old dog-eared stamp clinging to the interior, the cupboard, so to speak, was bare.

Bare. Hmm. That made her think. She looked at the desktop again, and her eye went to the diary. Why take up space with such a large one, even though it was rather beautiful and matched the chair which seemed to be his pride and joy? If you weren't going to use it, would you really keep it on your desk for almost a whole year? Potter didn't seem the pointless clutter type. Unless it was a present from Letty, and he had a sentimental attachment to it? The way he'd comforted his wife just now had been very touching. Beth'd been going off him more and more every day with each report she'd typed, but she had to say he definitely seemed like a caring husband. And father, helping Letty with the undoubted burden of breaking the bad news about their pet to the children.

Beth slid the diary across the desk and flipped through it again, then turned it upside down to see if anything would fall out. Nothing. But the book was surprisingly heavy. Yes, it was covered in leather, and seemed almost as well upholstered as the chair, with a lovely sponginess to the front and back that made Beth sink her fingers idly into its springy depths. She'd always wondered how they bound books like this. Was it actually foam rubber under the leather? She opened the back page to have a closer look.

There was a pocket at the back, helpfully labelled in gold tooling, *receipts*. The pocket bagged a little, as though it was used frequently. Her heart beat a little faster. She slid a finger in… tentatively. And felt for the bottom of the pocket. There it was, the smooth outline of a key. A very small one this time. That would fit the desk, which seemed to have a tiny lock, considering its impressive size. With a smile, Beth retrieved the key, fitted it into the lock, and turned. Now it was just a matter of guessing where Potter kept the cabinet keys. Surely he wouldn't hide those in the tiresome way he'd done with the other two?

But, it seemed, old habits died hard. Although most burglars would probably have died of frustration before they got to this point, or merely jemmied open all the doors in their way with a crowbar, Beth, of course, was all about covering her tracks. She rapidly opened and shut every desk drawer, the last key declining to leap out at her through the perfectly ordinary mixture of staplers, hole punchers, scissors, paper, and envelopes that greeted her very disappointed gaze. Honestly, why would he even bother to lock these drawers, when their contents were ordinary enough to send anyone into a coma? And where, for heaven's sake, would he hide the filing cabinet key? Once again, she sat and gave the matter some serious thought.

'Where would I put this key, if I were a seriously sneaky, paranoid bastard with an inferiority complex that I'm trying to make up for with a very, very big desk?' she pondered, asking the smooth cream walls, even addressing the Rothko, its colours quivering at her across the room.

'Aha!' she said, getting up from the tan embrace of the chair with a little difficulty, and speeding over to the picture. She reached up, up, and again was thwarted. The top of the frame was just out of her reach. Why did that always happen? Beth, who knew all too well that it was a height thing, pushed the thought as far away as it would go, and realised she'd have to drag her own office chair in from outside, to prove whether her hunch was right or not. No point trying to stand on Potter's own chair – it was too cushiony, and it also felt too hefty to shift. She wasn't sure if she'd even be able to shove it into position, and the same went for the chair she sat in for the dictation sessions. It was surprisingly solid, whereas her own chair outside, though it wasn't exactly lightweight, did have the bonus of being on castors.

All her labours were rewarded a few minutes later, when she was on her tiptoes on her chair, as was now almost beginning to feel like standard practice. Carefully, she reached up above her head and felt along the dusty edge of the picture. Just when her heart was beginning to sink, her fingers struck gold – in key form. The final lock. She felt as though she'd been playing her part in some obscure Dungeons and Dragons-style game, and had gone through endless levels before at last winning the chalice, gold coins, diadem, or whatever.

With a much lighter heart, she pushed her chair quickly out of the office again, whacking against the bin propping the door as she passed, and turning back just in time to see the office door shutting inexorably behind her with a very final clunk. With the office key locked firmly inside. Where had she even left it? She couldn't remember.

Beth stopped stock still, head clasped in her hands, as she desperately tried to visualise the state she'd left Potter's office in. Was there anything that would give away the fact that she'd sat in his chair, chucked his stuff hither and thither across his desktop, rifled his drawers and, most importantly of all, discovered not one but two of his secret keys?

Beth's heart plummeted into her stomach. Stupid, stupid, stupid. She'd been so carried away at her cleverness, she'd been careless.

But think. *Think*. What had she done? She'd emptied out the pen pot – and she'd chucked away the sharpenings, not left them on his desk. Well, it was good they weren't still strewn all over the place – but was it bad that they were in the bin? Only if he looked in it… and would he?

Mind you, the bin itself was going to be out of place – but only a little. She'd shifted it about a foot to wedge the door. With any luck, it might have been moved back nearly to where it started by the door as it swung back. The desk diary, the in-tray, the reports. All of those she'd replaced where she found them. There was a lot to be said, some days, for being a bit on the OCD side. But wait a minute. The desk itself. It was unlocked. And the filing cabinet key she'd taken from the top of the Rothko. That was still in her hand right now. And, much worse, the office key. For the life of her, she couldn't remember where she'd put it.

She'd unlocked the door, gone into the room, sat at the desk… had she just left it there, lying on the polished blond surface, in full view? She squeezed her eyes shut. But, try as she might, she couldn't quite get the key to swim into focus. She tried it in various positions on the desk, but none seemed right. It was no good. It was a bit like playing that game, Pelmanism, which Ben had gone through a brief but exhausting phase of loving beyond reason. Day after day, when he'd been five or six, they'd got out the cards, shuffled them, lain them face down, and battle had commenced. They'd each turned over two, then turned them back. The aim was to remember where the pairs lay, pick them up, have another turn, and maybe sweep the board.

But it was much, much more frustrating than that, of course. It was as though Ben were jousting with himself, or more accurately, with the gaps in his memory. Sometimes, even when they were down to just a few remaining pairs, he couldn't seem to remember which was which. As usual, she was faced with the parents' dilemma – to help or not to help. And by 'help', some would say she meant cheat. But it was awful to see your child struggling, and yet know you could end their agonies. Usually, she held out. He'd have fewer agonies if he learnt how to probe his own memory. If she nudged his hand, yes, he'd be happy this one time. But he wouldn't improve.

Now it was Beth struggling with the limitations of a mind which had never seemed so woefully inadequate. She pictured the desk, for the umpteenth time, as it had been (as far as she could recall) when she'd sat down. And how it had looked when she'd pranced off with her bright idea about the chair. Was there a difference? Was there a key-shaped anomaly left on that shiny surface for Potter to pounce on as soon as he entered the room? She just could not remember.

She was feeling a little sick now with the stress. She tried to take some deep breaths. What was the worst that could happen? Well, he could sack her immediately. And say he did, would she actually care? It wasn't really her job. She was just keeping the seat warm for Nina, poking into things on her behalf. It wasn't as if she loved typing reports, when it came to that. And she had a whole other job that was safe. Or was it? If he spread word that she'd been snooping, he'd damage her reputation, wouldn't he? Maybe even get Wyatt's to doubt her worth. And would Nina be tainted by association? She'd hate it more than anything if she got her friend sacked through her own carelessness. But Nina, small and bouncy, did seem almost as indestructible as the rubber ball she sometimes resembled. Losing her job was not in her plan; it would be a blow, there was no doubt. But she was resilience personified. Would it really take her long to find another?

Beth thought hard about this. Nina had known her by sight as someone who ferreted around, successfully, in mysteries. By this stage, was there anyone in Dulwich who'd be that surprised at the news that she was a bit nosey? She calmed down a little. Anyway, she reasoned, wasn't it quite likely that the Rothko key was Potter's spare? It had been dusty up there, and his Simpkin key in the mug cupboard was a just-in-case measure, too. He'd have those on his personal keyring, for sure. And it was more than possible that he could have fled the office without locking the filing cabinets.

The only thing she really had to worry about was the desk. It was not only open, but she was also sure she must have left the office key out somewhere on its surface. Before she started to hyperventilate again, Beth reasoned that today there'd been very unusual circumstances. He'd rushed out, with hardly a thought, to be in the bosom of his family at a difficult time. With any luck, he'd been doing the crossword just before, hadn't he? And he'd been annotating her report, probably using a pen from the pot. Nothing drawer-bound there. Maybe he hadn't used the desk drawers at all. She'd have to hope he wouldn't really be able to remember whether he'd left them unlocked or not, when he rushed away after the bad news. Just a niggle of doubt would be enough to keep her in the clear. For now. But she wasn't much looking forward to tomorrow morning, that was for sure.

It was with a heavy heart that she locked up the street door herself. She hadn't quite known what to do with the hard-won filing cabinet key, now rendered useless by her thoughtless action. Should she stash it in her desk? But no. If Potter did realise he'd locked his desk, and it was now miraculously open, then he might well be curious or suspicious enough to search her work area, as she had done his. She'd take the key home and have done with it, and hope for the best with Potter's office key.

She toiled back from Nina's later with a heavy heart. They hadn't really had a moment to discuss things, though the other woman had been able to tell that something had gone wrong. But Ben, perhaps now getting a little fed up with unfettered access to junk TV, junk gaming, and junk food, was a bit clingier than usual and was definitely ready to go the moment she appeared. Worst of all, Harry was finally coming over tonight, his schedule having at last allowed him a window when she wasn't either working or asleep. Normally, she would have been thrilled, but with an attempted breaking-and-entering on her conscience – and an unsuccessful one at that – she really wasn't feeling in the mood.

At least she didn't have to cook. Ben had already had his quota of frozen, reheated food and appeared quite satisfied with that. He didn't even resist bedtime much, for once. In fact, his docility was quite worrying, but she reassured herself that it was highly unlikely to last. As soon as he was off to bed, teeth cleaned, and a book selected from the teetering pile in his room, Beth nipped downstairs.

One advantage of being out all day was that the house remained fairly tidy. With only Magpie to roam around – shedding hairs wantonly, of course, but unable to shift the furniture around or do much other real damage, other than wage her long war of attrition against sofa legs and curtains – Beth could just whizz around, plumping up cushions, and everything was ready. Harry was bringing a takeaway, so she just assembled plates, glasses, and cutlery on a tray, moved that and a bottle of red into the sitting room, and turned on the telly, pressing mute on the remote just in case Ben was still awake.

She'd nipped up to switch off his light and tuck the duvet round him, marvelling as usual at the perfect fan of his lush eyelashes, so much nicer than her own, when the doorbell went.

As she ran down to answer it, she felt that flutter in her tummy that suggested that, despite everything, it was going to be a good night.

Chapter Twelve

The first thing Beth heard was Harry swearing beside her. Not a great start. She opened her eyes a chink, looked across at him, and realised the room was already light. Sitting up abruptly, she put her hand to her forehead. A little too much wine last night; she really wasn't used to it. And other things, as well. It wasn't just her head that was feeling a twinge this morning, she thought with a reminiscent smile.

Harry, meanwhile, was now on his hands and knees, peering under the bed.

'Bloody sock,' he growled.

Beth spread an arm over to the other side of the bed – now *his* side, she realised with a jolt – and felt a bump under the other pillow. She fished it out, held it aloft.

'Looking for this?' She couldn't keep the triumph out of her voice.

'Ah, you're amazing. How do you do it?' Harry, his shirt unbuttoned but his trousers on, snatched the sock from her hand and pinned her back down under the duvet with a long and thorough kiss.

'Just naturally talented, I suppose.' She could feel a smile right down to her toes now.

'As long as you're only looking for socks these days. Don't want you getting into any more trouble, do we? Took years off my life last time,' Harry said over his shoulder, putting on the sock. When the silence continued for a beat too long, he turned back to her, a frown on his handsome face. 'Beth? That was a joke. I know you're too sensible to put yourself in danger.'

Beth forced a smile. ''Course. Absolutely. I was just... miles away.' Miles might be overstating it, but she'd been down the hill, in a certain office in Herne Hill, watching the door close on that hard-won key. Harry had been a perfect distraction last night, but now the reality of her situation was crashing in again. This could be the morning that Paul Potter discovered he had an imposter in his midst. How was he going to take it?

He was unlikely to be thrilled, that was for sure. But would she be in *danger,* exactly, even if he did put two and two together? Potter was a middle-class, middle-aged dad, for heaven's sake. He wasn't The Terminator on the rampage.

Nevertheless, she wasn't much looking forward to the morning. And if she was honest, she was a bit uncomfortable. Unless she was much mistaken, she'd just lied to Harry. Maybe it was a white lie, but her very well brought up conscience told her that a lie was a lie, whatever the shade it came in. She bit her lip guiltily.

'Beth? Beth, are you ok? I said I've got to go. I'll sneak out, hope I don't wake Ben. What have you got on today? Just pottering, enjoying the holidays together?' He looked across at her, his blue, blue eyes merry and just a bit wistful at the thought of missing the fun. She knew there was nothing he'd love more than to be out and about with them, at the park, kicking a ball to Ben, sneaking the odd kiss when a kick went semi-deliberately wide...

Well, she'd be pottering, all right. Paul Potter-ing. And the closest they'd get to the park would be on the way back from Herne Hill tonight, when Ben would make his ritual demand to take a detour down Court Lane, and Beth would have to point out, for the umpteenth time, that not only was the park shut (as twilight would have long passed at this stage) but also that Charlie wasn't around to pop in on either, being either halfway up, or halfway down, a mountain.

Beth's colour rose at the thought of the deception.

'You look so pretty, those pink cheeks,' Harry said, leaning in for one last, long, lingering kiss, before leaping up decisively. He'd brought his coat upstairs with him last night, and his big biker boots, too. He was always so considerate, in case Ben wandered down for a glass of water, saw the clobber taking up the hall, and wondered what on earth was going on.

Beth didn't want to let on that Harry's tiptoe down the stairs was much more like the hippo from *Fantasia* than the Tinkerbell tread he seemed fondly to imagine. Luckily, Ben was capable of sleeping through even that.

But as soon as she heard the discreet click of the front door, Beth threw off the covers and went along to get Ben up. Time was already ticking on and, little though she felt like confronting whatever might be waiting for her at the solicitor's office, there was no point putting it off. Delay wasn't going to make things any better.

Ben wasn't exactly reluctant to troop off to Nina's, but she could tell that the delights of unfettered access to rubbish telly were definitely wearing off. It looked as though one great side effect of this little experiment might be that she'd performed aversion therapy on her son. Mind you, she might not be able to enjoy the consequences of it. If Potter spotted her snooping – as he was pretty much bound to do – she might well be spending the next few years behind bars. What was the penalty for breaking and entering, anyway? She would have asked Harry, but knowing him, he would only have flipped out. There'd be time enough for that when she'd been officially caught.

She arrived at the office, not quite creeping like a snail as Shakespeare's schoolboy did, but certainly plodding like someone approaching their own scaffold. So intent was she on keeping going, when all her instincts were telling her to run away, that she didn't notice Potter coming up behind her until she was unlocking the street door.

'Ah, great timing, Beth! We might as well get straight down to it. Bring your notebook through when you're ready.'

Beth, slinging her coat on her chair and grabbing some paper from the printer, made a mental note to chivvy the stationery suppliers... if she made it through this morning, that was. Suddenly, she had a brainwave. Potter had just about got his own office door unlocked when she bustled rudely past him with the wodge of paper, made for his desk, spotted the key lying where she'd left it, shining brightly right in the centre of the pale blond wood, and dropped the sheets of blank A4 accidentally-on-purpose all over the surface of the desk.

'Oh my goodness, how silly! Oh, I'm such a butterfingers,' she trilled, hoping she wasn't over-playing her hand. She started to gather up the papers, just about to snatch up the key with them, when Potter came over and joined in. This wasn't what she wanted at all.

'Tell you what, Paul,' she said, leaning forward and splaying her hands over the mess of paper. 'You don't want to bother with this mess. Just pop the kettle on, and when I've tidied this lot up, I'll make the tea and we can start the dictation in style!'

Potter hesitated for a moment. It was the first time Beth had been so decisive. She'd been content, over the last few days, to do exactly what she was told and keep her head down. She'd shown as little personality as possible, tried to be an office fixture, with as much definition as a smoothly functioning photocopier. But she had noticed, over the years, that men sometimes quite liked a bossy woman. Particularly men like Potter, who'd probably had a nanny, or at least a cleaner or housekeeper, who'd looked after him at some point.

There was a split second when their eyes met over the desk – his registering surprise, hers steely. Then, to her inestimable relief, he threw up his hands. 'You win. I'll go and check the answering machine.'

Sweat broke out on Beth's brow as she hastily swept the paper into a pile, the key now safely cutting into her rather damp palm. She straightened the edges of the stack, sat down in the chair facing the desk, and took a deep, slightly ragged breath. She couldn't quite believe she'd got away with that, especially as checking the answering machine wouldn't take more than a second. She'd eat her own woolly hat if there was a message on it. As soon as Potter came back in, she'd make an excuse, nip out, and replace the key under its Simpkin mug.

But what was Potter up to? She could hear him banging around in the kitchenette. That hadn't been part of the plan. He was only supposed to have filled the kettle, put it on. The last thing she wanted was him poking about there. She could feel a prickle of alarm running along her scalp.

'Paul? Um, that paper's all sorted now. We're ready to make a start. Or, er, I'll get the tea going, shall I? You can, um, gather your thoughts?'

There was no reply, but she heard the unmistakable sound of someone rooting around in the cup cupboard. Potter was looking for the key.

She bounded out in time to see him standing with the 'Dad' mug in one hand, and a furious expression on his face.

'What the hell is the meaning of this, Beth?' he said, drawing himself up to his full height. It was a long way up, but when she craned her neck, she could distinctly see the cat's whiskers of white standing out starkly against his dark tan. There was no trace at all of a smile any more and his eyes were boring down into hers.

Beth shrank back against the loo door, then edged back towards his office, trying to put clear space between them. Wrong way. Potter turned towards her, and she realised her exit was cut off. Beyond him lay her handbag, coat, and the outer door to the street. Behind her was only his office. There was the tiny patio beyond, but she didn't know if it led anywhere, and the door was doubtless locked. Potter did seem to have a thing about keys.

Chapter Thirteen

Letty Potter was doing what she did best. She was shopping with Belinda MacKenzie and a couple of the other girls. It wasn't that much of a novelty; they did it often, but they did it well. They drifted, like a flock of exotic birds, from shop to shop, picking things up, putting them down in the wrong places, unfolding jumpers and moving candles from shelf to shelf, driving the shopkeepers mad, though not a word could ever be said or they would all flutter away and alight somewhere else.

This time, the pretext was a little drinkies that Belinda was hosting. It was a pre-Christmas thing, and would shortly be followed by Letty's own after-Christmas thing. Both were Dulwich institutions. Everyone knew about them, though of course, not everyone was invited. Being asked was a signal honour, and just because you'd been on the list one year certainly didn't mean you were guaranteed a place the next. Everyone had to work to be included. You needed charm, witty conversation, hyper-sensitivity to the needs of your hosts and, of course, a hide tougher than ten rhinos as far as personal slights were concerned. Or just shed-loads of money. Or you could be in the position to bestow important favours – governors of Wyatt's or the College School were always in demand, somehow.

Belinda had already found a dress to wear to her own do. Letty, to her chagrin, had adored the frock the moment Belinda had picked it up and held it up against her. It was drifty, silvery, and basically screamed *Letty* in large capital letters, as far as she was concerned. In fact, she was pretty sure Belinda had only picked it up and made a show of loving it because she knew Letty would be bound to want it.

It was ironic. She knew that Belinda had spent the whole of yesterday teaching her children to share nicely, not to grab each other's things and to be mature. Belinda had told them all at great length that was her plan during lunch in Jane's and then a cappuccino or two over the road at Romeo Jones, while the nannies just took the children off their hands to give them a tiny break. Letty suspected that it had been Belinda's au pair who'd done the teaching, if any in fact had gone on at all, but it was all wasted effort because the biggest culprit in that house was always Belinda herself.

Letty shot a venomous glance at her friend, who'd draped the dress over the cash till now, ready to pay for it, and was making the harassed assistant open the glass display case for the jewellery, so she could try everything on and then loudly declare she wouldn't bother with costume, she actually preferred *real* diamonds.

Angrily, Letty sorted through the racks of dresses, clashing the hangers together at a pace which drew curious glances from the other two who'd accompanied them. She slowed herself down deliberately, took a breath, then found the perfect thing. It was severely tailored, knee-length, with a deep décolletage and was in a stunning deep midnight blue. It would not suit her one little bit. But it would look divine on Belinda. She pulled it out with a joyful little cry, and sure enough, Belinda's eyes swivelled to the dress and then stood out on stalks. She bustled over.

'Oh! It's just perfect for you,' Belinda said, through gritted teeth.

Letty absolutely knew this was a lie, not because Belinda's smile was rigid – it always was these days – but because the dress might have been made for Belinda herself. And Belinda was staring at it, as if mesmerised, drinking in the lines which would caress her own beautiful curves so well, showing off all that work her personal trainer had been doing on her, while the colour was exactly the foil that her Californian corn-coloured hair needed. Plus, that tiny touch of Christmas sparkle at the neckline. It had it all. Letty smiled like the cat that had got the cream.

'You know what?' Letty said, holding the dress up against herself, as Belinda had with *her* dress such a short time ago, 'I'm beginning to have my doubts. Is it really, really me?'

Belinda, so mesmerised by the dress that she barely registered Letty's words, just murmured, 'Lovely... er, what?'

'I tell you what, Belinda. I have a feeling this would suit *you*,' said Letty, as though she'd been hit by the most enormous brainwave.

'No, really? But I mean... you picked it. It's yours... if you want it?' The avaricious gleam in Belinda's eye told Letty her fish was hooked. She just needed to reel her in.

'Feel the material, isn't it gorgeous? Oh, actually, maybe I *will* just try it...' Letty teased, stepping back a pace and taking the dress with her.

Instantly, Belinda looked bereft. Was that a tear forming in her eye, or was it the result of one syringe of Botox too many? Letty wondered. Time to put her out of her misery.

'I tell you what, Belinda. Why don't you go and try it on? I think it might be exactly your colour. Really slimming,' she said, unable to resist a gentle twist of the knife. Belinda's eyes shot to hers, and Letty kicked herself. She might just have gone too far there. Belinda spent a fortune subduing her body. She would never acknowledge the need to wear something that disguised the pounds. 'But no, actually, didn't I read something saying sparkly fabrics are unforgiving? In that case *I* definitely can't wear it,' Letty said, with her best fake regret. It was enough to seal the deal.

Almost despite herself, Belinda's hand snaked out and grabbed the hanger. 'Maybe I'll just slip it on. Won't take a second. You won't mind waiting for me, will you?' she said over her shoulder, but didn't wait for an answer. Of course they wouldn't all mind waiting. People never did.

Quick as a flash, Letty was at the till, grabbing the silver dress and thrusting her credit card at the surprised assistant. 'I'll take it,' she said. 'No, I don't need to try it on. Just stick it in a bag, don't bother with all the tissue paper and stuff,' she said, keeping an eye on the changing room. She didn't hide her actions from the other two. In the grand scheme of things, they didn't matter, and they knew it.

The girl ran the card through the machine while Letty drummed her fingers on the counter. There was a nasty bleep. The assistant looked surprised, shook her head. 'The connection's playing up today, sorry,' she said, swiping the card again. Letty, her eye on the back of the shop, merely nodded. Then came another of those nasty beeps. 'Declined. I'm sorry,' said the assistant, meeting Letty's eyes reluctantly.

Letty's face flamed. 'What do you mean, *declined?* It can't be. There's nothing wrong with this card.'

'I've tried twice. It says to contact your branch. Do you have another one I could try?' said the girl. Letty looked in her purse. It was stuffed with cards, as usual, but as she scanned them, there was a flurry of movement from the changing room curtains and Belinda stepped out, dress over her arm, and a very smug smile on her face.

'It's just right,' she announced loudly to the whole shop. She strode over to the counter, looking at Letty in surprise. 'Are you getting something, too?' she asked.

'Er, no,' said Letty, fixing the assistant with a hard stare and stepping away from the counter – and her dress. As she turned, her forehead was knotted with a frown. What the hell was going on her with card? What was Paul up to? Why wouldn't he have paid the bill? It was usually erased, every month, like clockwork, by a direct debit that took her back to zero and gave her a lovely clean slate. Something must have gone wrong.

This wasn't in their deal. They'd be having a discussion, as soon as she could get away from prying eyes and ears.

Her face, as she shoved her purse, hard, back into her bag, was a long way from showing the ethereal snow queen expression she habitually adopted. In fact, only Potter would have recognised her now.

Chapter Fourteen

Beth, stuck in the office and with Potter towering right over her, his anger leeching out and seeming to colour the very air red, only had a moment or two to think. And in time-honoured fashion, she fell back on the plan that had saved so many women over the centuries. She played dumb. She'd once seen a cushion, in a Dulwich sitting room, embroidered with a little motto. It had been a decade or so ago, when such things were fashionable, at the home of one of her mother's more annoying friends. It said, *'Ladies, never underestimate yourselves. You can always get a man to do that for you.'* It was supposed to be hilarious. At the time, she'd merely marvelled at the fact that someone, somewhere, had had the time and patience to work this passive-aggressive slogan in meticulously dainty cross-stitch. Now, in her moment of need, it came back to her in a flash.

'I'm not sure what you mean, Paul,' she said, stretching her eyes as wide as they would go, and trying a small but wobbly smile. 'Are you cross because I cleaned out the mug cupboard? I had a bit of time to spare yesterday, and thought I'd do something useful, once you'd had to leave early because of the dog thing... I mean, the terribly sad death of poor, erm, Lancelot. I'm so sorry if I've done the wrong thing. I was trying to do something nice to cheer you up, you must be really sad about him,' she simpered.

If she'd had a lace hankie with her, she would have wrung it artistically in her hands, or maybe even dabbed it to her eye, which was wet with unshed tears. This was more the product of sheer terror than wounded feelings, but Potter was not to know that. Like many a St George before him, he could have slain a fire-breathing dragon on the spot, but he was no match for a damsel in distress.

His lance crumpled before her misty eyes. Yet still a dash of lawyerly doubt remained. Potter said nothing but ran a finger swiftly along the interior of the upper shelf, and showed her the dirty, dusty result.

'Well, I didn't get very far,' Beth said, lowering her eyes. 'And that cupboard is very high up for me. But the lower one is lovely and clean,' she said, crossing her fingers behind her. She hoped that, as it was so much used, it would at least be dustball-free. Potter gave it a cursory glance and grunted.

'That was, er, thoughtful,' he said at last, visibly seeming to collect himself. Beth breathed, for what seemed like the first time in several minutes. 'And yes, we had a terrible evening with the, er, children. They're heartbroken, absolutely devastated.' He shook his head sadly. Was she imagining it, or were his own eyes growing moist? If they didn't get a grip, they'd both be bawling in a minute, though for entirely different reasons. But Potter was speaking again. 'The thing is, Beth, there was, um, something on that upper shelf... I don't suppose you came across, erm, anything?'

He was being so cagey. One part of her mind was wondering why, exactly, Potter was so over-protective about his blessed office key. It all strengthened her notion that there really was something in those filing cabinets that it would be worth her getting her hands on. The other part was busily wondering how on earth she was going to extricate herself from this mess.

Beth thought fast, very fast indeed. She leant forward, awkwardly reaching around Potter, who leapt out of the way like John Cleese being scalded, and reached down a mug from the lower shelf. 'I did find something, I just put it in here for safekeeping,' she said, doing a bit of legerdemain that would, she thought smugly, have had the Magic Circle begging for her to join. All that practising with the ridiculously complicated set of tricks her mother had bought Ben for his last birthday had finally paid off.

Naturally, Ben himself had shown zero interest in the kit – and she could hardly blame him. But miraculously, when she shoved the mug under Potter's nose, there was the key, shining innocently at the bottom. If he'd plucked it out at that moment, he'd have discovered it was unpleasantly warm, having been clutched in Beth's clammy palm for all too many anxious minutes. That would certainly have been difficult to explain away. But, having had a very public hissy-fit about something which now seemed trivial, Potter was suddenly keen to distance himself from the whole key business as though it were all deeply unimportant and way beneath his lofty dignity.

'Right. Well. When you're ready, then, Beth,' he said gruffly, and stalked back into his office, shutting the door with a snap.

Beth, her knees sagging all of a sudden, remained where she was, pressed up against the loo door. She took a few cautious breaths, then gathered herself together. Potter's dictation was bad enough at the best of times. Now she was mentally and physically exhausted, and it wasn't even ten o'clock yet. Had he believed her about the cupboard-cleaning business? It was impossible to say. She'd been through worse moments – and she had a quick flashback to a nasty episode in a passageway in Camberwell not very long ago – but for some reason Potter scared her out of her senses. Was it because he was so tall? She'd always had a problem with people looming over her. Well, most people did, but some of them did it in a much more emphatic way than others. Potter, because he was so solidly built, not the sort of beanpole one usually got at his altitude, was extremely intimidating. She'd have to ask Nina if he had that effect on her.

Again, she had a flash of suspicion. Perhaps that was the reason she was sitting here – Nina just couldn't bear her boss. Maybe there was nothing more to the mystery than that.

But no. Beth knew there *was* something more, lurking in this building, that was the explanation to a lot of the strange goings-on here. The empty appointment book, the lack of clients, the tumbleweed that must, surely, be blowing through the accounts. And yet Potter's lifestyle was as lavish as anyone's in Dulwich, supporting not only him, but also a high-maintenance wife and some very expensive kids, with pricey habits like piano practice, ballet, and extra karate lessons on top.

At least they had one less mouth to feed, since Lancelot had gone to the big kennel in the sky. And what a mouth! That was going to be a huge saving in dog food. As Beth knew only too well, from her efforts to provide Magpie with dainties that she considered worthy of her notice, a discerning pet could be quite a drain on delicately poised finances. Lancelot must have eaten Magpie's weight in top-notch protein every day. Mind you, he was probably the least of poor Potter's worries. No wonder the man was tense. So would Beth be, with all that on his mind.

Feeling a new sympathy for him, Beth started to calm down. When she'd gathered herself enough to step back into his office, with her wad of A4 clutched firmly in her hand this time, she gave Potter as sharp a glance as she dared, then took her seat and braced herself for the endless spiel of dictation. She badly wanted to know what was going through his mind. But his eyes were blank, unreadable, no trace left of his earlier emotion. And he barked out his reports in mechanical style. It was impossible to tell whether she'd really got away with the key business or not. She was forced to admit that Potter might well be a much better actor than she was.

This time, when Potter started murmuring vaguely about coffee, once he'd dictated the first few reams of bristling legal jargon at her, Beth was all too glad to cotton on – finally – to his hints.

'We don't have a coffee machine, I've looked everywhere,' she said patiently, mentally laughing at the idea that one could have been hidden all this time in their miniscule kitchen area. She waited a beat. He looked expectantly at her. 'Oh, wait a minute. Here's an idea. Why don't I pop down to one of the shops and get us a takeaway each?'

Potter broke into a smile and she couldn't help reciprocating. He was definitely a scary man, but when everything was going his way, he really wasn't so bad, she decided, as she slung her bag over her shoulder and made for the door. And at least caving in and getting the coffees gave her a bit of a break from typing.

It was a huge relief to be out and about in Herne Hill. The office, for all its airy beigeness, was surprisingly claustrophobic – or maybe, again, that was just the inescapable presence of Potter. Anyway, it was lovely to be liberated, however briefly. She was getting to know and rather love the string of shops. Anywhere else, it would have been called a parade, but she'd certainly never heard that word used here. Instead, it was a loose collection of quite useful stores, something unheard of up the road in Dulwich, where you could buy a hand-fringed cashmere poncho for just shy of a thousand pounds any day of the week, but a loaf of white sliced was almost out of the question.

As well as a deli, a small wine bar, a Thai takeaway, and a hairdresser's she'd never seen anyone in, there were also two chemists here. They were positioned on opposite sides of the road and, according to Nina, were involved in a deadly rivalry going back years that was so arcane no-one quite remembered any more how it had started, though some people darkly mentioned a nit shampoo cartel. There were also two branches of Oxfam. This could have given the place a depressing feel, but one was dedicated to second-hand books, and the other was the unacknowledged drop-off point for plenty of last season's Anthropologie and Oska numbers, briefly worn by the yummy mummies up the hill. Beth certainly wasn't above having a rummage now and then, although you did run the risk of having an embarrassing encounter with your jumper's previous owner in the playground.

Though it was cold and there was a mean-spirited wind nipping at her exposed hands and face, Beth was happy to see one of those perfect December skies up above, only a few tones lighter than Matisse's favourite cerulean blue. The trees along the pavement pointing into this heavenly shade were nude as any artist's models, leaves shamelessly shed into the gutter long ago. But Beth still saw the promise of spring in the bright chill. Maybe it was her lucky escape this morning, maybe it was the lingering delight of the night before, maybe it was simply being outside, but she felt irresistible bubbles of happiness rise up, like prosecco in a chilled glass. No, like *champagne*, she decided.

Even waiting in the deli for a coffee for her temporary boss didn't put a dent in her good mood. It was nice to stand in a really varied queue for a change, with women over the age of 40, even the odd man, and a pensioner or two. She adored the Village, she really did, but during school hours, without a jammy toddler and the keys to a Volvo, she sometimes felt like a fish out of water. Herne Hill seemed a bit more real. Even the gritty floor beneath her feet, the steamed-up windows, and the smells of fennel, coffee and bacon, the shouts of the kitchen staff preparing orders, seemed a little closer to urban living. It was refreshing.

Conscious that much more time had passed than she'd anticipated, Beth bustled back to the office. She wasn't quite expecting a reprimand, but she wouldn't have been surprised if Potter had looked down his long nose at her, from his great height, and made her feel small – all too easy for him to do, of course. Getting the coffee had been his idea, but the fact that she'd enjoyed bunking off to do his bidding so much made her feel obscurely guilty. It didn't take a lot, she realised. She had to get better at shrugging stuff off. She was pretty sure other people didn't go through life feeling bad about things that really weren't their fault.

She braced herself, squaring her shoulders as she reached the frosted glass, and opened the door with some difficulty, due to the large cardboard cups in each hand. Only to find the place deserted. Talk about an anti-climax. 'Hello? Paul?' she called out. She dumped the drinks down on her desk, stepped over to Potter's door and knocked just to check, but wasn't surprised when there was no answer. The place had that deserted feel.

Had he left her a note? Nothing on her desk. She quickly looked at her phone. A line of kisses from Harry, which had her blushing up to her fringe, but nothing else.

She sat down, a bit deflated, and now with two cups of coffee to get through. She was damned if this cappuccino with extra chocolate on top was going to waste. She took a sip, but the liquid was still boiling hot. Should she just finish typing out those reports first?

Beth shook her head at herself. She was prevaricating. And the reason wasn't hard to divine. All the shocks of the previous day, and this morning, had damaged her nerve. But she didn't know how much time she had. Potter could be back at any moment, and she would have made no progress. How much time, she asked herself sternly, did she really want to spend typing in someone else's chair? This was Ben's Christmas holiday. She should be out with him, doing nice festive things, instead of letting him moulder away in front of a telly. And what about Harry? She hadn't quite broached the whole telling-him-what-she-was-up-to thing. He had no idea about the little plan she'd cooked up with Nina.

Well, they weren't at the stage where they were living in each other's pockets, were they? It wasn't as if she was blithely going off every morning, lying to him. She had just glided gracefully over her whereabouts, and he'd made a series of comfortable assumptions. That was his lookout, and she hadn't sought to disabuse him. But she knew, in her heart of hearts, that he would seriously lose it if he could see where she was right now. 'Under false pretences'; 'meddling where you have no business'; 'putting yourself in danger'. In some ways, she didn't even have to tell him – she knew full well what he'd say. And he had a point.

She had to knock this thing on the head, find out finally what on earth was going on. And the way to do that wasn't by drinking coffee and typing reports. But first, she had to cover her back. Carefully, she used her chair to fish out the Simpkin key, then she unlocked Potter's office and pushed her chair up against the Rothko. While she badly wanted to delve into the filing cabinets, she had no idea how long Potter was going to be out, and after their scary encounter this morning, she didn't want to risk it. She reluctantly put the key back on the top of the frame. She then shoved her chair all the way back into place at her own desk, and sat down on it, exhausted.

The minutes ticked by, and she cursed herself for her cowardice. If she'd just peered into that cabinet, she could have solved the mystery by now. What a stupid waste of an opportunity. She got up again, decision in every movement. Perhaps a bit too much decision, as she caught one of the cups with her elbow and the rich brown liquid burst out everywhere as one paper cup knocked the other, and both hit the desk. Damn.

Inexorably, as liquid split on a desk always will, the lake of coffee found its way to her keyboard. Her laptop screen, which had been showing the latest interminable legal report, suddenly went blank. Beth wailed aloud, the sound shocking in the quiet emptiness of the office. Even the pervading beigeness was under attack now, as the drips started falling busily off the edge of the desk and onto the seagrass flooring. Beth didn't know what to salvage first, the laptop or the carpet. She grabbed the computer and lifted it clear of the puddle, then threw a packet of tissues – still in their cellophane – from her bag onto the floor. Doing no good at all, she realised. She ripped them from the now coffee-soaked pack and trod them into the gathering puddle, mopping up the rich and deliciously-scented cappuccino. What a waste.

She was gasping for a drink now, parched – but there was still so much staunching to do. Frantically, she tried to remember all the internet cures she'd ever read for wet equipment. Cover with rice, bury in pasta? Or was that a half-remembered tuna bake recipe? She ran a tissue over the keyboard in despair – and was thrilled when the blank screen came to life immediately. Perhaps things weren't as bad as she'd feared. She turned the laptop over and shook it. Only a dribble of coffee came out, and she wiped it off straight away. To be on the safe side, she switched it off, then carried on dabbing the keyboard. There. It looked fine. Smelled a bit of coffee, but that wasn't a bad thing, surely? Well, not today, a little voice told her. Might not be so great down the line, when all that frothy milk started to go off. An even littler voice told her that might be Nina's problem, if she could possibly get all this mystery stuff wrapped up.

She turned to spill number two, under her desk, and pressed unenthusiastically at the small mound of damp, brownish tissue that was rapidly absorbing the coffee. Nothing much she could do there for the moment. She'd nip out to the Sainsbury's later, get whatever was the latest in carpet cleaning products. There was bound to be something. And on the bright side, it was all under her desk – not on show to the public at all. Not that there ever seemed to be any public in this office, anyway.

But no sooner had she had that thought than she heard a sound she'd almost forgotten. It was the bell of the street door, as someone pushed in from outside.

'Freezing out there. Oooh, you're nice and snug in here, aren't you, dear? And doesn't it smell nice. Lovely, always liked the smell of coffee, I have,' said a tiny bent figure. It was an elderly lady, wheeling a tartan shopper towards her over the carpet, and bringing in the very last of the autumn's leaves on her contraption's wheels.

She followed Beth's eyes down to the trail. 'Oh, I'm so sorry, dear, my basket's so useful, can't quite manage the shopping the way I used to, you see. But it does sometimes get in a pickle. I'll just see if I can…' She tottered forward, ineffectually brushing at the crushed leaves with her brogue shoes and stamping the leaf mould further into the carpet.

Beth hurried out from behind the counter. 'Don't you worry about that, let's sit here, shall we?' she said, guiding her potential client to the seating area and lifting her astonishingly heavy shopper over to put beside her. 'Oof.'

'Just picked up the cat's tins from the supermarket,' said the lady, smiling.

Beth returned a slightly more circumspect smile, wondering silently if her back was ever going to be the same again. The lady's cat must have an appetite as healthy as the late lamented Lancelot.

'And what can we do for you today?' Beth asked, though

she wasn't sure, truthfully, whether she could do anything at all for her. As Potter was out, the chances were that the firm was going to lose their first sniff at an actual paying customer for days. It was such a shame. She put on an extra-helpful smile and tried to look as though she knew everything there was to know about the law. She must try her hardest to land this job, whatever it might be. 'Did you have an appointment, Mrs...?' she said, trying to make it sound as though they were snowed under with clients, despite the yawning emptiness of the office.

'I meant to ring, but I thought I'd just pop in on my way back from fetching Orlando's bits. I live up yonder, round near the Sunray Gardens,' she added, dashing Beth's hopes that she might be trailing a huge fee. If she lived close to Nina's, she was almost certainly talking about a flat, not one of the large Victorian villas off Half Moon Lane. 'I'm in the sheltered housing,' she added, unconsciously confirming Beth's diagnosis. 'I expect you think I've come to make my will,' said the little old lady, with a beady look at Beth.

Beth had indeed rapidly run through and dismissed all the other possibilities in her head, but she decided to say nothing. Sometimes, as she'd found in her long-lost journalistic career, silence was much more effective than speech. Sure enough, the woman couldn't resist filling the vacuum.

'Well, it's not that, see. Lots of others in my block have done their wills with your Mr Potter, right enough. Oh yes, they all love him, they do. Sam Cooper, Bert Hazelwood. Even Prue Smith came here, she did, and she only had buttons to leave. But I made my will years ago, on one of those forms from the Post Office. Don't need a fancy lawyer for that, do you?' she added smugly.

Beth, who wasn't even a tiny bit of a lawyer, fancy or not, felt obscurely put out by this, but maintained a polite expression, reluctant to see off the slightest chance of a paying client, however unpromising they might appear.

'No, I've come about something completely different. See if you can guess what it is.' The lady sat back, gave a little self-satisfied wiggle in her chair, settling herself down more firmly as though she was bedding in for the duration.

As she did so, a faint smell of old-fashioned mothballs reached Beth's wrinkling nose, reminding her forcibly of her late, and much lamented, granny. She'd been a great aficionado of naphthalene, which Beth had always found hard to understand. Yes, the pungent chemical did deter insects – but it meant that little else with functioning nostrils would willingly approach you either. What use were immaculate woolly jumpers, if no-one wanted to hug you in them? But despite the heady vapours, Beth had been extremely fond of her granny. Now the smell, unpleasant though it was, reminded her of happy times with glasses of warm milk and an uncritical beam of affection.

Meanwhile, the lady opposite fixed Beth with mischievous eyes, set in a sea of wrinkles that even WH Auden would surely have slapped moisturiser on. She was wearing a tweed coat, buttoned up to the top, which she showed no sign of loosening despite the warmth of the office. Her legs appeared to be encased in thousand-denier tights, with as many folds as an elephant's trunk, and her sensible lace-up shoes allowed an impressive set of bunions room to roam.

Beth ran through all the possibilities she could think of that could have attracted a dear thing like this – conveyancing, litigation, libel? But even a nasty spat with neighbours seemed unlikely; this lady seemed so twinkly. And surely she must have passed the quarrelsome age some decades back? Nothing at all seemed to fit. Much to the merry little figure's delight, she admitted that she gave up.

'Come for one of them pre-nups, in't I? Like that Kim Kardashian.'

Beth was speechless for a moment. For one thing, she wasn't sure whether Kim Kardashian had even had a pre-nup, and for another... well, her mind just boggled gently for a while, while the little old lady looked on and transparently enjoyed the sight.

Eventually, Beth found her voice. 'Well, congratulations! May I ask, who's the lucky man?' And how old is *he?* Beth wondered, but just about managed not to say.

'Oh, I've got a couple on the go. Not sure which one it'll be, but one of them's going to pop the question in the next few days. That's if they don't pop their *clogs* first,' said the lady, cackling with laughter, which rapidly turned into a fearsome hacking cough.

Beth, getting up to fetch some water, sincerely hoped none of the members of this love triangle were going to tarry with each other's affections for too long. Delay could be fatal.

'I've shocked you, in't I? Bet you thought we was all too old for hanky-panky. Well, let me tell you, a Freedom Pass in't just for the buses, love,' said Beth's client. She took the glass of water from Beth in an alarmingly shaky hand, sipping gingerly at it. It seemed to do the trick, the ferocious cough subsided to an occasional ghastly wheeze.

'My chest's been a nightmare, ever since that doctor got me to give up smoking. I told him, I did, the fags were the only things keeping the phlegm down. Would he listen? Pah.'

'Oh, when did you give up?' Beth asked politely, imagining the lady puffing her last during the Swinging Sixties or thereabouts.

'It was just last week. Look here,' she said, holding out a trembling arm, pushing back her coat sleeve with some difficulty, and displaying a couple of dog-eared nicotine patches stuck to her skin. The mothball aroma was suddenly a lot stronger. Beth wondered why it didn't put suitors off, but maybe the sense of smell declined with the passing years?

She drew back in alarm. 'I'm pretty sure you're only supposed to wear one of those patches at a time.'

'Nah, one wasn't working. This is a bit more like it. But you haven't got a fag on you, have you, darlin'?'

'Er, no, and um, maybe we should talk about the pre-nup? The thing is, I'm not entirely sure we do them, and even if we did, we'd have to wait until you were actually engaged. That is, I think so.'

'So you don't know? I thought I could just take a blank one, fill in the details as I go along. That way I'd be ready for any of them beggars. It's like the January sales, sometimes, down at the sheltered housing. And I'm in a good position now that Ivy Penrose has passed.'

It was Beth's turn to cough now. On the one hand, this was the only potential fee she'd laid eyes on since she'd been at the solicitor's office. On the other, she was pretty sure this wasn't how the law was supposed to work. And were pre-nups legally binding anyway?

'If you don't mind me asking, do you have the sort of level of assets that would make an agreement of this sort necessary?'

'Well, no-one's ever complained about me assets before, dearie,' said the lady irrepressibly, looking down at her well-filled tweed coat, which did indeed seem to boast substantial bulges, even if they were at waist height. She immediately started to cackle again, this time more loudly than before. Beth wondered if she should pat her on the back, or feed her another sip of water, but when she got up to assist, the lady waved her away.

Just when Beth was starting to fear the pre-nup would be redundant and the old lady's beneficiaries would have much preferred her to concentrate on brushing up that Post Office will, the bell jangled, and Potter loomed in the doorway.

'Ah, glad you're holding the fort there, Beth. Had to pop out. Some trouble with Lancelot.'

'But isn't he dead?' Beth blurted.

Potter gave her a sharp look. 'Yes. Very sadly. But the vet wanted to discuss an… um, issue, that's come up, something to do with the circumstances. But there was a huge queue, then the same again in the chemist when I went to pick up my prescription… Look, if I give it to you, could you nip out for it? Meanwhile, I'll take care of Mrs, erm?'

'It's *Miss*,' said the old lady archly, recovering magically from her coughing jag now there was a man in the room. She got up from her seat as though she was on springs and allowed herself to be ushered ceremoniously to Potter's office, with him gallantly wheeling her shopping trolley, after momentary surprise when he felt the weight of Orlando's cat food haul. At the door, she turned and gave Beth a smirk. It looked as though she was going to get her pre-nup, even if she died doing it.

Beth was a bit reluctant to leave the office while this interesting side-show was going on, but now that it had moved into Potter's inner sanctum she was excluded anyway. She got up and couldn't help herself, stooping over to retrieve the largest bits of leaf that had been wheeled in and throwing them in her bin. As far as she knew, it wasn't her job to clean the office – Nina had been vague on this point – but she was incapable of sitting and staring at clumps of dirt. She took the slip of pink paper from her desk, threw on her coat and scarf, and looped her bag over her arm.

The cold was really biting now as dusk fell, the Matisse sky gone and replaced by a blue-black backdrop, the colour of the Quink ink cartridges Beth remembered from school. Wow, that seemed a long time ago. The bare fingers of the trees stood out starkly, but a couple of strings of clashing Christmas lights strung across the shop facades added an artificial glow, and reminded Beth she hadn't done a thing to get ready and the 25th was looming. She shook her head to try and banish such thoughts and walked quickly to the chemists, choosing the one on her side of the road. Maybe there'd be some stocking fillers here she could snap up while she was waiting.

It was a relief to get in out of the cold. The windows of the shop streamed with condensation, giving the interior a cosy fug, and she handed over the prescription to a smiling assistant and turned to see if there was anything here that might make a small boy grin on Christmas morning. Apart from a small stand of make-up, which she felt quite drawn to inspecting for herself, there was very little for Beth to pause over. Ben was too old for Minions bubble bath; too young, thank goodness, for the Family Planning section; would definitely not appreciate any of the nit-repelling sprays she was quite tempted to invest in; and would throw a toothbrush out of his stocking without even giving it a cursory glance. Things had been a lot easier when he'd been tiny and didn't have to keep one eye on 'coolness' and what other kids would think of his bag of swag.

The best Christmas, and almost the easiest (apart from the two-hourly feeding and changing rigmarole), had been his first. As doting new parents who greeted their miraculous child's every move as proof that he was a rare genius, she and James had bought him ridiculous quantities of toys and been mildly miffed when he'd spent forever playing with one tiny scrap of Rudolph-infested gift wrap, crumpling it in tiny hands, dropping it, picking it up, attempting to eat it, and then repeating the whole sequence until even his captive, captivated audience had had enough.

Beth felt the usual needle of guilt now, as she remembered James. She drifted over to the make-up display, picked up a mascara and unscrewed it, peering at the bristling wand without really seeing it. James'd been such a wonderful dad. And he'd been a lovely man. She'd had a moment recently when she'd wondered if things would have lasted between them, if he hadn't gone and died on her like that. She'd even decided that things had become a bit stale. But now, she realised that she'd probably needed to think that, in order to liberate herself from James's ghostly embrace. She'd had to turn away from the image of him as a perfect husband and father, see him as a flawed human being just like everyone else, in order to move on – into someone else's arms. It had been hard, and she'd probably been too harsh to James's memory. But she'd been too misty-eyed about him before. She hoped now that she'd finally achieved some sort of balance. It was hard getting perspective on things. And perhaps it was even harder if you weren't particularly tall, she thought, with a self-indulgent smile.

She put back the mascara, which was probably now a bit dry, and looked at an eyeshadow palette. Everyone seemed to do these at the moment – acres of tones of beige, sliding up gradually to muddy browns. It reminded her of the décor of the office, and she put it back. Next, she looked at a contouring kit. Blimey. She couldn't imagine how these brick reds and dark greys could ever translate to cheekbones and chiselled noses – well, not in her hands, anyway. She'd be safer with a lipstick. But no, even these were either too dark or too sparkly. Feeling pickier than Goldilocks, and a bit disappointed as it had been ages since she'd had new makeup to play with, Beth screwed the last bullet-shaped lipstick back into its case and turned sadly away.

'Um, prescription for Potter?' said the assistant at the counter. Beth walked up with a smile. 'Are you Mrs Potter?' the young woman said, the light glinting off a delicate gold ring in her nostril.

'Er, no, but he asked me to pick it up for him.'

The girl frowned and scanned the creased prescription, smoothing it out with her hands, pretty pink nails catching the light. She turned it over, then back again. 'I'll just check this. Won't be a second.'

Beth nodded a little blankly, wondering what the problem was, but content to wait. The shop was all but empty now, with just one forty-something woman pottering around the cold cures. There were a few little packets of sweets at the counter that might do for Ben, if she was desperate. And she pretty much was at this point, she admitted to herself, with Santa's sleigh so close she could almost hear the bells.

She quickly selected a couple of the bags and lined them up to pay for. There was some murmuring from the back office, and Beth was sure she heard the word 'Potter'. The door between the shop and pharmacy area wasn't completely shut.

It was too hard to resist. She sidled round the counter, trying to look as if she wasn't, and got as close as she could to the back-room door, pretending she was scrutinising the shelves closest to it. Unfortunately, as she soon discovered, these were generously laden with laxatives and their opposites which, she remembered from a long-ago crossword clue, were called costives. Her late father, who'd suffered from a dicky tummy (possibly due to the fry-ups which eventually did for his arteries), had bluntly called these 'cork pills'.

She picked up a box of Imodium and pretended she was desperately interested in the small print. 'Capsules to restore your body's natural rhythm,' read the euphemistic blurb. She turned the carton this way and that, while straining her ears to hear the muted conversation from the back room. *'...Sent someone else in for it this time.' 'Is it the usual? The Zimmer frame?'* Then the handle was turned, and the door abruptly clicked shut, cutting off the sound of voices.

At the same moment, someone came into the shop, out of the cold, and bustled over to the counter. It was a mother that Beth was on nodding terms with, her Year 1 child cavorting around her. Beth smiled at her, realising she probably knew Nina. The woman beamed back initially, then noticed Beth clutching the tell-tale jumbo pack and averted her gaze, embarrassed.

A second later, the shop assistant came out of the back room like a jack-in-the-box and almost bumped into Beth, who rapidly back-tracked and then bumped into the little Year 1 lad, who set up a fearsome wail. His mother stooped to comfort him and couldn't resist sending a daggers dart in Beth's direction.

Beth, by now scarlet and still clutching the massive carton of anti-diarrhoea treatment, sidled back to the proper position at the counter and tried to pretend lots of difficult things weren't happening at the same time. The assistant fixed her with a professional-looking smile, her eyes dropping only once to the medication. 'I'm really sorry, but Mr Potter hasn't filled in the part authorising you to pick up the medicine for him.' She shrugged her shoulders.

Beth blinked. Was this the only problem? 'Um, well, can I just fill that in now? What do you need, my name and address?'

'I'm sorry, no, he has to do it, and he has to sign it, too.' Beth thought for a minute. This was a pain, and Potter was not going to be thrilled.

'Is there any way round this? I can get him on the phone and he can authorise me? He's just up the road in his office.'

'Yes, I know,' said the girl sympathetically. 'But we can't really do anything, our hands are tied. Sorry. Would you like me to ring that up for you?' she said neutrally, studying the box in Beth's hands.

'Oh! No thanks, I was just, erm, looking...' said Beth, putting the packet down hurriedly. 'Are you sure you can't just give me the prescription?'

'I'm sorry, no,' said the girl firmly, her tone final, as she looked over Beth's shoulder to the Year 1 mum, saying a little sharply, 'Yes? Can I help you?'

Beth had no choice but to take the sheet of paper back and shove it into her pocket. As she turned to leave, empty-handed, the other mother steadfastly avoided Beth's eyes. Oh dear. That probably made one fewer friendly face to talk to in the playground when Katie was away, and on top of that, she had to make her way back to the office empty-handed. She'd concentrated so hard on her eavesdropping and been so eager to distance herself from the Imodium, that she'd ended up forgetting to buy the sweets for Ben. But just before she turned up the road to the solicitors, she'd remembered her earlier mishap – the coffee. She trailed down to the Sainsbury's, investing a much-begrudged fiver in a lurid, shocking pink aerosol that promised to get any stain out of any surface. We'll see about that, she thought with a harrumph.

Oh well, at least having a real client in the office might have cheered Potter up, though the prospects of making any money out of the lady and her pre-nup seemed extremely slim. Beth was pretty sure that off-the-peg forms weren't really a thing, in the UK at least, and even if they were, one of her prospective suitors would not only have to go down on one knee – quite possibly a perilous operation in itself – but also live long enough to sign on the dotted line, and then make it all the way to the altar as well.

Beth wasn't altogether surprised to find that there was no trace of their recent customer when she got back to the office, apart from a few remaining shreds of mulch. She could spray that with her aerosol while she was at it. And that might rather sneakily cover up the mopping operation from her coffee mishap, if Potter had failed to notice the lingering scent of the spilled liquid and the suspicious darker patch under her desk.

She knocked on Potter's door, popped her head round, and explained briefly what had happened in the chemists – leaving out salient points like the eavesdropping, the Imodium, and its impact on her social standing – and watched his face fall. He wiped a hand over his features, a characteristic gesture she was coming to recognise, then pulled himself together and said with false heartiness that it didn't matter a jot.

'Anything you need to finish up, Beth? If not, then why don't you make a move? And then tomorrow will be the last day before we shut up shop for Christmas. Not sure whether you'll be back with us after that, will you? Or will Nina be back in play?'

'Oh, I think Nina will be returning to the helm, don't you worry,' said Beth, equally jovially. 'I've got a couple of reports to finish, but if you don't mind, I might get to them tomorrow morning. First thing when I get in, of course,' said Beth. 'Just got to fetch my son from the childminder's now,' she added, not letting on that his office manager and her nanny were, surprisingly enough, one and the same person.

'Of course, of course, must be tricky juggling,' said Potter, trying to sound sympathetic but actually just coming over, as far as Beth was concerned, as insufferably smug. He didn't have her logistical problems, as he had a wife at home. Not for the first time, Beth wished she did, too. Or a helpmeet, she supposed; she wasn't too fussed about gender. Someone on her team who could take up the odd centimetre of slack every now and again. It would be a long time, if ever, before Harry played any part in her childcare arrangements. Until then, it was her and Ben *contra mundum*.

As Beth trundled off in search of Ben, she kept thinking that she'd missed something important somewhere. Was it something that their unexpected bride-to-be had come out with? Her mouth quirked irresistibly at the corners as she replayed that scene. And Nina would love it, too. No, it wasn't their new client, good value though she'd been. Was it Potter's terrifying, almost murderous rage, this morning? No, once he'd calmed down, that had all been fine. And so little else had happened. The deadening effect of office life crashed in on her.

She was lucky, she realised yet again, that her job at Wyatt's was so flexible. Much more so than her employers had ever imagined or wanted, she thought briefly, but she waved that airily from her mind. Even though, to all intents and purposes, it was just as much office-bound as her current post, it allowed her oceans of licence by comparison. She had *carte blanche* to nip out whenever she liked, sometimes with unforeseen consequences. And if any reports had to be typed, well, she only had herself to blame if they were dull, as she wrote every word herself.

She'd always tried to value her little job, but now she would be thanking her lucky stars every time she opened her office door, with her own key, that she hadn't hidden somewhere like a crazy fictional cat.

As she walked up the road towards Nina's place – realising that you only really appreciated that Herne Hill was hilly when you were walking up towards Dulwich, after a long day at work – a thought continued to nag away at her. There was something, somewhere, that she'd missed. What on earth could it be?

Just then, a mum in a hurry swerved past her, almost dragging her little girl by the arm. Either they were in one of the few after-school clubs that hadn't stopped for the Christmas break, or they were rushing for a train at North Dulwich station. Maybe a holiday treat, like one of the West End shows. Beth had taken Ben to see *The Lion King* a couple of years ago, and they'd both been mesmerised by the elegance of the drifting giraffes moving across the stage.

Just as they overtook, the mother clipped Beth's leg with a bulging plastic bag. 'Oh, I'm so sorry,' she said, as Beth inwardly winced but outwardly apologised back for getting in the way of the woman's collection of unfeasibly sharp objects. That was going to bruise, Beth cursed, as she rubbed her shin ruefully. But wait a minute. That white plastic bag had had a green cross on it. From the chemists.

What was that snippet she'd overheard in the chemists? Well, eavesdropped on, if you wanted to be strictly accurate. It had been something about Potter's prescription. Beth had barely glanced at the slip of paper which she'd handed into the pharmacist. It wasn't that she wasn't interested – she was interested in everything, all the time. But the drug, zopi-something, had meant nothing to her.

There hadn't been time to Google it between being handed the piece of paper in the office, in front of Potter and the lady, and getting to the chemists just a few doors down. She supposed she'd been counting on getting the box over the counter. Then, if she'd been curious enough (and of course she was), she could have read the insert with all the instructions and the usually hair-raising contraindications, at her leisure, and pretended she'd been stuck in a queue.

But, of course, she'd come back empty-handed. All she had to go on was the half-whispered, half-remembered conversation between the pharmacy assistants. *'Zimmer frame'*, that had been it. Or something very like it. And the word on the original form had definitely started with the letters ZOP. So that was what she was looking for. It might mean nothing at all. But Beth was feeling hopeful as she turned the corner where Nina's flats were located.

To her astonishment, despite the cold, there was a little knot of people gathered outside the block under a street lamp, including, she could now see, Nina, Wilf, and Ben. They were all bundled up against the chill, with Ben wearing one of Nina's own hats – a signature Dulwich number in thick cable knit with a furry bobble right on top. It reminded Beth of Letty's beautiful pale turquoise version – though she was willing to put money on the fact that Nina's was a more modest Primark knock-off, which probably meant the style had caught on a little too far and the Dulwich *cognoscenti* would be moving restlessly to find the next *It* hat very soon. Goodness knew how Nina had persuaded Ben into something a bit girly and furry – but Beth was glad she had, it was freezing out here. She dashed over.

'Nina? What on earth are you doing out here?'

'Beth! Great! I was a bit worried we'd miss you in the dark,' said Nina, grabbing her arm in greeting.

Beth hated to point it out, but Nina's ample embonpoint and white coat, today teamed with a neon pink version of Ben's hat, did mean that spotting her was not exactly a game of *Where's Wally?*

'It's all kicking off here. There's been another one,' Nina said, with a significant glance at Wilf. His little pixie face was alight with excitement and expectancy, and he was gabbling to Ben, who was patiently standing at his side.

'Another what?' Beth was baffled.

Nina, over Wilf's head, started to do a mime, sticking both hands behind her head and waggling them furiously, then staring at Beth as though she must know what that meant. Exasperated, she then turned round and started waving her arm low down at her side. This gesture Beth had seen often enough in the playground, when Ben or a friend had farted and found the whole business hysterically funny. But that had really only been in vogue when he'd been smaller. Beth backed away half a pace, put her head on one side, and wondered what she'd been thinking of letting this woman look after her son. Nina was now frantically mouthing a word. What was it? It looked like…

'Golf? Golf,' said Beth, her eyebrows disappearing into her fringe. Playing charades was all very well, and she was more or less braced for a few compulsory rounds of it after lunch on Christmas Day, but in the sub-zero temperatures of a Herne Hill housing estate? After a long day with the great dictator? Beth could feel her stocks of patience disappearing from the shelves like plasma tellies in a Black Friday sale.

Nina grabbed her arm again and hauled her off a few paces to the side, away from the boys and the crowd, which seemed to be growing. Ben watched his mum closely but seemed relaxed. Wilf continued to chatter away, oblivious.

'What is it? What's up?' said Beth urgently.

'I was saying *woof!* Honestly, what are you like? It's another *dog*,' said Nina, who still seemed to be expecting some sort of plaudits for her acting.

She'd be waiting a while, thought Beth, who was distinctly underwhelmed. 'I was going to guess elephant, if you'd had a gun to my head. But what's this about dogs?'

'Another one's been poisoned. Rosie.'

'No!' Beth felt cold. This was getting serious. 'How many's that, now? Roxie the dachshund, Lola the spaniel, Lancelot the Potter's Great Dane. And I heard about another one, Truffle, the other day, though apparently that was old age. And now one here? Are you sure?'

'They're saying it's a serial killer,' said Nina, her eyes round as saucers.

Beth was silent for a moment as it sunk in. Could you really be a serial killer of dogs? Was that glorifying a petty act of spite, probably carried out by a dreadfully maladjusted teenager? But on the other hand, these were blameless, loving, trusting pets, loved by their families, leaving broken-hearted children behind them. Whoever was doing this was not only destroying dogs, they were destroying childhood memories, too. It was evil.

'But I don't understand what everyone's doing out here?'

'Oh, this is what we do round here when something big happens. Bin lorry forgets to pick up the rubbish. Someone kills our dogs. Out on the streets. Solidarity. You probably don't get this round the posh bits of Dulwich.'

You certainly didn't, thought Beth. The worse things got in the outside world, the more Dulwich families seemed to close in on themselves. Yes, the Ocado deliveries started clanking more, the bottles of wine becoming a dire necessity rather than an occasional temptation due to the twenty-five per cent reduction on a half-dozen. But that was a secret between the householders, their extremely heavy recycling bins, and the exhausted supermarket drivers filling up GPs' surgeries with their complaints of chronic back pain.

'Whose dog was it this time?'

'Oh, that bloke over there. The one sobbing on that fat geezer's shoulder, can you see?'

Beth looked across and saw a chap whose head, covered with fine blond stubble showing up like a halo in the street light, was bowed as he leant into an equally shorn friend, and wept openly. It was shocking – you so rarely saw men give way to their feelings in public, even in this day and age, Beth realised. She certainly hadn't seen her own father cry. Her brother rarely seemed capable of any of the deeper emotions, so determined was he to skate blithely across the surface of life. Ben still cried, earnestly and heartbreakingly, when he hurt himself, but somehow he'd learned to control tears of rage, chagrin or sorrow. She certainly hadn't tried to teach him to repress his feelings – unless it was by example. It was a horrible thought, and Beth turned away from it and focused on the poor, bereft man in front of her.

He cried on, every now and then raising his voice incoherently then burying his head again in his friend's meaty shoulder. That T-shirt must be sodden by now, Beth thought, admiring the restraint of the pal on the receiving end of all those tears. The erstwhile dog owner, meanwhile, still had a thick leather leash, encrusted with silver studs, dangling uselessly from his hand, its one careful lady owner now gone for good.

'Poor man, he's absolutely in bits,' said Beth. It was an understatement. 'Did you know the dog?'

'We all knew Rosie. She was the loveliest Staffie. Looked tough but, like Bob, she was sweet as a nut, she really was.'

Beth didn't like to admit that she most dogs quite scary – they were usually at an unfortunate height for her and seemed to delight in snuffling in places she'd much rather keep private. She knew, though, that Staffordshire Bull Terriers had had an unjustified (and ironic) mauling in the press a while back, resulting in Battersea Dogs' and Cats' Home, where she'd got her beloved Magpie, being full to bursting with the sad abandoned creatures, big-hearted and affectionate dogs who adored their families, but maybe didn't boast the cuddlier appearance of a golden retriever.

'How dreadful,' she said sadly. 'But wait a minute, how does it help us all standing out here?' she asked, not daring to add, 'getting really cold.' It didn't seem very sympathetic.

'Oh, you know, we're just showing we all care. It's what

we *do*. Plus, the police are supposed to be on their way and we want to make sure they know we take this very seriously, very seriously indeed.'

Beth was starting to have a bad feeling about this. 'Are you sure it's a good idea for us to be out here with the kids?' she said, conscious of sounding lame.

Ben and Wilf were watching proceedings with big eyes, seeming to find it all as fascinating as Bonfire Night or any other outdoor evening activity. She supposed, at their age, there were few occasions when they were really outside for long periods on a dark winter's evening. And at six and at ten, novelty was always good. Plus, the mood of the crowd, part excited, part angry, part almost vengeful, was quite intoxicating. There might be precious little actually happening at the moment, but there was certainly an air of tense expectation, which was no doubt infecting the children. Beth felt it, too, and wondered with a stab of foreboding where all this was going to lead.

Just then, Beth thought she saw someone she knew moving through the crowd. His head was down, he was wearing a dark coat, but there was something very familiar about his gait. Wait a minute, could it be? Yes, he hurried past a street lamp, and she saw him clearly. It *was* him. Tom Seasons, the Bursar of Wyatt's. What on earth was he doing here?

He disappeared round the corner, and then Beth had something else to worry about. There was the distinctive flash of blue lights advancing up Red Post Hill, bouncing off the buildings, and a very familiar plain clothes police car drew up, followed by a patrol vehicle. The crowd started to move, pushing forward towards the cars for reasons Beth didn't understand at all. She immediately shrank back into the crowd, looking for Ben, grabbing his hand. He tried to shake her off, but for once she held on tightly, not caring a jot if he lost face or if she was being embarrassing. Nina, she noticed, dived for Wilf as well, and they stood together in the thick of the press of people. Beth's ears were on stalks, listening out. And then she heard him.

'Evening, ladies and gentlemen,' came Harry's voice, the very slight Irish burr always a little stronger when he was under pressure, though you'd never know it from his measured tones. Immediately, she felt a bit calmer. It was going to be all right.

'Now, I understand there's been an incident, and I'm here to look into that. I'll be talking to Mr Fletcher here, and we'll be doing everything we can to get to the bottom of this occurrence—'

'Occurrence? It's blimmin' murder, mate, that's what it is,' piped up a lad in a hoodie from the back of the crowd. Beth peered over.

Immediately, the crowd murmured approval. 'What you going to do about it then, eh?'

'What about our dogs, are they going to be next?'

'It'll be the kids after, that's what,' came an angry woman's voice from right behind Beth.

Beth ducked down, but too late. Harry York, a good six foot four in his socks, scanned the crowd, his eyes came to rest on her, widened incredulously and, to his credit, roamed on until he found the woman who'd just spoken, puffed up with her own aggression and busily gathering the approval of her neighbours.

'Madam, I'd like to say to you, and to every one of you here now, we are looking into this incident and will be treating it very seriously indeed. Very seriously,' said York, and if Beth wasn't mistaken, he narrowed his eyes directly at her. 'We'll be canvassing all of you, house-to-house, and that will be the moment when any of you can raise concerns directly with me, or one of my officers. Please do pass on any information you may have. We're going to get to the bottom of this together, aren't we?'

There were murmurs of assent now, and Beth thought admiringly how well her Harry – if she could call him that – had played things. There had been ugly moments when it looked as though feelings, already running high, were going to spill over into aggression and defiance. But they had been skilfully defused. Now Harry stepped forward and took

Rosie's owner to one side, and was handing him a wad of tissues and patting him on the back. His friend looked a little relieved to have had the sobbing weight removed from his shoulders and, sure enough, his thin T-shirt looked damp, even from this distance. How could he stand the cold, dressed like that? Beth thought, turning to make sure Ben's coat was done up to the chin and also calculating how soon they could make their escape and sidle away from Harry's inevitable disapproval.

At that moment, Harry clapped the bereaved dog owner on the back one last time and turned, inexorably, to face her. The crowd had thinned out disappointingly by now, Beth realised, people melting away almost as quickly as they had assembled, no-one wanting to linger in the freezing temperatures now that the show was so evidently over. Nina, her arm round little Wilf, smiled merrily at Beth, ignoring her beseeching eyes, and said, 'Tomorrow, yeah?' making for the door of the flats before Beth could remonstrate with her.

Beth turned back to Harry and tried a smile. He narrowed his eyes a little at her, despatched the PCs with him to the four corners of the estate, and then said, 'Beth. Fancy meeting you here.'

'Mm,' she squeaked, acutely conscious of Ben's ears flapping away as he sensed something very interesting going in the dynamic between his mum and her friend. 'I was just passing…'

'I'm surprised you're still up, mate,' said York, addressing Ben directly and, of course, going straight to the heart of Beth's ever-present, over-active maternal guilt gland. 'Quite late for a school night.'

'There's no school, silly. It's Christmas!' sang out Ben, pointing to all the decorations in the flats behind him. Sure enough, there was even a fake Santa straggling down the façade of the building, complete with a sack of presents, both of which looking as though they'd seen better years, let alone days. And reindeers, elves, stars, and trees blazed down on them from all sides. Outdoor decorations in Dulwich itself were restricted to the odd string of white fairy lights draped terribly tastefully over a hedge, but no-one in this postcode seemed to have got the memo, and the morass of twinkling electricity could probably be seen from Mars.

Beth, a little worried that calling a policeman silly was an arrestable offence even if you were extremely overexcited and ten, smiled as winningly as she could. 'We were just visiting a friend, got caught up in the whole thing... I'm not sure how,' she tailed off.

Harry, in his dark navy coat, with a thick cream scarf wrapped round his chin, looked tall, forbidding, very official despite the plain clothes, and not nearly as smiley as she'd have liked. Not at all like the last picture she had of him in her mind's eye, rumpled from a busy night and giving her a long, lingering kiss before sneaking out of her house without waking Ben.

'Funny how that seems to happen to you,' said Harry drily, unbendingly addressing her from his full height. 'Well, you off home now?'

'Yes, yes, I think it's time we got you to bed,' Beth said to Ben in the false-bright way that she knew he hated most.

'Fancy a lift?' Harry put his head on one side. The question was directed solely at Ben.

The boy nodded furiously for a moment, then thought of something. 'Can we have the flashing lights on?'

'Nope,' smiled Harry.

'Sirens, then?' asked Ben irrepressibly. Beth couldn't blame him for trying, but Harry just laughed, shook his head once and opened the back door of the discreet, dark saloon car to let him slide in. He then did the same for Beth, with a little more irony. But he touched her hand as she got into the car, and immediately she had the warm feeling that everything would be fine. He couldn't really be cross with her just for being in the wrong place, could he?

But already she had that feeling she'd sometimes got long ago at school, when the Headmistress was banging on about some minor infraction of the rules, like lying down on the lawn outside the science block where they would be – gasp – visible to people on the top decks of passing buses, or buying cigarettes from the newsagents opposite the school gates. Every time, from the woman's demeanour, you'd have thought murder had been committed, there in the hall. And despite herself, without fail, Beth had always started to feel guilty, no matter how clean her hands were of whatever the terrible crime was. By the end of those assemblies, her cheeks would be as scarlet as the culprit's should have been.

And now she felt as though she was going to be raked over the coals again. This time, though, she had a weapon at her disposal that she'd never possessed as a schoolgirl.

Harry did try to be stern with her, once Ben, inevitably protesting he wasn't tired but caught out in a colossal yawn, had been packed off unceremoniously to bed. 'Why is it that, whenever there's any trouble in Dulwich, you're in the thick of it?' he asked, sounding exasperated and pushing his hands through his thick blond hair.

'Well, this time, I think you mean *Herne Hill*,' Beth said, straight-faced. 'That's completely different, you know,' she added, ducking as Harry chucked a cushion at her. 'Here, mind out, you nearly got Magpie with that,' she said. The cat stalked off, deeply unimpressed, pausing only to dart a glance of profound dislike at Harry out of her emerald chip eyes before disappearing into the kitchen. She then wriggled herself out of the cat flap with some difficulty. It was hard making a dignified exit when you were getting to the comfortably fluffy phase of feline life.

Back in the sitting room, Beth was braced for more of a telling off, but luckily some of the fight seemed to have gone out of Harry.

'You know, I just worry about you, Beth. You're such a, well, you're not a trouble-maker, but my mum would definitely call you a trouble-magnet. You really don't need to have a finger in every pie in Dulwich – or Herne Hill, or wherever. You know what you should have done, when you saw trouble brewing? You should have called me. As it was, we got an anonymous tip at the station.'

'The thing is,' Beth said earnestly, 'I really didn't know there was anything going on, till I was in it. And it was all quite peaceful. People were just so upset. That guy's dog was some sort of four-legged saint, it turns out. Did you know about this awful poisoning business, anyway? Why didn't you tell me about it?'

'Excuse me, I don't have to tell you every crime that occurs in a one-mile radius of your favourite café, you know.'

She had to admit that was fair enough. And anyway, she wasn't really interested in lost bicycles and pinched iPhones – unless they tied in with a case. But that's what Nina's business had become, she realised with a jolt. It was a case, and for better or for worse (probably for worse, she thought with a slightly sinking feeling) she was investigating it. Not that she needed to trouble Harry with all that now. He had enough on his plate. Nevertheless...

'But this dog thing, I mean, it's so cruel, it's... just so awful. And I do have a pet, you know. I think you should have informed me, just to keep Magpie safe.'

Magpie, who'd stayed outside for long enough to realise it was exceptionally cold, even if you were wearing a nice fur coat, sauntered back in at that moment. She scrambled up onto the sofa, stepping delicately over Beth to stand on York's legs, staring at him for a moment as if to dare him to complain, and then proceeded to knead his legs enthusiastically with her unsheathed claws.

'She's wrecking my trousers,' he yelped. Both Beth and Magpie's surprised glances gave him to understand that to complain was to announce yourself as an irredeemable wimp. After he'd gritted his teeth in silence for a minute, Magpie settled herself down with a whump, like a hovercraft coming to rest.

'Magpie is a cat, not a dog,' said Harry, getting back on track and daring to move his legs a little. Beth watched as Magpie dug in a warning claw. She didn't tolerate a lot of fussing from her chosen cushion of the evening. She was bestowing quite an honour, and the best way to show you were worthy was not to move a muscle, unless it was your stroking hand, and that should be applied lightly and reverently.

Harry winced and continued, 'Magpie's in no danger. And she can definitely look after herself.'

'You say that, but this awful person could start on cats next. What if they're just warming up on dogs? And anyway, do you know for sure that it's poison? Is there definitely someone out there killing pets?'

Harry gave Beth a level look. 'You know I can't tell you anything about ongoing investigations. Where would that end? I know you love to be involved, and you somehow *get* involved, but it's not a good thing, Beth. You've got no legal status, you've no back-up if things go wrong. It's just asking for trouble.'

Beth gave him a reproachful look. 'I just want to keep my cat safe. And what about friends who've got dogs? What am I supposed to say to them? Presumably, if this goes on, there'll be some sort of guidelines, won't there? You could see the way feelings were running high, tonight.'

Harry sighed deeply. Beth could tell he was mulling things over. Her point about guidelines had to have struck home. There must be plenty of things people could do to protect their dogs, after all. And things to look out for.

'Is it similar poison in every case? Is that how you know these deaths are all linked?'

Harry rolled his eyes. 'Look, I will say this. It does seem to be the work of the same perpetrator, so far. But at this stage we don't want to whip up any hysteria.'

It was like sitting next to an official press spokesman, thought Beth. Dry as dust – and almost as much fun as that sounded. She didn't want to wreck their unexpected evening together entirely, but on the other hand, while Harry was here, she really felt she ought to pump him for every detail. She knew Nina, living so close to the unfortunate Rosie, would be full of questions for a start.

'There've been at least three or four dogs so far, haven't there? Roxie, the little dachshund; that was before school broke up. And Lola the spaniel, too. Then Lancelot, the Great Dane. Now Rosie. And possibly one called Truffle as well, though that's not clear. Is there anything linking all these dogs, apart from the fact that their owners are all in Dulwich or Herne Hill?'

Harry was looking at Beth in astonishment. 'How do you even know that much? We're just piecing things together. Honestly, I ought to just tap your phone line. It would cut our investigation time in half.'

Beth didn't like to admit that most of this knowledge was gleaned on the ground, as it were, in Potter's office. But she did rather glow at the thought that Harry admired the way she had her finger on the pulse.

Unfortunately, it turned out he hadn't meant it that way at all. He was, in fact, building up quite a head of exasperation, which suddenly erupted all over the sofa.

'Beth. Beth, you can't go on doing this,' he burst out.

Magpie gave him a look of total disgust. Honestly. You thought you'd found a nice comfy place to have a well-earned snooze after a frankly exhausting day, you'd finally got all that pointless shifting around sorted out, then there was this shouting. It was too much. She shot up, giving him a last jab with her claws for good measure, and settled on the other side of Beth, flashing him the merest glance to signify her hearty disapproval.

York immediately started brushing ineffectually at the impressive calling-card of shed hairs Magpie had left behind. The black ones weren't too bad, the white ones stood out against his dark trousers which, until very recently, had been his smartest pair. Somehow this seemed to crystallise his sense of frustration and annoyance.

'Look, you'll only end up getting hurt, and I don't want that,' he said, as though it had been wrung out of him, his face working.

For Beth, this was a far more effective tactic than any telling off. She herself had known the awful pain of losing someone unexpectedly. There was no way that she'd consciously put anyone else through that. She put out a hand and Harry grabbed it and squeezed tight. They exchanged a small smile.

But, thought Beth, on the other hand, she certainly wasn't

planning to modify her behaviour to suit someone who, to put it brutally, might not even turn out to be a permanent fixture in her life. She would never ask him to change careers and become an accountant, for instance, on the basis that numbers weren't going to hurt him, in the way that a machete-wielding maniac in Lewisham, say, was quite likely to. She knew that being a policeman was more than a job for him, it was part of who he was as a person. He knew the risks and accepted them because he loved his work. Or enough of it to keep the balance. Yes, it was scary, thinking he was out there, up against a London that was getting colder every day, and not just as far as the weather was concerned. But so far, she'd mostly been able to distract herself from worrying about what he might be up to, with her own little exploits. Even if that changed, she wouldn't feel entitled to ask him to renounce a career he loved.

She was quite clear that he didn't have the right, either – or, maybe, yet – to ask for big sacrifices from her. And on the face of it, her job as an archivist could hardly be safer. Short of a large stack of school magazines falling on her, or the very real risk that reading through the collected speeches of previous headmasters might bore her to death, she ought to live for ever, as far as accidents at work were concerned. But she knew that work wasn't the bit that worried him. It was life, life in Dulwich, which did seem to have taken a turn for the macabre recently.

Anyway, that wasn't to say that she accepted his charge that she was always getting into trouble. Was she a *trouble-magnet*? She didn't think so. She would plead guilty, yes, to having perhaps more than her fair share of curiosity, and sometimes that had led her to hair-raising places and situations, but she still thought that everything she'd done had been justified by the end results. It wasn't idle thrill-seeking, after all, that kept her pushing ever onwards, but the need to sort things out, clear up messes, make sure that things were better once she'd finished. And on that score, she really felt she was doing pretty well.

The jury was out on the whole situation at Nina's work,

though. She'd been there days now, poking diligently into things that, no doubt, Harry would think did not concern her, and she had yet to uncover real evidence of wrong-doing. But she had one day left. And she was damned if she was going to give that up.

No, if Harry was going to worry himself frantic about what she was up to, there was only one possible solution. She wouldn't tell him.

It wasn't *lying*, after all. It was just avoiding trouble. Maybe she was more like her brother than she'd ever known. He didn't make promises he couldn't keep, because he just didn't believe in making promises at all. No woman, so far, had been able to get him far enough into the commitment zone to make one in the first place.

She suddenly saw the charms of dancing around the truth, as though it was a maypole that she could garland with the bits that suited her, while ducking under and away when things were less appealing. Beth knew all about sins of omission and decided she didn't really like the sound of them. She'd be living by a different principle – that of the *need-to-know* basis. If Harry couldn't cope with the thought of her getting involved in things that didn't directly concern her, then such things could just glide away into an interestingly misty hinterland where, in his mind at least, she sat at home most of the time with her son, and did nothing more taxing with her brain than the quick crossword in the newspaper.

It was a little bit hard to believe that Harry would really prefer this Stepford Wife incarnation of her to the feisty, indefatigable woman who'd infuriated him and intrigued him by turns before – the person he'd found irresistible enough for them to get to this stage. But men, she decided, were strange creatures. She looked over at Harry, where he sat, visibly feeling diminished after having to admit he cared about her welfare. He didn't like to feel vulnerable. She understood that – no-one did. But most people accepted it as the price of love.

She'd come to a decision that ought to protect both of

them, though, and she was determined that the whole business shouldn't wreck their evening. She bustled to the kitchen, coming back with a bottle of red, then lighting the reasonably realistic gas fire and, after a moment's hesitation, a scented candle for good measure. In her scheme of things, this was tantamount to showering Harry with roses while a violinist played *That's Amore* behind the sofa.

Beth pressed home her advantage by leaning forward and puckered up. Someone had told her that if you did this to a man, he was automatically pre-programmed to kiss you, whether he wanted to or not. Sure enough Harry, after giving her a single, distrustful glance, accepted the delicious inevitable. After a prolonged bout of what she still couldn't help calling *snogging,* Harry was putty in her hands. Though some of him was not very much like putty at all, she thought with considerable satisfaction.

Chapter Fifteen

The next morning, Beth lay in bed feigning the sleepy aftermath of bliss while Harry bumbled about getting his kit together. He sighed again over the appearance of his Magpie-modified trousers, stumbled over his shoes and generally made enough noise, with his sneaking off, to wake anything except a small boy. Thank goodness, Ben was always immovable once he'd finally been coaxed into bed, and today didn't seem to be an exception, even when Harry almost tripped and fell on the stairs as Magpie, in a last bid to do him down, wound through his legs like an Olympic slalom champ.

As soon as she heard the gentle click of the front door, Beth threw back her flowery duvet – not for the first time, contemplating getting a more unisex cover, then rapidly dismissing the idea as she loved waking up in a bouquet of flowers – and leapt into the shower. She got the breakfast sorted, then woke a tousle-haired Ben and frogmarched him out of bed.

Luckily, Ben was too used to suffering the odd ways of grown-ups to bother asking why they were getting up earlier during the holidays than they did during term time. He yawned his way through a bowl of cocoa pops – Beth found that unfeasibly large amounts of sugar did help both of them put one foot in front of the other in the mornings – and off they went, trudging down the quiet street.

Pickwick Road looked as though it had also had a high sugar morning. There was a dusting of frost on every hedge, sparkling in the pale wintry sun. All the cars had been iced with it overnight, like a row of glistening buns. There'd be some grumpy scraping of windscreens this morning, that was for sure. Beth made a mental note to buy some de-icing spray.

She hardly used her little Fiat, now that Ben had pretty much finished with his tutoring, and the last time they'd had a frosty morning she'd been reduced to using her Tesco Clubcard to clear a little circle that she could see through. All her neighbours had, of course, been brandishing special ice-scraping implements, or at least Waitrose loyalty cards. She was determined not to be caught out again.

'Brrrr,' shivered Ben, and Beth picked up the pace. 'Come on, quicker we get there, the quicker you can be doing some fun things with Wilf,' she smiled.

'When's Charlie back?' asked Ben.

Beth turned to him, concerned. 'Aren't you having fun at Wilf's?'

Ben thought about it. He was a meticulously fair child. 'It's fine, but Charlie's my *real* friend. And we've got a lot of stuff we need to do. There's a new level we can get to in our game. You know the one, it goes like this, you turn the console like that and then press at the same time and a new screen comes up, and I really need to explain it to him…'

Beth effortlessly tuned out Ben's long explanation of the latest gaming techniques, and started worrying about the quality of his holiday instead. It hadn't really been fair to leave him with Nina and Wilf for so long. He wasn't going to be small forever; she should treasure these holidays with him while she could, exhausting though they could be. The time would be coming, very, very soon, when he wouldn't hang out with her for any money. And instead of capitalising on his current acquiescence, she was parcelling him off to a friend while she did, what exactly?

Maybe Harry was right. Maybe all this was just a silly, and potentially dangerous, waste of time. She remembered that moment with Potter with a shiver of horror. He'd really seemed capable of anything in those seconds. She had genuinely feared for her safety. And yet here she was, not only trooping back there, but getting there extra early. She really needed her head examining.

But it was the last day – her last opportunity – before Potter shut up for the holidays. She didn't know what his plans were for Christmas; they weren't exactly on cosy discussion terms. And if she were honest, her own state of denial about the rapid approach of Father Christmas didn't help much. She really, really needed to do a bit of shopping. And at least source some sort of turkey.

If Potter's financial state was as bad as Nina thought, he ought to be at home in Dulwich throughout the festivities, sharing a couple of crusts of dry bread with his nearest and dearest. But Beth could not see that appealing one little bit to Letty. She'd do her best to probe what the Potter Christmas would be like. It would be a good indication of the underlying state of affairs, she decided.

As they got to Nina's, Beth looked around at the other flats, remembering the garish lights and the jostling crowd last night. Today, everything was calm and quiet, the reindeers and snowflakes just outlines in the daylight, waiting patiently for their moment when darkness fell and they would be switched on again to such startling effect.

There were one or two posters taped to the lamp posts, Beth noticed. She wasn't sure if they'd been there yesterday. *REWARD: Anyone with information on the poisoning of our beautiful girl, Rosie, call this number.* Under the writing was a picture of the dog. The photo, which was a bit pixilated, had probably been taken on a phone, then blown up to a frankly unflattering size. Only a mother, or a father in this case, could call Rosie's slathering chops beautiful, though Beth thought her soft dark eyes did look very kind. Poor dog. She certainly hadn't deserved her awful fate.

There were a few empty beer cans rolling around in the gutter, and the place had the look of somewhere that had partied hard, and perhaps not wisely. Nina poked her head around the door, her strawberry blonde curls standing on end. She held a fluffy dressing gown up to her chin and looked as though she'd only just surfaced. From inside, Beth heard the theme tune of *SpongeBob SquarePants,* suggesting Wilf at least had been an early riser.

'You're keen to get to it,' Nina said through a large yawn, letting Ben sidle past into the flat.

'Last day before Potter shuts up for the break. It's now or never,' said Beth, unable to take her eyes off Nina's face. She'd rarely seen anyone look so sleepy, and yet be standing upright.

'Sorry, it was pretty noisy last night till the early hours. Turned into a wake-cum-disco. Apparently, Rosie liked a dance,' said Nina, rolling her tired eyes a bit.

'Really?' said Beth.

'Any excuse,' laughed Nina. 'It was fun but went on that bit too long. I thought we'd have the rozzers round again. There's lots of old folks round here who probably weren't that thrilled, but in the end I just fell asleep.'

'Was Wilf ok?'

'Oh, yeah. He'd snooze through the last trump, that one. Up at the whack of dawn like you this morning, more's the bitty. He'll be so chuffed that Ben's here. Not sure what we're going to do without him.'

'You're welcome to come to us any time you like,' smiled Beth, realising she'd become fond of Nina and would really miss her once this little investigation was over. 'I'm hoping I'll find something today, it's my last chance. If I don't, I'll feel I've let you down.'

'Nah, don't be silly. I know you've given it a really good go. Tell you what, if you don't find anything, that doesn't mean I'm giving up. I'll just take over and keep on digging. Get there eventually.'

Immediately, all Harry's warnings from the night before came back to Beth. She hated the thought of Nina stumbling into something that would get her into trouble. 'It might not be safe. He can be quite... threatening, Potter, don't you find?'

'Paul? Nah! He's a big softy. Maybe it's his size you don't like,' said Nina shrewdly. 'When you stand face-to-face, it can feel a bit as though you're talking to a mountain. I try and be standing while he's sitting, and sitting while he's standing,' said Nina, nodding sagely.

Beth, not sure she could remember this complicated ballet while also on red alert for funny business and carrying out all the normal office functions as well, was non-committal. 'Hm. Well, I'll certainly bear that in mind.'

Nina burst out laughing. 'Well, if that isn't shorthand for *not on your life*, I don't know what is. Anyway, I won't hold you up. I really need a coffee. Get to it, girl!'

'Sorry, I'll let you get on. See you this afternoon. And let me know if anything kicks off here again with the dog situation.'

'Oh, it should be all quiet, don't you worry. Ben will be just fine. Unless another dog gets done in, of course.' With that, Nina shut the door.

Beth could almost see her stumbling over Wilf's detritus to the coffee maker, like a drowning woman reaching for a lifebelt. She hoped she'd be all right, in charge of two energetic boys all day when she'd clearly been sleep deprived. But Beth knew from experience that a pair of children was often a lot easier to handle than one. They entertained each other, reducing the burden on the grown-up in a rather magical way. She hoped things would pan out like that for Nina.

As she carried on down the road to the office, Beth noticed this morning's hard frost was already disappearing, leaving the gutters awash with water and the pavements slick. She admired the colours teased from the humble paving slabs when they were wet like this, hues of violet and gentle taupe standing out amongst the standard London grey. There was so much to love about the place. That didn't stop her slowing a little as she approached the frosted glass of the office. She wasn't mad keen to go inside. But at least she'd be on her own for a bit. Potter never came in this early.

The longer she'd worked here, the less she'd liked this place, she had to admit. Why it was, she didn't quite know. There was nothing, in the bland, rather aseptic décor, to inspire dread. But she definitely felt a sense of unease as she let herself in and switched on the neon lights. Perhaps it was these, taking a moment to fizz into action, and then throwing a forensic pall of harsh, ugly light over the interior, which made it such an unfriendly workspace.

She hung her coat over the back of her chair, unwound the scarf from her neck and slung her bag on the counter. She was finally going to get into Potter's filing cabinets and see what on earth was going on. She'd be able to do a thorough search before he was anywhere near. It wasn't even worth sitting down in her chair. She just needed to march in there, unlock the door with the key from the cup cupboard, get down the filing cabinet key once she was in his office, and then bingo, she'd be there at last. On the case, doing a proper search, a thorough investigation that was bound to reveal what on earth was so strange about this place. She pressed her hands together, then gripped them into tight fists, willing herself into action.

But it was no good. For some reason, she just didn't want to get on with it. Had she finally found a quest that she wasn't willing to plunge into thoughtlessly? Was it Harry's warnings last night?

Or was it that she had a very bad feeling about… something. Beth thought hard. She'd gained new respect for her instincts over the past few months. In fact, that last time she'd ignored their jangling warnings, she'd had a sizeable clonk over the head and woken up in hospital. She pressed a hand to the side of her skull. There was nothing to show for it there now, but she remembered all too well the horror of those moments before she'd lost consciousness. She'd realised then, that by putting herself in the path of trouble, she'd risked making Ben an orphan.

Things were different now, though, weren't they? She had Harry. But no, what was she thinking of? If she were off the scene, he could hardly take over. He had no legal status, and she wasn't entirely sure what other right he had to become a quasi-parent to her son. They weren't even officially going out yet. They'd never so much as strolled into Jane's café together, let alone given Dulwich any other indication that things might be serious. No, all Harry would be, at this point, was another mourner at her graveside. While that might be nice for Ben, it was not going to get him through life. There was nothing for it. She had to be a bit more careful.

Beth hated to wimp out, she really did. But the confrontation she'd had with Potter, right here in this little space in the kitchen, had been very unpleasant, and that had been a situation she'd been able to talk herself out of. If he found her with her head right inside his filing cabinets, there was not much she'd be able to come up with which would justify such blatant snooping.

She had to admit it. She was just plain scared. So she did what she always did in moments of crisis. She flipped on the kettle, got her usual mug, then decided to pull her chair over while she was at it to get Potter's key from under his Simpkin cup – and discovered there was nothing there. But she'd put it back there only last night. Flummoxed, she searched the rest of the top cupboard, as best she could. She was at a huge height disadvantage, so it was a case of lifting her arms above her head, moving each cup then feeling under it, as this was all happening well above her eye-line. But after ten fruitless minutes of rooting, she was pretty sure: the cupboard was bare.

She hopped down from the chair and flexed her arms, sore from being held at such an odd angle for all that time. Where could the blessed man have hidden the key now? She was kicking herself. She ought to have expected as much. After all, he'd found out quite incontrovertibly that she knew where his beloved key was, and for a man so hooked on security, that was always going to be a problem. He'd probably moved it the moment her back was turned.

She paused only to slosh some boiling water into her mug and stir the bag absently with a spoon. No reason why she shouldn't have a cup of tea while thinking. She quickly scanned the office. Where else would she hide a key, if she was a ridiculously tall, paranoid solicitor? There weren't a lot of possibilities. He'd done well with his original Simpkin arrangement and was no doubt furious that he'd been forced to make changes. She let her eyes wander, looking for anything out of place, anything unusual, anything with space for a key... but that was pointless. The key wasn't exactly large; it could be anywhere.

She pursed her lips. The filing cabinet key in his room had been on top of the horrible Rothko. There weren't any posters out here – thank goodness – but there had to be some alternative hidey-holes. She turned on her heels. The frosted glass frontage. The small seating area with its leaflets. Her own small desk. The kitchenette... There was a mug upended on the draining board, which she definitely hadn't left out last night. She darted to it, turned it over, but there was nothing there unless you counted the high tide of a ring inside. She sniffed, unimpressed by the washing-up skills on display, but her gaze roved on.

Wait, could the key be in the fridge? She leapt to it, opened the door, but apart from the usual milk, and now a wrinkly apple, it was empty. The ice tray? She scrabbled open the door, but that's all it was inside – ice. Plenty of it. Enough for a small snowman, which was extraordinary given the matchbox size of the fridge – but definitely no keys. The cleaning cupboard? This was so low down, for Potter, that she would have been amazed if he'd even known it existed, let alone stashed something here. As she thought, there was only a bottle of Cif and a couple of mummified microfibre cloths. The cup cupboard she'd already searched.

She stared at the door of Potter's office, with concentrated dislike. The bloody man! Talk about making things difficult. If he wasn't looming over her, making her feel knee-high to an oompa loompa, then he was hiding stuff with a fervour that made George Smiley, with all his tradecraft, look like an amateur. It was blooming ridiculous. She wandered over to the door and rattled the knob in frustration. And it turned in her hand.

Wait, what? she thought. *It's open all along?* Aside from the tide of annoyance and frustration, mostly self-directed, that rose up unstoppably as she realised how much time she'd wasted searching for the key, Beth felt a prickle of alarm. Why wasn't it locked up tight? This wasn't like Potter. It wasn't like him *at all*.

But even though bells were ringing, she didn't feel she had a choice. She had to go inside. This could be her last, her very last, opportunity to search the files, after all. Yes, it had to be done. She carried on turning the handle and, softly, softly, opened the door.

Part of her was thinking, there's no need to pussyfoot. No-one here to see her or tell her that she was invading Potter's privacy, virtually breaking and entering. And she should get on with it all, as fast as she could. But despite that, she moved slowly, opening the door a centimetre at a time.

Later, she couldn't have said what she was expecting. Did she think someone would rush out at her? Or that the street door bell, silent for so much of the time, would finally burst into life and she would be caught out? Or maybe it was a more primeval sense that something, somewhere, was very far from being right, and she was about to find out what it was.

Whatever the reason, Beth was almost moving in slow motion as she finally twisted the door open and then pushed, advancing as though her feet were mired in treacle. She kept hearing Potter's voice in her head, barking at her to shut the door, go back to her work, get on with her last report and stop wasting time.

Chapter Sixteen

But when the door finally swung open, she realised she'd never be hearing from Potter again. His office was cold, still, calm, and had a curiously uninhabited air, all the more surprising as its owner was sprawled, unmoving, across the big blond desk.

Beth had a moment of cold horror, not just for Potter, but also for herself. She really, really, didn't want to discover another body. She put a hand up to the door frame and steadied herself as best she could. If she set foot in the office, then she'd have no choice but to put all those wheels in motion – again. If she just hovered here, maybe even shut the door, finished that cup of tea and then went home to Ben... maybe, just maybe, all this would simply go away.

But then she realised. He might still be alive. She darted forward, and time finally seemed to be moving forward again, after the slow motion of the last few minutes. She looked at the inert form. He was bent right across the shiny surface, head resting on the unusually cluttered desk, face first. All she could really see of him was a lot of hair, thinning slightly at the crown now she was being forced to study it, and with a curiously vulnerable-looking strip of skin at the back of his neck. It wasn't as darkly tanned as the hands splayed out on the desk, or the face, mercifully hidden. Was he dead?

She had a dilemma. She knew (who better?) that she shouldn't touch anything. But maybe he'd just passed out? Beth reached a tentative finger towards his neck and saw that her hand was shaking wildly. She tried to still it, but to no avail. She put her other hand up to steady it. At last she got herself under control enough to touch the inert form, very quickly. He was cold. Very, very cold.

She took a breath and turned her attention to the mess strewn across the desk. Right in front of her was a cup with some liquid in it. There were pills all around it, a bottle of rum with a sticky centimetre left, and a couple of medicine bottles – one lying on its side, label uppermost. *Zimovane*, she read. Where had she heard that before? Or something like it? The memory slotted into place. The chemist. Then she saw, with a thrill of horror, that the mug was the 'Dad' one made by his children. The uneven red lettering seemed to shout at her. How could he have chosen this cup, so lovingly if ineptly made?

But there were more urgent considerations. She had to call the police and report this horrible find. Poor, poor Potter. She hadn't been his biggest fan, true, but this? It was too grim.

She was dialling the third nine on her phone when she suddenly realised the world of trouble she was going to be in. Harry was sure to get wind of the situation. Much though she'd love this to be handled by some sweet but bumbling bobby on the beat, she knew the Met would call in the big guns straight away, and round here that meant Harry. He'd come down on her like a ton of bricks. Two tons, most likely. It would be worse than Potter at his most threatening. She'd concealed from Harry the fact that she was working here, and why, and he was going to be deeply unamused to find out when, yet again, her involvement in a situation led to the removal of a body bag.

But, thought Beth, it wasn't her fault. Who'd have thought that Potter would do something like this? He hadn't struck her as the type to carry out such a desperate act. True, he'd seemed preoccupied and worried of late – but if everyone in Dulwich who was a bit *distrait* was at risk, then they'd have to section every single person in SE21.

Besides, she had no choice but to ring. Potter had a family, and they needed to be informed. Her eyes filled with tears as she thought of his children. She didn't know them well, only as beautiful blonde creatures that were in the same playground as Ben, but seemed to inhabit a slightly different world – one that didn't involve mud, scraped knees, or any other messy side effects of being small.

And Letty! What was this going to do to a woman so ethereal that it was already a surprise that she walked on solid ground like the rest of them? At least she'd look amazing in black, thought Beth, then immediately chided herself and wondered how such a thing could have popped into her head at such a time. She completed the call, asking for police and an ambulance, though she knew it was too late, and stood there quivering gently for a minute. Gradually, she got herself back under control, reminded herself to breathe, then she backed away, closed Potter's door, and sat down in a heap at her desk.

But there was something she just had to do, no matter how dire the circumstances. When she'd arrived this morning, she'd had one last day to accomplish her task. Now, thanks to Potter, she probably only had a few minutes. But she was damned if she'd let them slip away, laying waste to all the time she'd put in for Nina. Her friend had been sure that something was badly wrong here, and it looked as though she'd been spot on. But they were still no nearer to finding the cause.

There was only one way to do that.

Beth put her hands flat against the desk and pushed herself up. She really didn't want to do this, but she had no choice. She'd have to go back into Potter's room. Yes, he was lying there dead. Yes, it was distasteful in the extreme, and would probably give her nightmares for ever, but it had to be done. She'd just have to think of him, not just as a recent corpse, but as – and here she really struggled to think of something that would get her back into the room in close proximity to a dead body – erm, a collection of chops. *Dead meat*. That's what they said, didn't they, in those lurid bestsellers like the ones in Nina's desk? Yes, it would be just like passing a butcher's shop window, and she'd done that often enough, hadn't she? What about those places in Chinatown, with grotesquely stretched ducks hanging from hooks? They were even pretty much the same laminated brick-red colour as

Potter.

At this point, Beth's rapidly-consumed early breakfast threatened to make a reappearance and she decided to drop the whole meat metaphor. It really wasn't working and, for the first time in her life, vegetarianism was seeming like an extremely tempting option. She'd just go for denial. It had served her well enough in the past for a multiplicity of issues.

Then, almost as though she were moving in a dream, she moved to the cleaning cupboard and fetched one of the fossilised microfibre cloths. Steeling herself, she opened Potter's office door again and tried to avert her gaze from the ghastliness on the desk. Practical issues would keep her focused. She reckoned it would be fine to have her fingerprints on the door, and maybe Potter's desk, as she'd been in and out for all those endless dictation sessions. But she had to keep traces to a minimum.

The cloth in her hand was stiff and unyielding. She looked down at it crossly, thinking she should really have words with Nina. It had clearly been an age since it had been used to clean anything. But then she realised all that was completely irrelevant now. The office was bound to close. Potter's empire was finished, crooked or not.

She crumpled the cloth in her hand as best she could, softening it up enough to be usable. Now for the key. She really didn't want to mess around dragging chairs in this time when she was up against the clock, so she jumped up and down in front of the Rothko, trying to swipe the hidden key with the edge of the cloth. It was lucky Potter was dead, she thought, otherwise she'd have to die of embarrassment herself, she must look so ridiculous. But just when she was completely out of breath and decided she'd be joining Potter by having a heart attack on the spot, she managed to flick the key with the edge of the cloth and knock it down onto the carpet.

Grabbing it, again using the cloth, she slotted the little silver key into the lock of the first cabinet and pulled out the top drawer. It shot out surprisingly fast, and when she got up on tiptoe again, she saw why. It was empty. Completely empty. She repeated the process with the other drawers – nine in total – with the same result. Every single one was cavernously, echoingly, rattlingly void.

She couldn't believe it. All this time and all that effort, and it had all been for nothing. So much for the secret that she had been sure had been lurking there at the heart of the office. And Nina, too. She had been sure there had been something going on. But, in fact, there'd been a big, fat nothing. It didn't make sense.

So transfixed was she that she whipped round without thinking, then confronted the dead Potter again, so still that she'd virtually forgotten he was there. She suddenly realised what she was doing, and how long she was taking. She had to hurry. It wouldn't look good if the police got here and she was poking around in the dead man's office.

She wondered what to do with the key, still shrouded in the horrible old cloth. She looked up to the top of the Rothko. Getting the key down had been one thing, but putting it back was out of the question. It was much too high for her to reach all the way up to the edge, and the thought of dragging her chair through from outside yet again made her feel tired, even if the police didn't catch her in the act. They surely wouldn't be long now.

She dithered, thinking how ridiculous her life sometimes was. Here she was, a blameless single mum, and yet she was standing in front of a corpse with a purloined key to get rid of, with a mind full of fraud, fingerprints, and DNA, instead of thinking about what Christmas present to get for her son. Could things get any more out of control?

Just then, she heard the faint wail of the siren. Even though so much seemed to have happened since she'd got to work, it was still early, and the sound travelled ominously in the quiet streets. God, that meant she had no time at all to get rid of the key.

She darted forward to the desk. Could she just dump it there? She looked over at the sprawl that was Potter. Should she put it near his hand? Or maybe *in* his hand? It would look very odd if something that was often used had no fingerprints at all on it. Beth studied the position of Potter's big, meaty paws on the desk. Could she slip the key under his hand? Maybe rub it across the pads of his fingers first? It was revolting, but she had to. Using the cloth and averting her gaze and looking determinedly at the rubbish bin, she swiped the key across the nearest hand. Even through the cloth, it didn't feel like flesh. The fingers were inanimate, like chunks of wood. Just as well, or she really might finally have been sick. She turned back and nudged the key into a better position, under the stiff, curled digits.

Now that she was at this angle, and altogether a lot closer to Potter than she wanted to be, she could see that he was folded over a piece of paper on the desk. It was close to the edge, so his head and torso had shielded it from view before. She knew she shouldn't look, but she couldn't resist a peep. Ducking down, and gazing along the plane of the desk, she could just about see the typed words, *'No more.'*

As suicide notes went, it was pretty crummy, she thought. No mention of the wife or children, no apology, absolutely no explanation. She'd give it a scant two out of ten. And not many points for effort, either. It wasn't even handwritten. It looked as though he'd run it off on the office printer. Well, if she were Letty, she'd consider that as the cherry on the top of a particularly rubbishy cake from Paul Potter. If he'd been on the *Great British Bake Off*, she sincerely hoped he'd have been drummed out even faster than that guy who'd chucked his Baked Alaska in the bin. Of course, being dead would have meant he had little chance of winning, she conceded.

But poor Letty. Beth knew what it was like to be left in the lurch by your husband. James had had no choice, but it looked as though Potter had bowed out for his own reasons. She felt a curl of anger rise in her stomach. No-one deserved this.

Just then, there came a thudding at the door. She took a last quick glance at the desk, checking nothing was out of place. The cloth. She quickly scooped it up, flung it into the cleaning cupboard as she ran past, and opened up the door to the police.

Sitting at home later, Beth thought it had been one of the longest days of her life. If she'd known what was coming, she definitely wouldn't have got up early. Hell, she might not have got up at all, though having Ben on the premises would have made that impossible. He was now happy as anything, on the sofa, inducting little Wilf into the mysteries of the PlayStation and very much enjoying winning every single game. When Charlie was clutching the other console, things were much more even. At last, there was an upside to Katie's skiing jaunt.

Beth, meanwhile, felt as used and gritty as that microfibre rag, hunched over her umpteenth cup of tea while Nina intoned, 'I can't believe it, I just can't,' at her side. Beth shot her a daggers look. She couldn't help it. She had every sympathy, and certainly shared the same sense of disbelief, but intoning it like a mantra was getting them nowhere fast.

First, she'd gone through the basics with the Constable, then it had been off to the police station to make a statement and, finally, her least favourite part of a really terrible day so far, the chance encounter with Harry just as he'd been coming in and she'd been let go. She cursed her bad timing, though she realised it was inevitable that he'd have found out about the whole business in time. But maybe he'd have dealt with it better if he hadn't bumped right into her. His face had been a picture – but not one she personally would pay to see in any gallery.

'What are you doing here, Beth?' he said, a momentary smile of delight disappearing instantly as he realised that Beth's unannounced presence in a police station could only ever betoken a major calamity. 'Anything you'd like to tell me about?' he tacked on with admirable restraint, given the circumstances.

Beth, looking back on the awkward encounter, could only wish her fringe was a metre longer and obscured her entire face. Of course, she'd started to blush guiltily right away, and of course, she couldn't look him in the eye. If she'd only been able to style things out, pretend she was just a blameless eyewitness. But no. It had taken him about a minute to ascertain that yes, she'd found another body, and yes, she'd filled in forms saying she was an employee of Potter's. It would be fair to say he then goggled at her incredulously.

'Can we have a chat?' he'd said pleasantly, for the benefit of his colleague manning the front desk. But anyone who knew him as well as Beth could identify a certain tautness of manner that was a dead giveaway for rage – not of the murderous variety, but certainly enough to make Beth wish she was dead anyway.

She had smiled back, despite her red face and darting eyes, and made an anodyne excuse about picking up Ben from the childminder's.

'*Childminder*?' said Harry, doing an excellent Lady Bracknell impression. Ah yes. Amongst the welter of half-truths and downright lies, Beth had forgotten Harry had known nothing of her peculiar arrangement with Nina. She ducked her head and strode for the door before he could stop her. And he'd let her go. What could he have done, short of arresting her?

But now, Beth almost wished he'd done just that. A couple of hours had since passed. Surely he must have read her statement and seen that she'd been masquerading as Potter's receptionist? He'd want to know why; she knew him. He'd want every spit and cough of the story. And yet, he hadn't been in touch. And though she was semi-dreading his call, this silence was equally unbearable. Possibly even more unbearable than a roasting, as she badly needed the comfort of reliable, strong arms around her and a reassuring pea coat to snuggle up to. Nina, with her constant refrain, was no substitute at all.

But as the day wore on and the sense of shock diminished, Nina's bouncy nature reasserted itself and Beth was glad of her presence. After brewing up yet another pot of tea, Beth went to the fridge.

'We've only gone and finished all the milk,' she smiled.

'I'll nip out and get some. Wilf and Ben are ok, aren't they?'

Beth nodded. To her shame, they were now glued to the

cartoons that Ben had become hopelessly addicted to during his days at Nina's. It certainly wasn't a triumphant childcare day for her. But then again, even for her, it wasn't every day that she stumbled over a body. Maybe she should cut herself a little slack.

It was kind of Nina to volunteer. She'd have to sprint down to the Sainsbury's Local and back, passing the office and the Potter home. But she seemed ok with that. Once she'd pulled on her snowman coat and wound a scarf round her neck, she looked ready for anything.

As soon as she'd left, Beth fished out her phone. It had been resolutely silent all day, nothing at all from Harry. She scrolled through his last messages, peppered with kisses and more, until they got to today, when their rolling words of love had come to an abrupt standstill. Would he ever trust her again? she wondered miserably. The minutes dragged on, but Beth was too jittery to settle to anything. She had the newspaper on the kitchen table, but there didn't seem any point in reading it when it had been so comprehensively scooped by events unfolding in real time. And she had her freelance work to do, but there wasn't a hope in hell of her getting down to that. She could barely muster the concentration to switch on her laptop, let alone formulate a coherent sentence.

She gazed out of the kitchen window, but instead of the wintry garden scene, with overgrown shrubs and a lawn where the bare patches had finally started to sprout only to be blighted by frost, all she saw was Potter, sprawled across his desk.

Finally, the doorbell shrilled. Beth was glad to get up from the table and push her gloomy thoughts aside. It was Nina, but not the somewhat subdued woman who'd left. This was Nina alive – and agog. She tiptoed theatrically past the sitting room, where the boys gawped as neon colours flickered over their vacant faces, and bustled into the kitchen, shutting the door that was so rarely closed.

'You'll never believe this, but there were police all over the Potter house. I thought I'd just go and take a look.'

Beth was confused. 'That's no surprise, though, is it? They must be investigating, trying to work out why he did what he, you know, did?'

'Yes, one constable with a notebook, maybe, probably one of those nice girl officers off the telly with the frown lines from looking sympathetic the whole time,' said Nina, while Beth wondered exactly which TV shows she'd been watching. 'But no, this was something different. The whole place was crawling with cops. There was crime scene tape across the drive, a policeman posted on the gate, great big vans outside the house. If it was like any telly show, it would be *Silent Witness*. I tell you, it was really creepy. I even saw a bloke in one of them white spacesuits. And I talked to the neighbours.'

Nina, who'd been gabbling so fast that Beth had a hard time making sense of her words, now leaned back in her chair, and Beth couldn't help leaning forwards.

'The neighbours? Who?'

'You know, that woman with the kids in Year 4 who always power dresses, even though she was made redundant? The one who hangs around laughing at Belinda's jokes?'

Beth thought. Laughing at Belinda's jokes was pretty universal. But yes, she did remember someone on the fringes of the group who always had a very corporate look. Beth rather envied her the sharp little ponte dresses and kitten heels.

'That's Lisa, isn't it? Was she made redundant? That's terrible,' she said absently. In normal times, she would have dwelt thoroughly on the impulses that had led Lisa to keep up her façade. Was she hoping to attract another job, somehow? Or maybe she just didn't have any casual clothes. But today, well, after a moment's consideration, it couldn't have seemed less important. 'What did she say?'

'You won't believe this. It's incredible. But it looks like he tried to do away with the lot of them.'

'What? What do you mean?'

'Potter. He drugged them. Kids, Letty, the lot of 'em.'

'What?'

Beth stood for a moment, holding onto the sink, feeling dizzy and trying to make sense of what Nina had said. Potter, the family man, killing his wife and children?

'No. No, I just don't believe it.' Beth shook her head, not just saying no to the idea, but almost trying to shake the very thought of it out of her mind. It just didn't compute. 'Are they all dead, then?' she whispered.

Chapter Seventeen

Nina pushed Beth into a chair and did what the English do best in a crisis – reached for the kettle, filled it, and turned it on. 'Sorry, didn't mean to spring that on you. It didn't work, for some reason. Letty and the kids have all been hauled off to the hospital to be checked over, but they're fine. Oh, and while I was talking to Lisa, guess who came past, looking all shifty? Only that guy from Wyatt's, the one everyone sucks up to.'

'What, Dr Grover?' said Beth faintly. She wouldn't have been surprised by anything at this point.

'Nah, that other one, the bruiser whose trousers always look like they're going to burst. The sporty one.'

Beth had to think for ages, but then it popped into her head. 'Tom Seasons. Are you sure? How do you know him?'

'Friend of the Potters, innit? Came by the office sometimes, when Letty was there,' said Nina.

Beth tried to process it all. It was astonishing, not only to hear that Potter had tried to kill his family – but even more so to hear that he'd failed. Everything she'd heard about these awful cases, when a husband snapped and did away with his nearest and dearest, suggested they tended to be pretty thorough. Stabbings, shootings, sometimes combinations of the two. Messy, awful, but invariably lethal. And then, an equally gory suicide at the end. Sometimes this last step was botched, true, and the man had to live with his crimes for the rest of his life, which to Beth seemed a fair punishment. But this? If Potter had managed to kill himself, why had it gone wrong for the rest of the family? It was all very odd.

And, in the middle of her horror, a part of registered that this was probably why Harry hadn't been in touch. He was going to be angry, that was for sure. But he must also be up to his eyes.

'This all seems wrong, don't you think?' Beth said to Nina, who was already taking the fiddly white film top off the new container of milk. 'You knew him much better than me, you'd worked for him for much longer. But from what I saw, he loved Letty and the kids so much! Everything was about *them*, the family. And the way he was with Letty! That time I saw them together, he mooned over her like they'd just met. It was…'

'Revolting?'

'I was going to say *sweet*,' said Beth reprovingly. 'But I know what you mean. It was a bit… over the top in a way. Certainly unusual.'

'I'm no psychopath, but couldn't that sort of mad love go sour? End up in a really, really bad way?'

Beth paused. 'Well, I'm no er, *psychologist* either, but I suppose it might. I just didn't get the feeling that Potter would ever hurt a hair on their heads. Though he could definitely be menacing. That time he was cross with me, I was terrified, I don't mind admitting.'

'Yeah, but you were poking around in his business, weren't you? Fair enough if he went a bit doolally about that,' said Nina. 'But we're talking about actual murder here.'

'Yes. And in a sneaky sort of way. If you'd told me he'd bludgeoned them all to death, then I would have been able to imagine that. Rage, loss of control. That red mist people talk about. He definitely looked as though he wanted to strangle me, and he was a big, strong guy. But drugging them?'

'Maybe he didn't want to mess them up,' Nina raised her eyebrows. 'My Wilf, he looks so peaceful when he's asleep. No way I'd want to wreck his little chops. Even if I was going to murder him, if you know what I mean.'

Beth, who'd had her own moments of gazing in wonder at Ben as he dreamed, knew there was nothing on earth so lovely as the face of your sleeping child. She could forgive Ben any daytime mischief, when she saw him in his dino-print jim-jams. Surely Potter would have been the same? But who could ever know?

'You might be right, Nina. But this is silly. We'll never be able to put ourselves into his head. He must have gone to a very odd place, to be capable of this.'

Nina nodded sadly. 'First the dogs, now it's people. What's the world coming to, eh?'

Beth put down her cup. She flicked her fringe to one side impatiently and leaned forward again. 'What did you say?'

'Just what's the world coming to? It's the kind of thing you do say, at times like this, in't it?' Nina said defensively. But Beth didn't stop staring.

'No, before that?'

'Um?' Nina looked upwards, her red-gold curls catching the light from the garden, where Magpie was staring hard at a robin in the apple tree. 'About the dogs?'

'The dogs. Exactly,' said Beth. 'Nina, I've got to go out for a while. Are you ok to watch the boys?'

Nina shrugged. As far as she was concerned, they didn't need much watching.

'You could go and sit with them for a bit,' Beth suggested.

Nina peered into her tea and sighed. The excitement of her revelation about the Potters had definitely worn off, and she suddenly seemed pretty down. It was an understandable reaction to the day's events.

Beth thought for a second, then rummaged in a cupboard and brought out a selection pack of crisps. It was supposed to last them weeks, but today seemed to be developing into an emergency – for the grown-ups more than the children. Nina brightened a little at the prospect. 'You could take it through to the sitting room, have a rest on the sofa with the boys,' Beth suggested. It might be better than being alone with her thoughts.

'But where are you going?' Nina eyed Beth, who was suddenly full of energy. 'Not got one of your mad ideas?'

'They're not always mad. Thanks for your support, Nina,' Beth said as loftily as she could from her starting point.

'Don't suppose you want to tell me, do you?' Nina said idly. Her expectations were as low as her mood.

'You'll think it's silly. I'd rather just get on and do it, then tell you in a few minutes if it pans out.'

'As long as it's not dangerous,' mumbled Nina, who'd already inserted her head into a packet of cheese and onion and looked as though she was quite unlikely to go through with Beth's suggestion of sharing this new bounty with the boys.

Beth smiled then headed out to the hall, popped her head briefly round the sitting room door, and waved to Ben who hardly looked up from the telly. She pulled on her pixie boots and coat, slung her bag over her shoulder, and shut the door quietly.

It felt very odd to be retracing her steps to Herne Hill, and she instinctively chose the other side of the road to walk down, though she couldn't resist glancing over at the frosted glass door as she passed the office. There was nothing there now to show that a tragedy had taken place so recently. No crime scene tape, no police officer on guard. She supposed the office had just been locked up once the body had been removed, and that was that. She couldn't help her mind flashing, yet again, to the sight of Potter sprawled over the desk. Thank God she hadn't been able to see his face. She still had the key to the office in her bag, but there was no way that she would ever willingly go back in there again, after what she'd discovered that morning.

She picked up her pace and tried a bit of an unconcerned saunter. But she needn't have bothered. People were going about their business as though it were a perfectly normal day – and for almost everyone, it was. Even those who knew the Potters well had to get on with things. And for the vast majority of humanity in south east London, nothing had changed when Paul Potter had sat in his office last night and drunk the bitter dregs from his Dad mug.

Beth shivered and gave up on the saunter. She knew exactly where she was going, and the sooner she got there, the better.

Her destination was in the little pedestrian-only shopping area close to Herne Hill Station itself. She looked around quickly, found the shop she wanted, and went in, wincing slightly as a bell rang when she opened the door. It could have been the twin of the one in Potter's office. She went up to the counter, where a girl with long dark plaits was wearing a white overall with a little insignia on the pocket.

'Can I help you?' she smiled.

'Oh yes, I hope you can. Paul Potter sent me to collect the report you had for him?'

The girl looked confused, which wasn't good. Beth's heart sank. Her little plan relied entirely on this girl believing everything she said was the gospel truth, and as usual she had precious little in reserve should the girl turn out not to be a total fool. Flying by the seat of her pants didn't even cover it. It was more like flying with a thong, not that she'd ever attempted such a thing. Although, assuming Harry didn't dump her flat after this escapade – and there was still radio silence from his end – maybe she should reward him by giving one a go? She shook such thoughts away and tried her widest, most guileless smile.

'Mr Potter said it would be all ready. And, um, I'm a bit pressed for time.'

The girl looked doubly unsure. 'I'm so sorry, I'm new here. Intern, you know, I just started this morning, I don't know where anything's kept. If you leave your name, I could probably email you later?'

She almost rubbed her hands in glee at the intern bit, but the emailing? Not so much. Beth didn't quite snort in disbelief, but she put her head on one side and gave the girl a bit of a mummy look. She knew when someone was trying it on. It was like the times when Ben insisted he'd cleaned his teeth while she'd been in the shower. And his toothbrush, on inspection, turned out to be drier than the Gobi Desert. No way would this girl be searching around on her behalf later on. Once Beth left the shop, her query would vanish from her mind like – well, like cheese and onion crisps disappearing into Nina's face.

The girl's resolve crumbled, aided by the jangling of the bell as another customer came in behind Beth and shifted noisily from foot to foot, signalling plenty of very useful impatience. 'Um, look, I'm sure I shouldn't be doing this, but as you're a good customer…' Beth nodded and tried to look as though she was never out of the shop. 'Well, I don't suppose you'd know where this letter actually was, would you, so I can serve this gentleman?' said the girl, stepping out of the way so that Beth could slide round to her side of the counter.

Beth didn't need asking twice. She was there like a shot, and began leafing through a pile of ready-stamped envelopes which should, no doubt, have already gone into the post, if someone had been more efficient. Meanwhile, the girl fixed the next customer with her best smile.

Beth pounced on a white A4 envelope, and only just resisted giving a whoop. It was addressed to Paul Potter in a scruffy hand. She folded it quickly, stuffed it into her handbag, and was thanking the girl and out of the shop before the door had time to shut.

Thinking about things later, Beth realised this was the moment when all the pieces had really fallen into place for her. There'd been moments before, when she'd had a feeling that she was missing something, that there was a scheme afoot that she just couldn't quite see. But this envelope, as far as she was concerned, was the first real proof that pointed her in the right direction.

But back at the house with Nina that afternoon, Beth was faced with a decision. She had to discuss everything with Harry. It was going to mean coming clean about what she'd been up to all holiday, but in the interests of justice, it absolutely had to be done.

That didn't mean she was looking forward to it one little bit.

With a heavy heart, she packed Ben off for a last airing at the Sunray Gardens playground and then a final session in front of Nina's jumbo telly. After today, Beth promised herself, she'd devote herself to Ben. There'd be no more cartoons. There might even be some practice exam papers, which was not going to make her the most popular mummy on the planet. But there would certainly be quality time, and what was more, she'd buy all the Christmas presents she'd so far neglected as well. Quite how she was going to get Ben's presents when they were going to be joined at the hip, was something she hadn't sorted out yet.

She rang the familiar number as she walked back home from Herne Hill, not surprised when it went to voicemail. Harry was bound to be swamped. But as she rounded the corner into Pickwick Road, her heart sank. There, outside her house, was the familiar car, windows steamed up. Damn and blast. Harry had beaten her to it. He was sitting in the car. They hadn't got to the key stage. Maybe now they never would.

Her steps dragged as she made her way up the little path, noticing despite the cold that the weeds were wriggling their way into the gaps in the crazy paving. She was going to have to get at them. She could never bring herself to use a spray, just in case Magpie broke the habit of a lifetime and sauntered round to the front of the house and, unlikely as it seemed, finally deigned to eat something that wasn't her preferred stratospherically expensive cat food.

Beth was just fitting the key into the lock, realising that she was trying to distract herself from the looming encounter, when she sensed Harry behind her. One look at his granite face told her everything she needed to know.

She'd been counting on having time to get in, sort herself out, maybe even look at the envelope in her bag before they had to have this… whatever it was going to be. A dressing down. A shouting match. A possible dumping. Well, she hoped not that, but she was braced.

'Harry,' she said. 'I was just ringing you.'

'Were you now?' he said, still wearing the expression he'd had at the police station. Disbelief, disappointment, hurt, anger. It was like a Pick 'n' Mix of horrible emotions. She felt for him, she really did. But she'd had her reasons. If only she could make him understand.

'You'd better come in,' she said sadly.

It was twenty minutes before they were through the worst

of it: twenty minutes when Beth had sat silent, while Harry had paced up and down the small kitchen, alternately shouting, trying not to shout, or speaking in a low, insistent voice that was a shout in everything but decibels. Finally, Beth had had enough.

'Look, I'm sorry if you feel let down, upset, worried, whatever. But the thing is that I don't have to run all my decisions past you. Why would I? Even if we were *married* —'

'God forbid,' shuddered Harry.

'Well, thank you, but even if we *were*—'

'Which we are not!'

'Well, at least we're agreed on that,' said Beth, pretty exasperated herself now. 'But I don't have to ask your permission to do anything, now or at any time in the future. Yes, I could have discussed things more with you, told you a little of—'

'—your crazy, hair-brained, deluded plan…'

'Yes. Maybe. But I'm not under any obligation to. And as you seem to think I'd be safest sitting at home doing a bit of needle-point, and even then, ooops, I might prick my silly little finger, why would I risk all this bullying behaviour by letting you in on what I was up to?'

Harry gave Beth a look from under lowered brows. 'Look, I don't want to come over as bullying. It's the last thing I am or want to be. But I *do* want to keep you safe. And I'm not going to apologise for that.'

Beth looked up at him and shook her head.

Harry sat down at the table, his hand reaching across for hers. Feeling childish, Beth got up, removing herself from such close proximity. Part of her wanted to feel the lovely reassurance of his touch. But quite a lot was still angry, and very determined to assert her right to act as she saw fit.

'Look, in the last few months, you've been burgled, hit on the head… chased by some true weirdos. I've sat in the hospital, wondering whether you were ever going to wake up. Do you really want to keep doing that to me, or to Ben?'

Beth flushed with anger. This was underhand. Of course,

she didn't want to put Ben through any unnecessary worry. But nor could she see things going awry in her beloved Dulwich, be sure of what was going on, and stand idly by while the guilty prevailed and the innocent suffered. What was the quote from Edmund Burke? *'The only thing necessary for the triumph of evil is for good men to do nothing.'* Well, as far as Beth was concerned, that went for good women, too. And the one thing that worried her about Harry – a policeman, for goodness sake – was that too often he seemed to be on the verge of letting things go. Given half a chance, he'd close a case if it was wrapped up neatly. And this current attempted murder/suicide? She was willing to bet he'd take it at face value for budgetary reasons.

She stared at him and couldn't help letting him see how far he was falling short, in her eyes.

'Don't you even want to know what I've found out this time?' she asked him defiantly.

Harry sighed deeply. 'Go on, then. I suppose you're going to tell me anyway.'

'Not if you don't want to listen,' said Beth, now on her high horse. But as her highest possible horse was only really a Shetland with attitude, not the majestic Shire with fluffy fetlocks that Beth would have much preferred, Harry couldn't help smiling at her fondly.

'You know I think you're wonderful,' he said, reaching out again.

Beth, reluctantly, touched her fingers to his, and found them clasped warmly. Against her will, something in the region of her heart melted, and she returned his smile. Just a little.

Harry smiled more and said with the faintest Irish lilt that he knew she couldn't resist, 'Please tell me what on earth you were doing at Potter's office in the first place. And we'll take it from there.'

They ended up, side by side on the sofa, with a glass of wine shared between them, though there probably weren't many countries in the world where the sun was over the yardarm. 'You know, you could have said that there was something fishy about Potter's business,' said Harry, much more mildly.

'And you would have said, "I bet there isn't, don't worry about it",' said Beth, rolling her eyes. 'At least now you can finally find out what was going on. And why he bothered with all those fake reports that I had to type. I think it was something to do with the sheltered housing. Maybe he was ripping off his clients? Not that he seemed to have many.'

'Yep, we'll have to look into that. There's usually a financial motive for these familicide cases.'

'Familicide, what a horrible word. But I'm still not convinced that Potter is the type who'd do that. He *loved* his family.'

'They usually do, Beth. They decide that the family is better off dead than struggling with the aftermath of a business failing, or whatever. Losing the house, the status they've all grown used to.'

'But that's so arrogant!' she protested. *And not that much worse than a man insisting he be kept informed of his partner's movements at all times*. But no, she thought a second later. Even if the two attitudes were on a sliding scale, there was still a yawning gulf between them.

'Yes, terrible,' said Harry, seemingly blind to nuances that Beth was finding as subtle as multiple slaps in the face with a wet fish. 'If you're right about the state of his business, then that could have been a trigger. And his wife, what's she like?'

Beth thought. 'Well, extremely high maintenance. Looks as though she might break if you coughed loudly in her direction. And the kids must be costing a fortune. Three of them. So, with private tutors, riding lessons—'

'Wait a minute, riding lessons? In the middle of London?'

'Haven't you ever been stuck in that traffic jam on the South Circular chugging past the stables? Oh no, I forgot, you're always dodging round that with your blues and twos on,' said Beth, quite pleased that she was now so in with Met Police slang.

'Only on urgent official business,' said Harry with a careful look at her.

She peeped a smile. Heaven forfend he should ever have any fun. If she had a siren at her disposal, she'd never queue in traffic again, she thought, conveniently forgetting that she'd nearly thrown up when he'd first taken her on the terrifying dodgem race that was high speed pursuit in London traffic. But back to the Potters' finances.

'They've got a skiing chalet somewhere, and a holiday home in the country here as well... where was it? Suffolk or Norfolk. And they have constant holidays in very hot places, if Potter's tan is anything to go by,' said Beth with a shudder, remembering the dark flesh of the man's hands splayed on the desk. She wrenched her mind back to the family's outgoings. 'And there will be school fees with a vengeance. Letty will do what Belinda does and Belinda is going for Wyatt's...'

'Ok, you're losing me there, you've gone into mummy-speak, but I get the picture. Expensive lifestyle, a wife with lots of expectations and no income, and kids on top. Poor bloke. It's enough to make anyone want to top themselves,' Harry said, shaking his head.

Beth looked at him incredulously. 'He could just have said, "*Let's economise.*" Anyway, you're assuming he did actually do it.'

'It's going to take quite a lot to convince me otherwise,' said Harry, with a shrug.

'Well, perhaps this will help,' said Beth with a flourish, producing the envelope she'd picked up earlier. She felt like a magician who'd just yanked a satisfyingly chubby bunny out of a silk topper. But she hoped that Harry wouldn't ask the inevitable question...

'Where did you get this?' He looked up for long enough to direct a searching glance her way, but luckily the contents of the envelope were electrifying enough to push all such thoughts out of his head. For now. Beth adopted Ben's 'innocent' look: wide eyes, head ever so slightly on one side, an expression of total guilelessness. When Beth was on the receiving end of this, it was tantamount to a red alert that skulduggery was at hand. She'd just have to hope that Harry was less well-versed in the ways of mischievous boys – and their mamas.

He looked down at the single sheet of paper, covered with what looked like a printed shopping list of ingredients with tiny numbers by each one, and a handwritten comment scrawled at the bottom.

'Good grief, is this what I think it is?' said Harry, after staring at the paper in silence for some moments.

'It is. Interesting, don't you think?'

Harry raised his eyes a little reluctantly to Beth's. 'And it was Potter who requested this? No-one else?'

'Absolutely. He was going to pick it up yesterday afternoon... but he got distracted. And he wanted me to get him a prescription from the chemist, too.'

'Don't tell me. Let me guess,' said Harry, scrambling to his feet the moment she'd given a brief nod to his suggestion.

'I'll see you later,' he said.

And this time it was a promise, not a threat. He turned round and stooped to give her a tiny kiss. She felt the pressure of his warm lips. It was all too brief, but it was still a sign of reconciliation. She put her hand up to touch the place as he strode out of the house with his phone clamped to his ear.

She heard his car speed off into the afternoon, then picked up her handbag again and slung it over her shoulder. Was this, finally, going to be her last trip to Herne Hill this holiday? She couldn't help hoping it would be.

Chapter Eighteen

The street lamps were lit, the day fading fast. As Beth watched, the sky slipped from the navy blue of her long-ago school uniform to the coal black of a Wyatt's blazer. There might well even be stars up there, studding the darkness, but you'd never know here in Dulwich. She'd always felt so safe, as a child growing up in the reassuring yellow glow of the city, where electricity from the millions of houses and businesses provided an accidental nightlight for the anxious. Tonight, she was more conscious than ever of the passions that burned behind these curtained windows, spilling out over the edges of lives like chinks of uncontainable brightness. What had been going on at the Potters' home?

Like Nina, she couldn't resist making the slight detour that would take her past the house. It was a huge slab of a place, standing proud in its own grounds – one of the few along this stretch of the village to do so. It looked as though she wasn't the only one who was curious. You'd never get anything as vulgar as a rubber-necker here, but to Beth it looked as though there was an unusual volume of people on the streets, even if one of the commuter trains at North Dulwich Station had just disgorged its load of weary wage slaves. Most seemed to be sprinting past and making for the Crown and Greyhound, though, no doubt to share an enjoyable frisson of horror for half an hour before moving on with lives that, briefly, would seem successful and happy by comparison with the Potters.

For a second, she hesitated, but then decided to cross the road so she could saunter right past the house. Why not? She did actually have a reason to be curious, unlike most of these people. Wait a minute, she knew that PC at the gate. He was the one who'd questioned her at Wyatt's that time, and now that she was effectively dating his boss, she decided they had even more of a bond.

The yellow and black crime scene tape, draped from one square box hedge to the other, looked incongruously like the sort of clever, edgy designer tinsel that Letty might well have bought, and Beth was forced to remember, yet again, that she'd done precisely nothing so far on the Christmas front. But it was coming, and the goose from the old rhyme was now so obese it could barely waddle. She'd have to get her head around it. For now, though, there were more important things on her mind.

She said a carefully casual hello to the policeman, who smiled awkwardly, while she peered past him through the open gate to the big windows of the house. There was no attempt here to hide behind blinds. The tall hedges on all sides acted as solid green net curtains, but once you were within the front garden the place was like a doll's house. She could see the spectacular staircase, the deserted living area, and the cavernous hall.

'How are *you*?' asked Beth, pretending fascinated interest, though all the while she was edging forwards until she was through the gate and peering over the policeman's shoulder, like a social-climbing guest at a duff cocktail do. The PC shuffled his feet and looked awkward. She was now on the wrong side of the tape, and he didn't really want to have to remind her of that. Not when the boss was so smitten, and all. He was just clearing his throat when the front door of the house was flung open, and Letty rushed out.

Beth's inadvertent prediction earlier was spectacularly confirmed. Letty looked amazing in black, her silver-blonde hair flying as she rushed forward and, to Beth's consternation, spat in her direction.

'What are you doing here, you bitch? You drove him to it,' Letty screamed.

Beth couldn't help it. She looked over her shoulder to check whether someone who actually deserved this treatment had loomed up behind her. She herself had done nothing,

nothing to warrant this. But apart from a short, startled businessman, briefcase in hand, who'd been peering in their direction and now hurried by as quickly as he could, there was suddenly no-one else in sight.

'I don't understand, um, Letty, I hardly knew your husband. I just came by, well, to see if there was anything I could do…'

'Don't lie, you're curious like the rest of them. Worse than curious, you're a vulture. You're disgusting, disgusting, and you're to blame,' Letty shrieked, throwing herself to the gravel and covering her face with her hands. If she hadn't just been widowed in horrible circumstances, Beth would have sniggered at her audition for the part of Lady Macbeth and urged her not to give up her day job. Not that she had one.

Unfortunately, the commotion brought two of the tiny Potter children to the front door, their usually radiant little faces blotched and red with crying for their daddy. Beth felt terrible for causing them more grief with her crass gate-crashing. And then she felt worse still, as Harry himself emerged from the house and gave her a long, level look in which pleasure at seeing his *inamorata* lagged an awfully long way behind disapproval, anger, and even a dash of disgust.

'I'll talk to you later,' he said to her with a significant stare, and carefully helped up Letty Potter. The distraught woman leant her lissom frame against him, wound her arms around his neck, and allowed herself to be gently guided back into the house.

Beth suppressed a harrumph. She realised it wouldn't go down well with anyone, not even the PC, who usually had a twinkle for her. She strode away from the house as quickly as she could and was soon outside Nina's door.

'You look a bit crushed,' said Nina, as the familiar and comforting sights and sounds of her flat rushed out to envelop Beth – a combination of chips and cartoons which, though it wasn't going to make Ben into the lean intellectual warrior she should be fashioning, at least had kept him safe and happy these past few days. She contrasted the life and cheeriness of Nina's home with the super-stylish yet chilly look Letty seemed to go for. She hadn't been inside Letty's house yet, but she was willing to bet it was all angles, just like the woman herself.

'Bloody Letty Potter only shot out of her house and accused me of all sorts as I was passing,' said Beth, disgruntled. Ben looked up briefly from his beached-whale position on the well-stuffed sofa, but the demands of the plot of this particular cartoon dragged his attention straight back, possibly because it was a Japanese animation that seemed to have cut and pasted its voiceover wholesale from Google Translate.

'What? That's so weird. What did she say?' Nina's brows knit together in the centre of her smooth forehead.

'She seemed to blame it all on me! I mean, I know she's in shock and everything, but that's so bizarre, isn't it? I mean, I hardly know either of them really. *Knew*. Oh, you know what I mean,' said Beth thoughtfully.

'Really strange. But then, Letty is, isn't she? Gives me the willies. Always has done. The way she's always lurking behind Belinda MacKenzie, with that little smirk like she's perfect and you're not. What's she even got to accuse you of?'

'She said I'd driven Potter to it. But how could I have done? I'd only just met him.'

'That makes it sound like you might have done, if you'd known him better,' Nina pointed out with the ghost of a smile. 'Maybe it's that thing, protesting too much.'

Beth looked at her, arrested. 'You could be right. I thought of Lady Macbeth, but maybe it's *Hamlet* after all. There's definitely something rotten in the state of that house.'

'Nah. It's new-build, in't it? Under guarantee.' Nina bustled around in the tiny kitchen area, getting everything sorted out for the supper.

Beth raised her eyebrows but said nothing, starting to clear the tiny table so they could all sit, knees jammed up together as usual. She stopped abruptly. 'Sorry, have you got enough for us? I was making an assumption…'

'You're all right, babe. Always enough for you two.' Nina turned back to the cooker, and missed the tears springing to Beth's eyes.

Whatever happened, she'd managed something over this holiday that she'd always found a struggle before – she'd made a friend. And that was worth so much, particularly as she could feel her phone vibrating with angry texts, which she had to assume were from Harry. It was like having a pocketful of bees. She didn't want to read them, to feel their sting. For the moment, she could do fine just imagining his irritation. And just when they'd seemed to have sorted things out, too. She cursed herself for poking her nose in again. But if she didn't, things might never get untangled. An injustice might be done. And she couldn't have that. She just couldn't.

As Beth settled in bed later that night, Ben safely tucked up along the corridor, she realised she'd come to something of an impasse. Without access to Harry, she had no idea how the police investigation was progressing. And if the one text she'd worked up the courage to read was anything to go by, at the moment that access was definitely denied for the foreseeable future.

She had her own ideas about Potter. She was absolutely certain now that Nina had been right in her suspicions. Something illegal had been going on, for quite some time, in that little office. Potter was certainly guilty of that much. Would that corrosive emotion, coupled with the fact that it had not been enough to shore up the great edifice of expenditure that was his showy Dulwich life, have been enough to push him into suicide? Maybe. And trying to polish off his family first? Well, it did happen. Beth had to concede it was all possible.

Maybe it was time to do what Harry had so forcefully said. Just duck out of the whole business and concentrate on things that did concern her. At the moment, unfortunately, that was a welter of undone Christmas chores, enough to make even Santa and his full team of elves feel a little daunted.

But there were ways to make everything fun, and having an excited ten-year-old at your side was perhaps the easiest way to inject some joy into Christmas shopping. Beth decided that central London would be a step too far, so they set off the next morning for the shopping centre at Bromley.

Beth knew from previous less-than-festive pre-Christmas experiences that taking the car would mean waiting in a queue snaking around central Bromley until someone else got bored with shopping. The alternative was a quick train journey – but from Herne Hill Station. She had no wish to keep on passing the office, the scene of so much unpleasantness, but in the end it was fine. They stayed on the other side of the road, and Ben was so bubbly that they'd passed it before she even had a chance to start dreading it.

Bromley's shopping centre was the closest Beth's pocket of south London got to a mall, unless you counted the Lewisham Centre which, with the best will in the world, was not really possible.

This place had a tendency to switch names, seemingly at random. For a while it had been The Glades, rather reminiscent of air freshener; then lately it had become InTu, a little like Sainsbury's clothing range; but now it was back to The Glades again. Though the name seemed wildly inappropriate for a large chunk of concrete set in the middle of a dual carriageway, Beth remembered that years ago it had been chosen by Bromley residents in a competition, maybe harking fondly back to prehistoric times.

Wandering the wide, shiny walkways, Beth realised that she could judge the passage of Ben's childhood by the shops they now sprinted past. Build-a-Bear Workshop, where he had once thrown a rare tantrum when she'd declined to buy his teddy a skateboard – 'I'm a deprived child,' he'd yelled at her – and the Disney shop, which he now seemed not to see at all, had once absorbed ridiculous amounts of pocket money. She'd thoroughly resented them. Now she looked at them rather fondly, and spent her time trying to finagle him out of Game and HMV instead.

'We'll never find a present for Granny in here,' she said

firmly at last, and frog-marched him to the more fertile hunting ground of the toiletries aisle of Marks and Spencer. Just when Ben was about to expire with boredom, it was lunch, and she let him choose, even though another burger was probably the last thing he needed, nutritionally speaking. At least at Byron they did put a slice of tomato and a scrap of lettuce beneath their buns. She wasn't particularly surprised to see Ben weeding these carefully out and laying them on the side of his plate, as carefully as a pathologist at a post mortem.

With a last stop for Christmas cards, their bags were satisfyingly bulgy by the time they got back to Herne Hill. This time, the morning's exuberance having worn off, Ben was full of tired questions. 'Why aren't you working at Nina's office any more? Don't you like Mr Potter? Are we going to Wilf's?'

Beth thought hard. She knew that, in this mood, he wouldn't really be listening very hard to her answers, it was more his way of showing his exhaustion. But, nevertheless, she wanted to answer him as honestly as she could.

'I won't be working there any more, Ben. That job has finished, so Nina will be looking for something else, too.' It was the first time this point had occurred to her and she realised, with a stab of guilt, that her friend had been thrown into a very difficult position which she just hadn't considered before.

'And we're not going to Wilf's. We've got loads of wrapping to do, all this lot,' said Beth as brightly as she could, shaking her bags with their rolls of robin-infested paper poking up into the chilly air.

'Oh *great*,' said Ben, echoing Beth's own gloomy thoughts.

'We can put on a nice Christmassy movie, get ourselves in the mood, and have a carpet picnic, too,' Beth said encouragingly. For some reason, eating on the floor always cheered them both up.

But as she fitted her key into the lock and swung the door open, all thoughts of Christmas, food, and presents flew from her head. On the tiled floor, right in front of them, was Magpie, lying on her side, very still, near a pile of cat vomit.

'Oh my God,' said Beth, darting forward and stroking Magpie's head. She scanned her anxiously for signs of life, wishing beyond anything that Ben was not with her, seeing this.

'What's this?' said Ben, picking up a small golden tin of incredibly fancy cat food. It was even pricier than Magpie's usual, and the sort that Beth privately suspected was only bought by ladies who loved their pussies that bit too much.

'Don't touch it!' said Beth – too late. Ben obligingly dropped the tin and gobbets of food went everywhere, adding to the rich smell of vomit in the air. Magpie made the cat equivalent of a groan. 'Can you get her carrier, darling?' Beth said urgently.

Normally, getting Magpie into her deluxe wicker basket involved both Beth and Ben working as a tag team, and wearing gardening gloves into the bargain. All four of Magpie's limbs would move in wildly different directions as she clawed frantically at her hapless humans. Today, Beth lifted her in tenderly in a few moments, and they ran for the car and sped down to the vet's. Luckily, it was still open, and Beth double-parked outside, her hazard lights flashing. There was no time to waste. They rushed in and Beth plonked the carrier on the counter, the tell-tale smell wafting up.

'I think my cat's been poisoned,' said Beth, and promptly burst into tears. Ben, at her side, buried his head into her jacket but she could tell he was crying, too.

Chapter Nineteen

Beth had to hand it to the vets. They were amazing. As she sat and sniffled, with Ben at her side doing the same, behind the closed door she knew important stuff was going on which she certainly couldn't bear to watch. She gazed at the posters about dog biscuits and vaccinations, not seeing anything except Magpie as a kitten, jumping in their back garden to catch insects. She'd been amazing, leaping so high in the air, her zebra-crossing coat so striking against the shabby green of the shrubs. Then Magpie as a teenage cat, pretending to be stuck up a tree so that Beth would risk life and limb to rescue her, only to climb up to the same spot again immediately afterwards. And Magpie, every day, providing the company and counsel that Beth had so badly needed, alone with her boy. Even in the past few tremulous weeks, with Harry on the scene, Magpie had had secrets whispered into her fur that Beth never wanted to say out loud. She was part of their family. She *was* their family.

The door to the surgery opened and the tired-looking vet put her head round the door. 'Mrs Haldane?' she said.

Beth scanned her face, trying to work out what to brace herself for. Ben made to get up with her, but she pressed his arm and asked him to wait, keep an eye on her things, then followed the vet, taking a deep breath.

On the table in the centre of the room lay Magpie, still and quiet. Beth ran over and stroked her fur, so silky and warm. She bit back a sob. 'Is she...?'

'She's going to be fine. She's had a very lucky escape, though,' said the vet, shaking her head. 'I hate to see things like this. It's so worrying.'

Beth put her hands up to her face and the tears came,

unbidden, washing hot over her fingers. 'I'm sorry. It's the relief, I think.'

The vet pressed her shoulder. 'I understand. Don't worry. We'll keep her in overnight. I'm going to put her on a drip just in case; she's lost a lot of fluid. Let's talk in the morning.'

'Can my son just say hello?'

'Of course,' the woman smiled.

She opened the door and said, 'Ben?'

Beth had never seen Ben look so bereft, and that alone brought a fresh wave of tears. He stared up at her, seeing her distress, and his face crumpled. 'No, darling, she's going to be fine, look, I promise,' said Beth, leading him over to Magpie, docile for once. They both stroked her, and Ben got a tiny tickle from her whiskers, making his smile spread from ear to ear.

Beth felt dazed by the time they stood outside on the street – all the more so when she saw the car that was double-parked behind her Fiat, still merrily flashing its hazard lights into the night.

'You know, you really can't park here,' said a familiar voice, and then she was engulfed in a hug from a big, navy blue pea coat. Ben was swept up, too.

'How… how did you know we were here?' Beth was bemused.

'A little bird texted me,' said Harry, his eyebrows up in his hairline.

'Ben? What? How did you do that? And when?'

Ben looked at his shoes, a mass of scuffs one term into the school year. 'While you were in with the vet. I thought it was a police matter,' he said defiantly. 'It could have been a *murder*.'

Beth shook her head. Time for her to change her phone password. But on the other hand, she was so glad Harry was here. She didn't have the heart to be cross. And Ben was so right. It could have been the end of their Magpie. Now that the shock and fear were wearing off, anger was rushing in to take their place.

'This has to stop, Harry.'

'I couldn't agree more, darling. Let's get you home. Then we'll get everything sorted,' he said, reminding her with a look not to say more in front of Ben.

Beth, suddenly feeling warm to her toes, thought what pleasure a single word could give.

As they sped back to Pickwick Road, a quick glance at the Potter house showed that the crime scene tape was still fluttering in the breeze, but the place looked dark, deserted. Beth stored up yet another question to ask Harry, the moment Ben's head touched the pillow.

In fact, after the alarums and excursions of the evening, including a quick and unpleasant clear-up operation in the hall, it wasn't until late that bedtime was finally achieved, and then only by Harry eventually reading Ben into submission with his dullest *Captain Farty Pants* book. Beth, listening to Harry snort with laughter upstairs – the oeuvre was still a novelty for him, if not for her – smiled and poured them both huge glasses of wine, and sat down for a moment on the sofa by the fire. She woke up, three hours later, with a rug tucked round her and a note from Harry propped on her chest saying he'd be back when he could, and that he'd taken the cat food for testing.

She ground her teeth in frustration but trailed up to bed, still worn to a frazzle, and overslept the next morning. So there was no opportunity for a call with Harry to put her out of her misery before Ben's ears started flapping. There were so many questions she was dying to have answered – chiefly, was she right in her suspicions?

Picking up Magpie from the vets was the highlight of the day, though the journey past the deserted Potter house and the closed office was a little surreal. It was already as though none of the turbulent events of the last week had ever happened.

Back at home, and with the little doorway of her wicker cell released, Magpie sauntered out, plonked her still well-upholstered backside down in the middle of the hall, and proceeded to give her chin a leisurely scratch with her long back leg, shedding copious drifts of black-and-white fluff onto the pristine tiles. Beth and Ben looked at each other, eyes shining. Normal service had been resumed.

By the time Harry finally arrived that evening, there was a sizeable pile of wrapped presents underneath the slightly ratty Christmas tree, which had been one of the few left at the florists in the Village. And there were paper chains, tinsel, and baubles hanging off everything except Magpie, who sat in front of the fire radiating feline contentment.

He took a seat and the glass that Beth had poured 24 hours earlier – though she didn't advertise that fact – and looked at her expectant face.

'I must say, I rather like it this way round, with you asking me the questions, instead of dragging me off to some crime scene just to do a bit of arresting for you,' he said with a smile.

'Come on then, tell me. What's happened?' said Beth, not bothering to hide her impatience.

'Well, you're going to love this, but yes, you were right. It was the piece of paper that did it.'

'You mean the report from the vet's? The post mortem on poor old Lancelot?'

'Exactly,' Harry said, shaking his head. 'The levels of zopiclone in his bloodstream were off the scale.'

'And zopiclone, that's also known as zimovane, right?'

'Yes,' said Harry.

'That's what I heard at the chemists – I thought it sounded like *Zimmer frame*. But it was enough to get me wondering. Why Potter needed the prescription, and why he was bothering to get a report on the dog as well.'

'He must have suspected that it wasn't natural causes, even though Great Danes aren't a long-lived breed – about eight to ten years, usually.'

'And what about the office scam? Was I right that Potter was diddling all those old folk at the sheltered housing?

'Yep. I don't know how you got onto that, but he was indeed siphoning off the money, rewriting the wills to include little, or not so little, bequests to a certain solicitor. And he was always careful to make sure it was the old folk without a lot of inquisitive relatives that he picked on. Mind you, there weren't enough of them hereabouts to support his lifestyle by the end. He was in serious financial trouble. The mortgage hadn't been paid for three months, the bank was about to foreclose, even the car was on a lease that wasn't being serviced.'

Beth was silent. Among the larger victims of Potter's fraud, there'd also be the smaller casualties – the flute teachers and dog walkers, who'd no doubt be out of pocket with no recourse. She felt for them.

'So that it explains it, really. Poor man. No wonder he did what he did,' Harry said, throwing back the last of his wine with a smile. 'Bed time?' he said hopefully.

Beth looked at him, agog. 'You're kidding, right?'

Harry looked at her, baffled.

'You know he didn't do it?' asked Beth slowly.

'What do you mean? He offed himself with the sleeping stuff, same as he used on the dog. No question.'

'No, no, no,' said Beth, head in her hands. 'Don't tell me they've got away with it. They haven't, have they?' she peeped up at Harry, through her fringe and her fingers, in consternation.

'What do you mean? It's all done and dusted, thank heavens. We can think about Christmas. Do you want to come over to my mum's?'

As taken as she was with this idea, though she now had an immense turkey squatting in the bottom of her fridge, Beth couldn't help shouting.

'Don't you see? Potter didn't kill himself. Why do you think all those dogs died?'

'You're not asking me to investigate pet killings now, are you? Don't you think I've got enough on my plate?' Harry was suddenly getting fed up.

'Look, think about the dogs. First a dachshund. Then a spaniel, then a Staffordshire. Each time a slightly bigger dog. Then, finally, the Great Dane. What does that tell you?'

'Nothing. Or, maybe that the poisoner was getting more

ambitious?'

'No! That they were adjusting the doses. Finding out how much of the stuff was lethal. Calibrating it carefully. And how big is a Great Dane?'

'Erm, about up to here?' said Harry, his hand shoulder-height from the sofa.

'Exactly. Big. As big as a child. And two Great Danes are as big as…'

'As a man,' said Harry, a light unwillingly dawning. 'It was all a dry run.'

'From someone who doesn't like to make mistakes. And who was very serious about what they were up to. And very angry. *Very* angry – with Potter. Because they knew about the finances going down the tubes. And they weren't happy about it. And maybe they wanted out.'

'His wife.' Harry sat up, electrified, and slowly met Beth's eyes. 'But why wouldn't she just get a divorce?'

'From a lawyer? Who'd stitch everything up for years? She might have ended up getting nothing that way, if he'd carried on losing money the way he was. No, she had to get rid of him quickly, stop the wealth haemorrhaging away. Preserve her lifestyle.'

'But she had no job. What did she think she was going to do?' Harry was baffled.

Beth thought for a moment. Then remembered Tom Seasons, the Bursar, slinking about the Village the other night. He was separated from his wife, thanks to earlier events. And he had admissions to Wyatt's in his pocket. 'Get married again,' she said in a flat voice. There would probably never be any proof, but Beth was as sure as she could be. 'Where is Letty now?' she added, urgently.

'Gone to the holiday house. In Norfolk. I'd better make a few calls,' he said, shooting up off the sofa. The next thing she heard was the car firing up outside and driving off into the night.

Chapter Twenty

Beth, as she hefted a perfectly-cooked turkey out of the oven on Christmas Day (if you didn't count singed legs and a distinctly crispy bit on the side where the bird had touched the oven wall), realised she'd learned many things this year. A new job could bring huge satisfaction. Persistence paid off. And sometimes, it was worth taking a chance, whatever the risks. Particularly if it was to preserve the things you loved – in her case, truth, justice, and the Dulwich way.

She felt a pang for the Potter children. They were with their grandparents, as Letty had been refused bail. It was probably just as well. Pet owners were up in arms about her cynical testing of sleeping pills on different sized pooches, to get the right dose to kill a man but not his wife and children. The fact that she had sacrificed her own pet, poor Lancelot, made it all the more horrifying. Letty, everyone said, wouldn't have stood a dog's chance out on the streets.

Somehow, there was much more outrage about the deaths of Roxie, Lola, Lancelot, Rosie, and possibly Truffles, too – though Letty wasn't yet admitting to that one – than about poor old Potter himself. Beth thought it was a tad unfair. Aside from that time when she'd thought he might hit her, or worse, she hadn't really disliked him. She'd certainly been furious when she'd realised all that dictation was fake, just the regurgitation of favourite old cases.

He'd been in a very odd mental state, knowing that ruin was round the corner. Either the work was going to dry up entirely or someone would notice the will fraud, but either way, he was seemingly caught in the headlights of oncoming disaster, helpless to prevent it. In some ways Beth understood Letty's frustration. And, let's face it, a lawyer was probably never going to seem as lovable as a miniature dachshund.

Both the Potters had been intent on protecting their family, though in different, equally disastrous ways. She could feel some compassion for both, but by killing pets to get what she wanted – and by trying to poison poor Magpie in an act of pure spite that was nothing to do with her dosage experiments – Letty had crossed all the lines. Sure, her dream was probably common where they lived – a miraculously smooth future, with substantial property assets bringing in an income, and a man waiting in the wings to take up the slack – but most women accepted they might have to work a little harder to achieve it than Letty had, either by putting up with a husband or by getting a job. She'd attempted to jettison the first and avoid the second, via the simple method of stockpiling her husband's untouched prescriptions of antidepressants.

As far as Beth understood, the bathroom cabinet at the Potter house had been bursting with packets of zopiclone, from the prescriptions that Paul was bringing home but not taking. It would have been the work of a moment for Letty to crush them with the bottom of one of her vast wine glasses, sprinkling the powder on dog treats, which she'd sneaked to dogs of the right size in the park in her cruel experiments. How she'd induced Potter to take his overdose was a secret that, for the time being, she was refusing to tell, though Beth remembered that mug upside-down on the draining board when she'd got to work on the fateful day she'd found the body. And the office key had been missing. Maybe she'd let herself in, surprised him by making them both a lovely cup of tea, even laced his with the rum Beth had found on the desk to disguise the taste, and he'd drunk it because he loved her.

Why Beth herself, or Magpie, had become the target of Letty's extra malevolence, she didn't know, and she was happy to keep it that way. Maybe Letty sensed that Beth was about to uncover the shaming secret of Potter's empty, fraudulent business. Or maybe she'd just got so into killing pets that she couldn't stop. But Beth couldn't help feeling a little satisfaction that, after her attack on Magpie, Letty would be off the streets for the next ten to fifteen years at least – Her Majesty's guest in the sort of minimalist interior she'd always seemed to enjoy. Only this time, she wouldn't be able to customise it with those little touches of silver she so adored.

Thinking of silver reminded her of the two photos she'd been sent this morning. The first was a lovely selfie of Katie, Charlie, and Michael, grinning wildly into the camera on the side of an expensive mountain, the perfect snow behind them glinting while the gold and silver paper hats they were wearing added a cheesy, festive note. They were having the most wonderful time, and she was glad – but she was happier still that they'd be back in a few days. She'd have a lot to tell Katie over their next cappuccino. Maybe even while poor Ben finally did a practice paper or two for the Wyatt's exam. He'd hate that less if he could do it with Charlie.

The second picture was equally lovely, and perfect for this day of all days. It was a modern Nativity, with Janice perfect in the role of Madonna. There she was, sitting up in a hospital gown as fetching as any cashmere, wearing a beautiful new silvery heart-shaped necklace and with a tiny pink rosebud of a daughter furled in her arms. Dr Grover gazed at them both with the slightly stunned look of a man whose life had just changed forever. Beth smiled. Her first goddaughter. She was looking forward to getting to know her. Janice would be on maternity leave, but Beth would pop in whenever her work on the Wyatt's slavery book allowed. Which was going to be pretty often, let's face it.

Beth glanced round the table at her mother, brother, and son. None of them, including herself, were perfect, or within a million miles of it. Their foibles were many and glaring but were balanced and smoothed out by deep affection and love. They might have rows. They might drive each other mad. But they were essentially good people. She could understand some of the frustrations that had driven Letty; Beth saw the pressures and stresses, as well as the pleasures, of a certain lifestyle every day on the streets of Dulwich. But no-one who truly felt compassion or affection towards others could deliberately hurt an animal. Unless, of course, it was a Christmas turkey.

She plonked the roast down to satisfying oohs and aahs, and heard a tiny ping from her phone. Sauntering over to the counter on the pretext of picking up the sprouts, she saw it was a message from Harry.

Beneath her fringe, she wrinkled her brow. That was another thing she'd definitely learned over the past few months. People didn't always like it when you were smarter than them. Though, in her view, if they had any character at all, they really ought to try to rise above that. Steeling herself, she clicked to open up the text. '*Happy Christmas xxxx.*'

A sudden glow of contentment told Beth that maybe she'd just found herself a little Christmas miracle after all.

THE END

Fantastic Books
Great Authors

CROOKED CAT

Meet our authors and discover
our exciting range:

- Gripping Thrillers
- Cosy Mysteries
- Romantic Chick-Lit
- Fascinating Historicals
- Exciting Fantasy
- Young Adult and Children's Adventures
- Non-Fiction

Visit us at:
www.crookedcatbooks.com

Join us on facebook:
www.facebook.com/realcrookedcat

Printed in Poland
by Amazon Fulfillment
Poland Sp. z o.o., Wrocław